THE
DEVIL'S
GATE

MALCOLM RICHARDS

STORM
HOUSE

By Malcolm Richards

Devil's Cove Trilogy
The Cove
Desperation Point
The Devil's Gate

Standalone
The Hiding House

As M.J. Richards:
The Emily Swanson Series
Next To Disappear
Mind For Murder
Trail Of Poison
Watch You Sleep

Cover Design by www.jcalebdesign.com

For more information about the author, please visit
www.malcolmrichardsauthor.com

For Mum & Dad

THE
DEVIL'S
GATE

PROLOGUE

LINDSAY CHURCH SAT at the dining table in a grand room with impressive bay windows and an ocean view, picking at her dinner. Her mother had said it was chicken in some sort of sauce that Lindsay had already forgotten the name of. But to her ten-year-old eyes it looked like chicken dumped in vomit. Lindsay thought she'd rather take a walk into town and grab a burger from that nice little place on the seafront. After all, they were supposed to be on holiday, but her mum and dad had insisted on a nice family dinner, something that was a rare occurrence these days.

Lindsay looked around. Her father, Paul Church, a greying man in his early fifties, sat at the end of the table nearest to the door—no doubt so he could make a quick exit—ignoring his food and his family as he thumbed the screen of his phone. She wasn't quite sure what he did for a living, something to do with science, but she knew he was rich. She also knew that he spent most of his days at work and hardly any time at home with his family; especially his two children. Lindsay didn't mind so much. She didn't particularly like her dad. He was moody and bossy, thinking he was in charge even though he was never around. And he was never interested in anything that she had to say. Sometimes she wondered if he forgot he even had a daughter.

It hadn't always been that way. There had been a time when she was younger, when he'd get home in time to read her bedtime stories. There had been a time when he *had* been interested in her thoughts and ideas, even the strange ones. Then there'd been all that trouble last year and her dad's face had been in the newspapers and on the television. He hadn't been the same since.

Lindsay's gaze shifted across to the other end of the table, where her mother, Donna Church, sat not eating and staring unhappily at her husband. Lindsay wondered if her mum felt the same as she did: what was the point of a family holiday if they were all going to continue ignoring each other? That was just another day in the Church family.

She'd overheard her parents arguing last night. Her mother had wanted to know why they even owned a second home in Cornwall when it sat empty fifty weeks of the year. Her father had called her mother ungrateful, which hadn't gone down well.

Sitting across from Lindsay was her brother, Todd, who had recently turned seventeen, which apparently made him think he was an adult now, even though everyone knew you weren't an adult until you turned eighteen. Being seventeen also made Todd think he was better than Lindsay. She sneered in disgust as she watched him shovel food into his mouth, his eyes on his phone just like their father. She didn't much like her brother, either. All he ever did was whine and complain at her. *Don't go into my room! Don't touch my stuff! Don't interrupt me!* Et cetera, et cetera. Moan, moan, moan. Lindsay didn't know what else he expected from her. She was ten years old.

Anyway, she still hadn't forgiven him for the dead arm he'd gifted her with yesterday when their parents weren't watching. He was always doing that—giving her a quick jab to the ribs or a punch to her upper arm, all because he didn't like her playing with his phone. It wasn't her fault that her parents wouldn't let her have a phone of her own, and it certainly wasn't her fault that he'd taken puke-inducing naked photographs of himself and left them in the pictures folder for anyone to see.

Lindsay stared at her food again. Puffing out her cheeks, she set down her fork and turned to gaze out the large bay windows at the far end of the room. In the near distance, the sky was turning all shades of orange, red, and purple. It looked like a big bruise, Lindsay thought. Like the one on her arm thanks to her stupid brother. Beneath the sky, the sea was calm and flat and growing darker by the second.

They'd been here for three days now and still hadn't gone to the beach, even though it was just across the road. Dad had spent most of the time working in his study, while all Mum wanted to do was explore boring towns and go to boring galleries. Lindsay only ever got to see the ocean once a year and she desperately wanted to dip her toes in it. Living in London, she got to see the River Thames sometimes, but it wasn't the same. The Thames was dirty and disgusting and surrounded by concrete, and if you dipped your toes into it, you'd probably never see them again.

The ocean was like a mysterious beast, rising and shifting as far as the eye could see. If she had to suffer a week's holiday with her annoying family, couldn't they allow her, just for once, to do something *she* wanted?

"Mum?" Lindsay said.

Donna heaved a shoulder, shifted her gaze to her daughter. "Hmm?"

"Tomorrow, can we go to the beach?"

"I thought we could go to Truro. Do some shopping and visit the Cathedral."

"We can go shopping any time."

"Oh, Lindsay, you know I don't like the sun. It brings me out in hives. Besides, what about sand flies?"

Lindsay sank into the chair and stuck out her lower lip. She didn't care about sand flies. She wanted to go swimming.

"Maybe your brother can take you," her mother suggested.

Across the table, Todd glanced up from his phone and snorted. "Don't get me involved."

"I thought you'd be first on the beach," Donna said. "I thought that's why you've been working out so much lately—so you can show off your abs to the girls."

Lindsay wrinkled her face. "Gross."

"Shut it, brat." Todd shifted his attention back to his phone. "Anyway, I can't tomorrow because I'm meeting some friends."

"What friends?" Lindsay said. "You don't know anyone down here."

"Mind your own business."

Lindsay sighed and picked up her fork again. "Must be a girl, then. Maybe *she'll* take me to the beach."

"What girl?" their mother asked. "When have you met some girl?"

Todd rolled his eyes. "There's no girl! We've been coming here for five years now. There's a bunch of guys I'm friends with and tomorrow we're going surf—"

Lindsay sat up, eyes sparkling. "Surfing? You're going to the beach? Then I can go with you."

"No way. I don't want you hanging around and bringing down the mood."

"I won't, I promise. I won't even talk to your so-called friends! Mum, please say I can go with him?"

She stared at her mother with begging eyes. Donna sipped her wine.

"Take your sister with you," she said.

Todd shook his head. "Forget it."

"Please, Todd!" Lindsay whined. "I promise I'll be on my best behaviour and I won't try to embarrass you or anything."

"You'd embarrass me just by being there."

Lindsay narrowed her eyes. Why did big brothers always suck?

At the far end of the table, Paul Church, who had been quiet until now, glanced up from his phone.

"Take your sister with you," he said.

Todd's face reddened. "No, that's not fair. I—"

"It's not up for debate. You want to be treated like an adult, you need to act like one. Take some responsibility."

Lindsay watched as her brother's face crumpled, then twisted into a grimace. He glowered at her across the table. Lindsay swallowed and stared at her food.

Great, she thought. *Now I'm going to get another dead arm.* But at least she was going to the beach.

Picking up her fork again, she speared some chicken and popped it into her mouth. It tasted gross but she swallowed it down. Tomorrow, when she was at the beach, she'd go to the burger bar on the seafront and use some of her pocket money to get a big, fat, greasy hamburger. Maybe she'd even get one for Todd, so he didn't hate her so much for ruining his day.

At the end of the table, Donna picked up her wine glass and returned to staring unhappily at her husband. Todd sat, silently seething and staring at his phone like he wanted to smash it into smithereens. Paul had already zoned out from his family and still hadn't touched a bite of his meal.

The drone of the front door buzzer cut through the silence.

In unison, the Church family looked up, stared at each other, then turned their heads in the direction of the open dining room door.

"Who could that be?" Donna said but made no move to find out.

Paul shook his head. "Probably charity collectors. They'll try their luck anywhere. Just ignore it."

Lindsay didn't want to ignore it. No one ever came knocking at the door of their holiday home. Probably because it stood empty fifty weeks of the year. She wondered who it could be. She stood, scraping her chair on the polished floorboards.

"I'll get it," she said.

Her father arched an eyebrow. "You'll do no such thing. Sit down and eat your dinner."

Lindsay sat down, glancing at her father's untouched plate.

The door buzzer sounded again.

"What if it's one of the neighbours?" Donna said. "I don't want to seem rude. . ."

Her husband heaved his shoulders. "You don't even know the neighbours. Besides, half of the houses around here are holiday homes. They're probably empty."

Whoever was at the door started knocking, making them all look up again.

Paul muttered something under his breath and shook his head. "Todd, make yourself useful and answer the door."

Todd opened his mouth to protest. A withering look from his father made him shut it again. Huffing, he grabbed his phone from the table and stood up.

Lindsay watched him stomp across the floorboards, then listened to his feet stomp along the hall. A second later, she heard the snap of the door latch as Todd opened the front door.

And then . . . nothing.

She waited to hear voices. But there were none. Which was weird. She waited a few seconds more, then glanced at her mother, who shrugged a shoulder and stared at Lindsay's father. The silence continued.

"Who is it, Todd?" Donna called.

All eyes were fixed on the open dining room door. A stillness fell over the room that was as hot and stifling as a blanket on a summer's day.

Lindsay shifted uncomfortably, suddenly feeling as if her clothes were too small and her skin had been stung by nettles. She looked at her mother and father again, noticing their faces shared the same perplexed expression.

"Todd?" Donna called out. She shot another uncertain look at Paul, who shrugged but made no move to get up.

Lindsay's gaze returned to the open door, the silence rushing in like rolls of thunder. Her mother got to her feet.

They heard movement from out in the hall; footsteps coming towards them. Todd was not alone.

Lindsay watched as her brother entered the room.

Except it wasn't Todd.

It was the Devil.

Eyes growing wide, Lindsay stared at the man standing in the doorway, taking in his dark clothing and the terrifying mask that hid his features. It was the Devil's face. Red skin. Yellow, reptilian eyes. A wicked grin brimming with shark's teeth that stretched all the way up to two barbed horns.

The Church family stared at the man. Confusion quickly turned into fear. Fear into terror. Then Lindsay's mother's hands flew up to her mouth and her father's jaw fell open. Frozen, Lindsay just stared, her eyes moving from the horrific mask to the glistening butcher's knife in the man's hand.

More footsteps. Three more people entered the room. All dressed in the same dark clothing. All wearing the face of the Devil. All clutching sharp blades.

Paul slowly got to his feet.

"What is this?" His voice trembled and he didn't sound at all like Lindsay's father.

The four devils stood silently in the doorway, their red masks grinning from ear to ear.

Across the table, Donna's complexion had turned a deathly grey.

"Todd?" she whispered. "Where is Todd?"

"I said, what is this?" Paul's voice was louder this time. He was trying to regain some control. "Where's my son?"

Lindsay's eyes flicked back to the four intruders. An invisible hand pressed down on her bladder.

Slowly, their leader lifted a finger to his masked mouth.

"Shhhhh. . ." His finger moved from his mouth and pointed at Paul's chair. "Sit down."

Donna let out a strangled cry. Paul remained standing, his eyes flicking uncertainly from masked face to masked face. In the doorway, the four devils grinned.

"I will not sit down!" Paul said, puffing out his chest. "I don't know who you are, or what you want, but you don't come into *my* house, making demands."

The pressure was building in Lindsay's bladder. Her temples had started throbbing. Realising that she was holding her breath, she let it out with a gasp, then sucked in more air. The devils remained, unmoving.

"If it's money you want, there's some in my wallet upstairs," her father continued. "But that's all you'll find. This is our holiday home. We don't keep anything of worth here, so—

The Devil darted forward. In one fluid movement, he brought the hilt of his knife smashing down on Paul's nose. There was a sickening crack and a spurt of blood. Paul stumbled backwards, crumpling into his chair. Across the table, Donna drew in a sharp, horrified gasp.

The intruders moved into the room now, grinning red masks burning nightmares into Lindsay's mind. Their leader—the Devil himself in her eyes—nodded. One of the intruders left the room, while two more circled the table until one stood behind Donna and the other behind Lindsay.

A scuffing sound came from the hall. The sound of something being dragged. The intruder who had left just a moment ago returned with two more—three red devils dragging Todd's semi-conscious form into the middle of the room.

Lindsay saw her brother's bruised and bloodied face. She watched mutely as he was forced onto his knees. Then she felt a hand roughly grab the roots of her hair and wrench her head back.

Tears stung her eyes. Cold metal bit at her collarbone. Her bladder released itself. Her legs grew warm and wet as she shifted her terrified gaze towards her mother. Lindsay saw that she was in the same horrific predicament.

"Please!" Donna hissed. The devil who had hold of her hair gave it a short, sharp tug. "Please, don't hurt my children!"

Paul was leaning forward on his chair, hands pressed to the bridge of his nose, blood spilling over his fingers. The Devil leaned over him and tapped the top of his head with the hilt of the knife.

"Paul Church," the Devil said, and Lindsay was immediately struck by how young he sounded; not like a grown-up, more like a teenager. Someone Todd's age. "You are charged with the murders of three young children. Luke James, Carla James, and Isiah James. Three innocent lives stolen before they'd had a chance to shine."

Paul looked up, red eyes growing wide and round. "Please," he begged through his hands. "It's not true. I was found innocent!"

The Devil grinned. "Three innocent lives smeared across the pavement beneath the wheels of your flashy car."

"The court ruled their deaths an accident! A stupid, tragic accident!"

"Please," Donna begged. The intruder who held a knife to her throat, pulled her hair so hard that she screamed.

"An accident!" the Devil roared. "Three innocent children are dead, while you sit here in your fancy second home. Unpunished."

The Devil straightened. Lindsay watched him turn and nod to each of the intruders. Then she felt blinding pain as the devil behind her twisted her hair at the roots, tearing the scalp. The burning pain was quickly followed by a sharp sting as the tip of the blade pierced

18

her throat. A single drop of blood dribbled over her collarbone.

"Stop!" her father cried. His hands were in front of him, pleading. His nose had swollen up like a balloon. "Don't hurt my family. It's not their fault!"

The Devil stood watching him, the frozen grin seeming to come alive. "Then choose. Your life as penance for the lives of those poor children. Or the lives of your flesh and blood."

Lindsay's father stared up at the mask in wild bewilderment. "What? No, you can't—"

"Five seconds or I'll choose myself."

Lindsay's mother started to wail and beg, the knife against her throat scoring a thin red line into her skin. Lindsay stared at her brother, who was still kneeling on the floor, his swollen eyes spilling tears over blood and bruises.

"Please!" Paul Church begged. "Please, don't do this!"

Donna was shrieking now, the knife pressing deeper into her throat. "Oh God, please don't hurt my babies!"

The Devil slowly lowered his head. "Out of time."

Lindsay's father sucked in a ragged breath. When he spoke, his voice was hysterical and high, stretched like elastic. "Why are you doing this? I don't even know you! I didn't go to prison—that means I'm innocent! Innocent!"

The Devil nodded to one of the masked assailants, the one who had brought Todd to his knees. Then he leaned down until his face was inches from Paul's.

"You are a selfish, disgusting man. Letting another child die to save yourself—your own flesh and blood." He stood up again and straightened his spine. "We are the Dawn Children! This is our New Dawn!"

Lindsay caught her brother's gaze and it chilled her to the bone. He no longer looked seventeen. He was a scared little boy, sobbing and dribbling. Behind him, the masked assailant raised his knife. Todd squeezed his eyes shut. His mother continued to scream and thrash.

Lindsay watched the knife cut through the air and plunge into her brother's neck. She saw it pull out again, saw arterial sprays of blood arcing through the air and raining down on the floorboards, the table, her father. Then she watched her brother crumple to the ground.

Her mother shrieked hysterically. "No! No! Oh, Jesus, no!"

Lindsay tried to turn away. Squeezed her eyes shut just like her brother. Because she knew what was coming next. She heard the *swish* of steel slicing through flesh, followed by the choking gurgles of her mother's dying breaths. She heard her father whimper and wail, his screams reaching up to the ceiling. She squeezed her eyes shut, tighter and tighter, until the blackness began to sparkle with lights. Then everything went blank and silent. Like she'd fallen asleep without realising.

When she looked up again, she felt strange and empty. As if someone had pulled the plug on her emotions and they'd all drained away.

A young man's face swam in and out of her vision. He was kneeling before her, bright eyes burning through the fog like storm lanterns. She didn't know if she was still at the dining table or if she was floating through space. All she saw was the young man's eyes and all she knew was that he was not her brother.

"We have spared you," he said. "You're an innocent. A child of the New Dawn. One of us."

The young man smiled and everything went dark again. The last thought Lindsay had before she fell back into the void was: *now, I'll never go to the beach.*

1

SUMMER CAME TO Porth an Jowl on a Tuesday morning in mid-June, bringing warm sunshine and a clear blue sky that hung over the cove like a tapestry. There was only one way in or out of the town and that was via Cove Road, which was shaped like a hangman's noose. To drive along it would first take you past the caravan park on the left, now open and booking up fast, and Briar Wood on the right. Then you would descend, passing tiered rows of old stone cottages, until you reached the heart of the town, veering around surf shops, gift boutiques and ice cream parlours, before finding yourself traversing along the pink slabs of the promenade and drinking in the view of a sandy white beach and a calm green ocean, wedged between two sheer cliffs.

Winter had been cruel to the people of Porth an Jowl, in more ways than one. Spring, not much better. But now that the weather had changed and the first wave of tourists had descended in surprisingly decent numbers, the townsfolk could taste hope in the air, mingling with all the sea salt.

Maybe when school ended next month and the holiday season entered its peak phase, all the horrors from the past year would be forgotten.

Or maybe not.

Carrie Killigrew stood at the counter of Cove Crafts, the tourist gift shop she'd been running for the last six years, staring through the glass storefront at the town square beyond. Tourists sidled up and down, stopping to take pictures of the quaint little shops, while eating ice cream or munching on pasties. But Carrie didn't see them. She was lost inside her mind—a jumble of thoughts and worries all knotted together and growing increasingly tangled. It had been hard to focus on anything lately. The lack of sleep wasn't helping, either.

Pulling her gaze back to the store, she watched a handful of potential customers peruse the shelves of nautical knickknacks, boxes of flavoured fudge, and traditional Cornish fairings. Although the holiday season had only just begun, business was already doing well, which was a huge relief. With all the terrible things that had happened in the past year, Carrie had fully anticipated customers to stay away in droves, leaving Cove Crafts to run into the ground. But it seemed that all those terrible events had instilled these early holidaymakers with morbid curiosity, tempting them into her little shop so they could lay eyes on the mother of a teenage killer.

She felt someone watching her now and turned to see a head bobbing over one of the shelves, then furtive eyes flicking away. It had irritated her at first, the constant staring, making her feel somehow worse. But she'd gradually learned to shut it out, to even use it to her advantage. Now, whenever she caught someone staring for too long, she'd guilt-trip them into buying trinkets from the shop. And they almost always did.

The bell over the front door tinkled, making Carrie turn her head. But instead of seeing another prospective customer, she saw her neighbour, Dottie Penpol. Dottie may have been an elderly woman, but it was as if her brain had forgotten to tell her body. She could always be seen marching through the streets of Porth an Jowl, arms and legs swinging as if she were powered by engine oil, her furtive, keen eyes searching out gossip. Which was no doubt why she was here now.

"Afternoon, Carrie," she said, flashing a yellow-toothed smile as she approached the counter. "How's business?"

"Business is good." Carrie waved a hand at the aisles of browsing customers, but Dottie was clearly uninterested. She hovered from one foot to the other, her nervous energy screaming that she had news to tell. "What brings you to Cove Crafts?"

Dottie's lips curved slightly at the edges. "You mean you haven't heard?"

"Heard about what?"

"Why, the *murders*!"

Her voice rose on that last word, making curious heads turn. Carrie had been expecting some sort of salacious gossip about one of the cove's townsfolk; it was usually Dottie's favourite topic of conversation. No one was safe, not even Carrie. She was well aware that her neighbour had been most helpful in spreading the word about the horrors that had taken place at 6 Clarence Row all those months ago. Carrie had resented her for it, at first. But wasn't that just the nature of small towns? Everyone knew everyone else's business. It was almost like a God-given right; an expectation that if you lived somewhere like Porth an Jowl, you had to be prepared for your insides to be ripped open and spread across the street for all to see.

Right now, Carrie felt no irritation towards the woman, only mild shock and confusion.

"What murders?" she asked, dropping her voice to a hush.

"It's been all over the news," Dottie said, almost gleefully. "A family was murdered over in Falmouth. Down on holiday, they were. Staying in one of those second homes that all the city folk seem to own down here—never mind it driving up house prices for us poor locals. Their cleaner found them. The husband and wife had been stabbed to death. The son, too." She glanced over her shoulder. Carrie followed her gaze to see that shoppers had all stopped browsing and were now staring in their direction. Dottie turned back, leaning in closer. "They had a daughter. Whoever killed the family took her."

Carrie was finding it hard to breathe. "Do they know who did it?"

"The police aren't talking. Only that the girl's missing and there's a search party looking for her." Dottie shook her head. "It's a terrible business. The last thing we need after everything that happened here. No offence, of course."

Irritation stabbed Carrie's chest. There it was. The accusation that every bad thing that had happened here in the last year was her fault.

If only she'd watched her son that day. If only she'd kept him in the hospital and not taken him home.

It didn't matter that her son had been held in captivity for years by a deranged serial killer of children, had been starved, beaten, broken down to nothing and built back up into something terrifying and dangerous. No, according to local gossip, the very fact that Carrie had given birth in the first place made her solely responsible.

Forcing a smile, she stared at Dottie, then at the tourists, who returned to browsing the shelves.

"It's a terrible business," the older woman said again. "Let's just hope it doesn't affect the festival, eh?"

"Oh yes, the festival. Because heaven forbid a family being murdered should take precedent over a marching band and a few waving flags." Dottie's eyes widened and her mouth fell open. Carrie forced down a smile. "No offence, of course."

"Yes, well, I think this town is due a bit of good luck, don't you? And Devil's Day will certainly bring in money. Maybe this year it'll bring some welcome distraction, too."

Here's hoping, Carrie thought. "Is there anything else, Dottie? Only I have customers. . ."

The elderly woman stiffened. "Just dropping by to see how you're doing. How's that mother of yours? All recovered now?"

There it was again. The pointing finger.

"She's doing much better, thank you. Fully recovered, in fact, and back on the yacht with Dad. Somewhere near Malaga, I believe."

"Some people have all the fun, don't they? Well, I best be off. Can't stand around all day gossiping, can we?"

Carrie smiled. The shop door opened again, setting off the bell.

"Oh look, it's Dylan," Dottie announced, as if Carrie was blind. "And little Melissa."

Melissa dashed forward, locks of blonde hair falling across her face as she headed for the counter. "Mummy!"

Carrie stepped out and swept her daughter up into her arms.

"Hi sweet pea," she said, planting kisses on the child's face. "How's my soon-to-be five-year-old?"

"I'm good! How many days until my birthday?"

"Two whole weeks yet, snuggle bum." She rubbed her nose against Melissa's and they both laughed. Her smile wavered a little as she glanced at Dylan, whose tall, muscular frame was still hovering near the door, dark eyes watching their exchange.

"Hi," she said.

Dylan lifted a hand. "Hi."

A clearing of the throat pulled their attention back to Dottie.

"How are you, Dylan? And those parents of yours? Haven't seen much of them at church lately. And have you heard about what happened over in Falmouth? A family mur—"

"Okay, Dottie, thanks so much for stopping by," Carrie interrupted, her voice loud enough to make Melissa flinch.

Dottie narrowed her eyes and smiled. "Well, I'm sure you two have a lot to catch up on, so I'll be off. Don't be a stranger, Carrie."

Pretty much impossible in this town, Carrie thought as she waved.

The three watched Dottie march out of the shop, followed by a couple of holidaymakers seizing the opportunity to escape without making a purchase. Arms swinging, the elderly woman crossed the square and was gone, no doubt desperate to share her news with anyone else who crossed her path.

"What was that all about?" Dylan said, finally moving away from the door and towards the counter. His eyes fixed on Carrie before glancing away again. "What happened in Falmouth?"

Carrie shrugged, staring at him uncertainly. Then she turned to Melissa and playfully pinched her nose. "Go get yourself a juice from the back."

"And a lolly?"

"Just one. I've counted them, so I'll know if you take more."

Screwing up her face, Melissa made her way along the nearest aisle, heading for the storeroom. Carrie watched her go, eyes flicking

27

between her daughter and the browsing shoppers. She turned back to Dylan and they both stood in silence, bodies shifting uncomfortably.

"How's she been?" Carrie asked.

Dylan ran a hand through his mop of dark hair, which was in need of a cut. "She's good."

"Any nightmares?"

"One or two."

"Has she . . . has she mentioned—"

A middle-aged couple dressed in matching shorts and t-shirts, sidled up to the counter and placed an ornamental lighthouse in a glass bottle on the counter. Carrie smiled and said hello. Dylan stepped back and stared listlessly at a shelf of porcelain anchors. As Carrie wrapped the lighthouse in tissue paper, she felt the couple watching her. She glanced up and they both looked away. The transaction complete, the couple nervously brushed past Dylan and went on their way.

At the back of the shop, the storeroom door opened and Melissa came trundling out, a carton of juice clutched in one hand and a bright blue ice lolly in the other. She smiled at her parents then awkwardly scrambled onto a stool behind the counter.

"Anyway," Dylan said, his smile fading as he glanced at Carrie. "I'm off to sea tomorrow for a few days. I won't be back till Tuesday, but Mum will pick Melissa up from school on Monday afternoon. That okay?"

"Of course. Why wouldn't it be?"

Silence settled between them again, prickly and uncomfortable; a reminder that they were still new at this separated life, still working on behaving amicably. They made small talk for a minute more, until the conversation dried up. Dylan leaned over the counter to ruffle Melissa's hair.

"See you after the weekend, my little pirate."

Melissa beamed at him. "See you, Daddy. Bring me back a mermaid."

"I'll see what I can do."

Dylan leaned into Carrie, and in that brief moment it was as if he'd forgotten they weren't together anymore, and she inhaled a heady mixture of his sweat and aftershave. He pulled away and shook his head, admonishing himself.

"Sorry. Old habits and all that."

Carrie watched him go. Saw him pause outside the shop door and slowly hang his head. Then he was gone.

"Mum?"

The weight in Carrie's chest grew heavier, threatening to drag her to the floor.

You're doing the right thing, she told herself. Besides, he'd been the one to call it a day. Although she hadn't fought to keep him.

"Mummy?"

Melissa sat on the stool, dimples creasing her cheeks as she sucked on the lolly.

"Yes, sweet pea?"

"I'm hungry."

Carrie smiled, ran fingers through her daughter's hair.

"We'll be going home soon. You want pasta?"

"No, ice cream."

"Um, what's that in your hand?"

"That's a lolly. Not an ice cream."

"Well, ice cream is for dessert. How about risotto?"

"Grandpa Gary and Nana Joy let me have ice cream first."

"Do they now? Well, in our house it's dinner first." Carrie stared at her daughter, feeling a stab of envy. "How about pizza?"

Melissa's eyes lit up. "With pepperoni!"

Laughing, Carrie turned away, fixing her gaze on the single customer left in the store. Her smile faded. Anxiety sprang up in her chest and trickled down to her stomach as her thoughts returned to Dottie Penpol's news.

2

TWENTY MILES SOUTH of Porth an Jowl, a train was pulling into a station. As it ground to a halt, Nat Tremaine opened the carriage door and stepped onto the open air platform. The seaside town of Penzance was twice the size of Porth an Jowl and just as stagnant in her mind. But just like Porth an Jowl, she supposed it wasn't entirely ugly. She took a moment to enjoy the view of the large swathe of sandy beach that stretched all the way to Mounts Bay, where St Michael's Mount rose up from the water; a tiny rock of an island with a handful of houses at the bottom of a sheer slope, and an impressive-looking castle at the top. She didn't know much about the Mount, only that a wealthy family had lived in the castle for hundreds of years, and that local legend would have unsuspecting tourists believe that a giant had once resided on the island and still lay buried beneath it.

Moving down the platform, she entered the station, her eyes taking in its impressive iron rafters, before scanning the empty concourse. Warmth rushed through her as she spied a tall, young man hanging back by the ticket office. To Nat's surprise, he was not alone.

She moved closer, forcing down her smile. Growing serious, she tipped her head in Jago Pengelly's direction. "Hey."

"Hey," he replied, dark eyes peering out from beneath a mop of equally dark hair. He was thinner than the last time she'd seen him, his tall, sinewy frame lost beneath baggy jeans and an over-sized black t-shirt.

Nat glanced down at the young boy beside him, this time allowing her smile to break free.

"Hello, little dude," she said, bending her knees. "I wasn't expecting to see you."

Noah Pengelly peered up at her with wide, round eyes that were even darker than Jago's. Instead of saying hello, he pressed into his brother's side and stared at the ground.

Nat straightened up again. No one spoke. It had been almost eight months since the Pengelly family had moved out of Porth an Jowl. Nat hadn't seen Jago since. She had tried, but Jago was always coming up with some sort of excuse. His mother needed him. Noah needed him. He had too much college work. He was broke. Nat had just about given up on their friendship when, out of the blue yesterday morning, Jago had sent her a text message, asking if she wanted to hang out.

"So, are we standing here in awkward silence for the rest of the afternoon, or what?" Nat said, flashing him a wry smile.

Jago shrugged. He stared down at Noah. "You want ice cream?"

Noah was silent, his eerie, haunted eyes fixed on the ground.

"He wanted some earlier," Jago said, and a strange expression passed over his face that Nat couldn't quite discern. Frustration? Helplessness?

She shrugged. "So let's go get him some."

They exited the station, bright sunlight assaulting their eyes as they crossed the car park and followed the road along the seafront.

Penzance was a popular tourist destination in the summer, which meant the pavement was currently bustling with holidaymakers dressed in shorts and t-shirts and colourful dresses, all meandering along, as they took pictures and ate pasties and ice cream. Nat pushed her way through them, clearing a path for Jago and Noah. They passed the harbour on their left, where the tide was out and a handful of boats rested awkwardly on the wet, slippery bed. Crossing the road, they strolled by a nautical-themed gift shop and a restaurant boasting a menu of locally caught fish, before coming to a stop in front of an ice cream parlour. Jago bought them a cone each, then the trio walked on in silence, Jago holding onto Noah's hand as they crossed a bridge and passed by warehouses and a shipyard, until the road veered around a corner and opened on to the pink and grey paving stones of the promenade, which stretched all the way over to the neighbouring fishing village of Newlyn.

The trio came to a halt outside the gates of the Jubilee Pool, an Art Deco style saltwater lido that extended off the promenade and had only recently reopened after violent storms had left it in near-ruin. Nat stared through the gates at the children and parents splashing about in the pool. Her initial joy at being re-united with Jago was swiftly disappearing.

"So, did you invite me here just so you could ignore me in person as well as over the phone?" she said, letting out a heavy breath. "You've barely spoken a word since I got here."

Jago shrugged, his eyes coming to rest on his little brother's face. "Sorry."

Nat waited for him to say something else. When he didn't, she followed his gaze until she was staring at Noah, who was deathly silent and far too pale to be considered healthy.

"How's your mum?" she asked.

Jago looked away, peering past the swimming pool, out to sea, where a passenger ship called *The Scillonian*, had left the harbour and was making its daily voyage towards the Scilly Isles.

"That good, huh?" Nat shook her head. She wondered which prescription medication was filling the void this time, then immediately felt guilty. Tess Pengelly had been to hell and back this last year, and even though Noah had been found alive, unlike the other poor kids who'd been murdered by Grady Spencer, the entire ordeal had broken her. Judgement wasn't what Tess Pengelly needed right now. What she needed was help.

"How about you?" Nat asked. "College going okay? Made any new friends?"

"Some," Jago said. "No one special. Anyway, it doesn't matter, does it? In a few weeks, it'll all be over. Everyone will be going off to university. Everyone except me."

"What do you mean? I thought you were London-bound."

"I can't. Not with…" He stole a glance at his brother, who stood by the gates of the swimming pool, tiny fingers wrapped around the bars as he watched the other children splash about. Jago smiled and ruffled Noah's hair. The boy didn't react. "Anyway, I'm taking a year out. And we're moving again. This time out of Cornwall."

Nat stared at him, mouth hanging open. "Where to?"

"Wiltshire. We have relatives there. Mum's sick of all the staring. Me too."

"When are you leaving?"

"In three weeks."

"Oh." Her heart was pounding. Tears pricked the corners of her eyes. She turned away, fighting them back. Pushing them down.

"Well, maybe it'll be good to get away. You can press reset. Get focused."

Jago nodded. "Here's hoping. How about you? How's life in the cove?"

"You know, the same old shit. Except now we have this stupid festival to look forward to. Rose has decided it would be good for me to get involved this year. She thinks I can use my art skills to impress the natives and make them less afraid of me."

"Cool."

"Not really. I mean, I guess it's good to be doing art. I just wish I was doing it elsewhere." Nat's eyes drifted downward once more, watching Noah cling to the bars like a ghost clinging onto life. "Is he okay?"

Jago shot her a glare. "Keep your voice down. He's not deaf, you know."

"Sorry."

He grasped his brother's hand and gently pulled him away from the gates. They continued along the promenade, weaving between crowds of tourists. As they walked, Jago stole worried glances at Noah, who remained silent beside him, his gaze blank and unreadable.

"Anyway, he's still working through it all," he told Nat in a hushed voice. "Getting abducted and locked in a cage for months isn't something you just get over."

"I guess not. Which reminds me, did you hear about Cal? Apparently, he's been moved from the young offenders place to a mental hospital while they wait for the trial. Apparently, he's not coping."

Jago stopped dead, pulling his brother behind him. "Don't ever say his name in front of Noah," he hissed. "Ever."

Shocked, Nat stared at him. "Sorry, I—I wasn't thinking."

"No, you weren't. And I heard about it. Honestly, I can't wait to get away from here and forget the whole fucking episode."

Lowering his shoulders, he started walking again. Noah hurried alongside, stumbling over his feet. Nat stood still, head lowered, lump in her throat. Every word that came out of her mouth was pissing Jago off. But she was no one's emotional punch bag. She thought about turning around and getting the next train back.

Like he would care, anyway. He's leaving. Just like everyone always does.

She hurried to catch up with the brothers. Jago glanced at her, then looked away.

"Sorry," he said. "I can't think about . . . about *him*. He took my brother and gave him to that psychopath. I don't care if he was a victim first. I don't care if he was brainwashed like they're saying. He gave my brother to a monster."

"A monster who's dead now," Nat said softly.

"Because I killed him."

"Because you had no choice. Because he deserved to die."

Jago stared at her through cold eyes. "Yes, he did. And I'd do it again in a heartbeat."

They both stared at Noah, who peered up at them with haunted eyes. Jago's shoulders sagged. "How are you doing, buddy?"

Noah shrugged.

"Can I have another ice cream?" he asked, his voice barely audible above the noise of the crowds.

Jago smiled. "Mum said only one. But I'll see what I can do."

They walked on, leaving the crowd behind as they headed for a small play park, where children climbed frames and sliced through the air on swings. On their left, the ocean stretched out in a wide green swathe.

"How about you?" Jago said, pushing open the gate to the play park and ushering Noah inside. "Are you still heading to London?"

"Not right now."

He looked at her, a frown creasing his brow.

"You're not the only one who had a bad year," she said.

"What will you do instead?"

Nat curled up her lips. What *was* she going to do? Because she sure as hell wasn't going to piss her life away in Porth an Jowl. She was supposed to be leaving. She'd promised herself that as soon as she was done with college, she was taking the next train to London. Or Manchester. Anywhere that wasn't here. But that was before the events of December. That was before what happened to Aaron Black.

"I guess I'll stick around for a bit," she said, avoiding his gaze, instead watching Noah cautiously approach the climbing frame.

"Why? I mean, what's holding you back? It's not like you have anyone to keep you here, so why would you stay?"

Nat flinched, feeling the sting of his words like cuts to her skin.

Jago's mouth hung open, then snapped shut. "Sorry. I didn't mean it like that. It's just that—"

"It's just that what?" Nat glared at him.

"Well, it's just that you're really talented. You should be in a place where you can meet other artists. Somewhere with culture, not some dead end town in the ass end of nowhere." He leaned forward. "Bad things happen in that place, Nat. You know that. So why are you choosing to stay?"

There was that question again. Why?

Nat already knew the answer. But she couldn't tell Jago. If she did, he'd finally understand what kind of person she truly was. The kind who ignored others in crisis. The kind who ignored pleas for help and let people die. People like Aaron Black.

Out of nowhere came an unbearable ache inside her chest that threatened to drag her down to the ground. She fought against it, pushing away with all her strength. She cleared her throat, felt the sting of tears in her eyes once more.

"Rose needs me right now," she said.

"Rose wants you to go to university and you know it."

Nat said nothing. She watched Noah, who was still beside the climbing frame, silently watching the other children play. She thought about going to London. She thought about staying in Porth an Jowl, where she'd never felt welcome and the locals stared at her short hair and tattoos with wide-eyed curiosity reserved for circus freak shows.

In London, she would be able to disappear. No one would judge her because in the city, weird was wonderful. And yet, the idea of being lost in a population of millions terrified her.

"You should go to London," Jago said.

"So should you. Wiltshire sounds boring as hell."

"I will. Eventually. But you should go now."

Nat glanced at Noah. The other children were staring at him, whispering to each other.

"You should come to the festival," Nat said. "You should bring Noah. Rose is organising all kinds of fun stuff for kids. It would be good for him."

Jago clenched his jaw as he continued to watch over his brother. "I'm never letting him near that fucking town again."

Shrugging, Nat pulled a tobacco pouch from her pocket, then remembering where she was, pushed open the gate to the play park and stepped back onto the promenade. As she stood, slowly rolling a cigarette, she watched Jago guide Noah over to the swings, where he lifted him onto the seat and began pushing him through the air.

The ache in her chest intensified. There had been a time when all she and Jago did was smoke cigarettes and stare out at the sea as they talked excitedly about their plans for the future. Everything was different now. Jago was leaving. Maybe that was a good thing. Their friendship had been waning for months now. Perhaps it had run its course. It happened sometimes; suddenly you ran out of things to say.

She lit her cigarette and drew smoke into her lungs. What did it matter that Jago was leaving? She'd been on her own for most of her life. It was easier that way. Besides, one less person in her life was one less person she had to worry about getting killed.

3

CARRIE SAT IN the living room with the curtains half drawn, nursing a mug of steaming coffee. Caffeine at this time of the day wasn't going to help with the insomnia, but sleep had started to feel a lot like a luxury meant for other people. At least she'd quit the booze.

With dinner done and Melissa playing upstairs in her room, Carrie watched the early evening news on television. The murders were dominating the show. A stern-faced newscaster in an expensive suit introduced the story, before the camera cut to idyllic images of Cornwall and the seaside town of Falmouth.

"Paul and Donna Church, along with their seventeen-year-old son, Todd, were found dead at their holiday home early this morning," a voice said over the visuals, which now cut to a shot of a modern, white house with a wide balcony overlooking the ocean. Police vans were parked outside. Tape cordoned off the area with uniformed officers standing guard. Crime Scene Investigators, dressed in imposing white coveralls and face masks, could be seen entering a large white tent that was pitched over the garden, suggesting that at least one of the bodies had been found on the lawn. "Devon and Cornwall police have yet to release any details of the killings other than the victims' names and this photograph of

Lindsay Church, who is still missing."

The programme cut to a school photograph of a feisty looking girl with wavy brown hair and a smattering of freckles across the bridge of her nose. Carrie's fingers tightened around her coffee mug. Aware that she was holding her breath, she gasped for air. The story continued, showing a group of police officers spread out and walking slowly in a perfect line as they scoured nearby fields and woods. Carrie had seen it all before, experienced it herself all those years ago when Cal had first disappeared. And again, last year, when Noah Pengelly had vanished. She suddenly felt dizzy and off-kilter, as if her own memories were being projected on the television screen.

"A search for the ten-year-old is now underway," the reporter continued in his monotone voice. "Meanwhile, the police are appealing for witnesses. Anyone with information should call Crime-stoppers on the following number. . ."

The field report ended and the camera cut back to the studio, where the newscaster continued the story. "Thank you, Charlie. Although we're still waiting on that statement from Devon and Cornwall police, there is some speculation that the Church family murders may be connected to the murder of former local councillor John Beaumont in December of last year.

"Beaumont and his young son Luke were abducted from their home. Mr Beaumont's burnt remains were found at an abandoned farm in January, following the discovery of video footage that captured his murder at the hands of Callum Anderson, as part of what appears to be a bizarre cult ritual. The footage was shot by crime writer Aaron Black, who was allegedly investigating Anderson's involvement with the group known as the Dawn Children. Mr Black subsequently vanished. His body was later recovered by local fishermen.

"As previously reported, Callum Anderson is a surviving victim of serial killer Grady Spencer, although it's now widely believed that Spencer had in fact been grooming Anderson to continue his deadly legacy. The seventeen-year-old is currently awaiting trial for the murder of John Beaumont and the attempted murder of his own grandmother, Sally Nance. Meanwhile, Luke Beaumont, who turned five in February, is still missing. We'll have more news for you later tonight. Now over to Susie for the weather. . ."

Carrie sat in stunned silence, mouth hanging open, heart thumping in her chest. Hearing her son's name mentioned on television again—in yet another murder report—sent waves of nausea coursing through her body. She leaned forward, fighting for air. Cal's crimes were old news now. Everyone in town—hell, the whole country—knew exactly what he'd done. They all knew what he'd been subjected to as well, but that part—where *he* had been a victim, where he'd been broken down and brainwashed—they'd all seemed to have conveniently forgotten about that. Now, here he was on television again and they were suggesting that these new murders were somehow connected to the man Cal had *allegedly* killed.

Carrie caught her breath. She was doing it again. Denying that her son was a killer. Even though she'd been there when he'd driven a knife into her mother's chest. Even though there was *video footage* of him killing Councillor Beaumont in a violent frenzy.

Guilt washed over her. Memories rushed in. She remembered being abducted by the Dawn Children from her home. Being locked in a cage at Burnt House Farm and left to die. But Cal had saved her life. He'd set her free. Chosen her over the Dawn Children.

And what had she done for him in return?

She'd driven Cal down to Land's End, where they'd sat on the cliff top and stared out to sea, her arm wrapped around him, pressing him into her side. They'd watched the sunset together in silence, mother and son. Then she'd driven him to the police station in Penzance, but it had been unmanned and she'd had to drive fifteen miles to the next station in Camborne. She had waited for Cal to jump from the car. For him to escape. But he'd just sat there in the passenger seat, head bowed and lifeless, as if he had already accepted his fate. And when the police had put him in handcuffs and taken him away, Carrie had collapsed on the ground and wept uncontrollably, screaming after him that she was sorry. But she had still felt hope for him. She'd still believed that Cal might one day come out of this intact.

Until Aaron Black's video footage had been discovered.

"Mummy?"

Carrie twisted around on the sofa. Melissa was in the living room doorway, eyes glued to the television screen. Carrie snatched up the remote. The television screen faded to black.

"Yes, sweet pea?" she said, aware that her voice was shrill and breathless. She cleared her throat. Forced a smile.

Melissa entered the room, her eyes still fixed on the screen. Carrie patted the empty seat beside her, but the girl didn't sit down. She stood there, staring listlessly, fingers twisting her hair in knots.

Carrie reached out to stroke Melissa's face. The girl flinched. "It's almost bedtime, sweet pea. What are we reading tonight?"

"Were they talking about Cal?" She had that look in her eyes again. Haunted and tired. Not the kind of look that should be seen on a child's face. "Is he coming home soon?"

Carrie tried to speak, but it was as if her throat had sealed up. She didn't want to have this conversation. Just the mention of Cal's name seemed to make Melissa regress to toddler age again, making her suck her thumb or talk in gibberish.

"I—" Carrie tried again. "I don't know when he's coming home."

The widening of Melissa's eyes told her it was not the answer she wanted to hear. And who could blame her? 'I don't know' didn't tell her anything. 'I don't know' said it could be tomorrow, next month, next year, or it could be never. There had been so much uncertainty in their lives lately. Far too much for a girl of Melissa's age. And everything she had witnessed—including her brother stabbing her grandmother in the chest—meant that all Melissa needed right now were cold, hard facts.

"We have to wait for the judge to decide what will happen with him," Carrie said, running fingers along Melissa's cheek as she tried to ignore the sting of her own words. "But I do know that whatever happens, Cal won't be coming home for a very long time."

Melissa's shoulders softened a little. She let out a long, shaky sigh.

"Good," she said.

It was like a slap to Carrie's face. Yet it was understandable. In the brief time that Melissa had known Cal, all he'd done was rip her family apart.

Carrie swallowed. Her eyes flicked to the drinks cabinet, which she'd emptied months ago, then back to her daughter.

"So, which story? And please, don't say Frozen."

Melissa was quiet, staring at her with an intensity that made her squirm.

"If Cal does come back home," she said, "I'm going to go and live with Daddy and Grandpa Gary and Nana Joy."

Another slap. But Carrie took it. How could she not? Wrapping her arms around her daughter, she brought her close and kissed the top of her head.

"Everything's going to be fine," she soothed, as her gaze wandered back to the television screen. "Everything's going to be as right as rain."

4

THE SPOT WHERE Grady Spencer's house had once stood was now a flattened expanse of soil and stone, cordoned off by temporary metal fencing. It was as if the earth had suddenly swallowed the house whole, leaving behind a dark stain as a reminder of all the unutterable horror that had been inflicted within its walls.

Forensics had put the final body count at fifteen; fourteen of whom had been children, the other a journalist who'd unwittingly stumbled upon Spencer's lair. All the identified victims had now been returned to their families to be laid to rest. There were no set rules about what to do with unidentified remains. The National Crime Agency recommended recording dental information and extracting DNA before burying them in single, marked graves, in case later exhumation was required. But with these unidentified children, it seemed no one wanted to rob their parents of a proper burial, so their remains continued to be stored at the morgue.

Before Spencer's house had been destroyed, Nat had come close to burning it down. Living next door to where children had been tortured and murdered right under her nose had left her feeling sick every time she walked by. One night in January, she'd downed most of a bottle of vodka, then filled the bottle with oil. She'd made her way to the back of Spencer's house and stood in the yard, lighter in one hand, Molotov cocktail in the other, rage and horror burning in her veins. It was only when a moment's sobriety had forced her to realise how close Spencer's house was to her own, where Rose slept inside, that she quickly tossed the bottle away.

The bulldozers arrived in March and made quick work of the house. The abandoned Mermaid Hotel, where remains of Spencer's victims had also been found, was next to go, leaving behind an empty space at the top of the left cliff that Nat couldn't help but notice every time she made her way into town.

Finally, the labyrinth of dark tunnels that connected both sites was filled in with rubble, erasing all traces of Grady Spencer from Porth an Jowl. All except one.

Nat stood at the edge of Grenville Row, staring at the plot of dark earth. The town council was still trying to decide what to do with the empty site. Someone had suggested building a memorial park, but the thought of sitting on top of the place where multiple children had been murdered had vetoed the idea almost immediately. For now, it remained an empty space next to Nat's home, which in some ways felt more of a reminder of what had happened than when the house had still been standing.

Nat was in a foul mood. She'd been excited to see Jago, but the realisation that their friendship was no longer the same had left a bitter taste at the back of her throat.

And now he was leaving.

She didn't even know if she'd see him again before he and his family were gone for good.

Rose was in the kitchen, her portly frame moving back and forth between the cooker and the table as she prepared dinner. As Nat entered, Rose glanced up, then busied herself with stirring a pot.

"Do my eyes deceive me? Is that Natalie Tremaine *on time* for dinner?"

"That joke's getting almost as old as you."

"How was Penzance?"

"Fine, I guess."

"You don't sound like it was fine. How's Jago?"

"Skinny. He had Noah with him."

"That dear little boy? How's he doing now? And Tess? You want to set the table for me?"

Nat dumped her backpack on a chair. Normally when she came home, Rose would greet her with big warm smiles, but right now it was as if the woman was struggling to look at her. Slouching her way over to the cutlery drawer, Nat frowned. "Noah's not looking so good. From what Jago said, their mum is still self-medicating."

"Well, that woman's been to hell and back," Rose said, wiping her hands on her apron. She glanced up, then away again. "As for that little boy, it's going to take time to get over it."

"I guess. Anyway, they're leaving. Moving to Wiltshire of all places."

"They are? Well, that's some news. But good news, I think. A fresh start is probably best."

Finished setting the table, Nat looked up to see Rose staring strangely at her again. "Is everything all right? You seem . . . weird."

"I'm fine, girl. It's you that's got a face like a wet weekend."

"That's my natural expression. It's called resting bitch face." Nat rubbed the back of her neck. "Seriously, what is it? You look worried."

"I told you, I'm fine. Now wash your hands. Dinner's ready."

Nat did as she was told. Rose served up plates of lamb stew and dumplings; not one of Nat's favourites, but she accepted it gratefully.

She wasn't feeling particularly hungry though, thoughts from the afternoon souring her appetite. Rose was right, of course; after all the horrors the Pengelly family had endured, it was a wonder they hadn't lost their minds. As she speared a chunk of meat, she thought about Jago. He'd taken a life. Sliced Grady Spencer's throat wide open. Even though that sick bastard had deserved it, Nat couldn't help wondering if killing him had affected Jago in some profound, permanent way. Was that why he was so different now? So distant. Was it the reason their friendship had drifted off course and crashed onto rocks?

"I was telling the new neighbours all about Devil's Day, this morning," Rose said, pulling Nat's focus back to the room. "They didn't seem the slightest bit interested. I suppose they're not from the cove, so they don't understand our traditions. Still, it's nice that someone's finally living in the Pengelly's old house. Between them moving out and . . . well, everything to do with next door, it's nice to have some new faces on our street, don't you think?" She paused for a sip of water and peered across the table. Nat stared back, saw Rose flinch and glance down at her plate. "Are you going to eat that food I spent the last hour cooking for you or are you just going to play with it?"

Nat blew air through her nose, leaned forward and speared a chunk of potato with her fork. She held it up for Rose to see, then swallowed it. She didn't care what Rose said out loud. The way she kept looking at Nat was making her worry.

Maybe she was just concerned about Jago leaving. She did always fuss over Nat, like her feelings were made of glass. Sometimes she wished Rose didn't care so much. At least she wasn't like Nat's parents, who had cared so little that she had the scars and burns to prove it. Social services had taken her from them with no question of ever being returned. She'd been moved from foster home to foster home, with each carer complaining that her attitude and temper were unmanageable.

And then she'd been housed with Rose. Nat had hated her to begin with. She had strict rules and terrible taste in home decoration. But she had allowed Nat to have bad days. She'd given her space when she'd needed to be alone. And when Nat had acted up—breaking the rules, calling Rose every terrible name she could think of, doing all that typical teenage shit multiplied by a thousand—Rose had forgiven her.

The woman was stubborn and superstitious and had a worrying obsession with floral print, but she was also kind and thoughtful and full of love. It made Nat uncomfortable sometimes. It made her want to lash out, to scream at Rose that she'd got it all wrong—that Nat Tremaine wasn't someone you cared about but someone you were meant to hate. Other times, Rose's love for her was overwhelming to the point that just thinking about it filled her eyes with tears. Like recently. Nat had turned eighteen two months ago, which meant she was no longer a ward of the state. Rose had told her in no uncertain terms that this was her home now. It would always be her home, no matter whether she chose to stay or go.

Which was why Rose's odd behaviour was making Nat increasingly concerned.

"When are the Pengellys off, then?" she asked, if sensing Nat was unsatisfied with her brush off.

"In a few weeks."

"So soon? You'll miss Jago when he goes."

"Not really. I mean, it's not like we hang out anymore."

"I don't believe that."

"Some friendships run their course. Jago's got his hands full with his family. He doesn't have time for me anymore, I get it. Anyway, now that he's leaving it doesn't matter."

"People always need friends," Rose said. "People always need someone they can depend on."

Nat shrank in her chair as Aaron Black's face flashed in her mind. He'd depended on her. He'd needed her help, but she hadn't given it to him. Now Aaron was dead.

"I have a feeling your friendship with Jago ain't over yet," Rose said with a smile. "I have a feeling your paths will cross again when you both move to London."

Nat grabbed her glass of water and gulped it down, wishing it was something stronger. But alcohol was off-limits right now. Getting caught drunk on campus had sent Nat straight to the college principal's office. There was concern that she and her grades were slipping off the rails, and while it was understandable that recent life events had affected her deeply, ruining all the hard work she'd put into the past two years was not an acceptable outcome. Nat had turned down the offer of counselling but had promised Rose no more drinking.

At least, not until college was over.

Rose set down her fork and rested her hands on the table. She was watching Nat again, making her neck muscles twist and knot.

"I know you don't like hearing it," she said, "but I honestly think the best thing you can do is get out of this place. Go to London like you planned. I've got some money saved. We can find somewhere for you to live, get you a little job. I know you don't want to go to university, and maybe you don't need to, but sitting around this place, growing old and bitter won't do you any good." She watched

Nat carefully. "And stewing about what happened to Aaron Black will only drive you mad."

Nat sat up, shoulders stiffening and her breath catching in her throat.

"I'm not stupid," Rose said, eyes softening. "I know you blame yourself. I know we never talk about it. But I can see it in your eyes, girl. They've had a dullness since he passed. That's understandable, but no matter how much you think you're to blame, you're not. Bad people are. And you are not bad."

Tears were filling Nat's eyes fast.

"You don't know what you're talking about," she said through clenched teeth.

"Yes I do, and you know it."

But the truth was that Rose didn't. She had no idea.

"Anyway," Nat said. "If I left, what would you do without me?"

"I expect I'd manage. I'd miss you, but I'd be happy knowing you were doing something with your life."

"London's expensive. You couldn't afford to send me there."

"Good job you're saving all that money from your job then, isn't it?"

Nat sank lower in her seat. She was feeling bad enough without having to be reminded of the caravan park, which was about to become a full-time summer job from hell.

"Maybe I'm saving up for a boob job."

Rose rolled her eyes. "And I'm Marilyn Monroe. Finish your dinner, then you best get upstairs to study. You've still got one more exam to go."

"Not for another two weeks, I don't."

"I'm being serious."

52

Nat clenched her jaw. "Is that what this is all about?"

"What's what all about?"

"This weird mood you're in. The way you can barely look at me right now. Trying to send me off to London. Don't you want me around anymore?"

"Don't be ridiculous! You know how I feel about you."

"Then what the hell is it?"

Rose set her cutlery down with a clatter. She stared at Nat, square on this time, and heaved her round shoulders. "I didn't want to tell you—but you'll find out sooner or later. Some people have been killed. Over in Falmouth. A family was murdered and the daughter was taken."

Nat's blood ran cold. Images flashed in her mind. Grainy video footage captured on a mobile phone. "Why were you trying to hide that from me?"

"Because on the news they're saying they think it's connected to that group. The one Mr Black filmed."

Nat's heart was racing, her chest growing tight. More images assaulted her. The interior of a barn. Children gathered in a circle. A beaten, bruised man begging for his life.

The desperate pleas of Aaron Black's voicemail filled Nat's ears. She stared at Rose, who had taken to wringing her hands.

"I didn't want to tell you because I don't want you to worry," Rose said. "There's no evidence. It's just speculation. The police haven't even released a statement. Anyway, I'm sure it won't be long before they catch whoever is responsible. Cornwall is small— whoever did it will soon be running out of places to hide."

Except Cornwall is remote, Nat thought. With hundreds, if not thousands, of places to hide. And she already knew who was responsible. Rose did, too. Aaron Black's video had revealed their name.

The Dawn Children.

"Try not to worry," Rose said.

Nat shrugged. "I'm not worried."

Her pulse was racing. Pins and needles were pricking the inside of her skull.

"Good. Because I don't want you getting any ideas."

"What do you mean?"

Rose leaned in. "You know full well what I mean, or have you forgotten about the stress you put me through when you disappeared like you did?"

Guilt stabbed Nat in the chest. "Don't worry, I'm not going to do that again."

"I want you to stay away, you hear me? I don't want you to even think about what I've told you. You've been through enough and I don't want you fretting over this whole awful business any more than you already do. What's in the past is in the past. All you need to do now is keep your head in those study books and your eyes on the future. Got it?"

Nat's heart was pounding. She stared at Rose across the table and slowly nodded. "Got it."

"Then eat up and I don't want to hear any more about it."

"Sure. Of course."

Nat ate, mechanically chewing each mouthful. The inside of her skull was itching. Blood rushed in her ears.

Was it true?

Had the Dawn Children slaughtered that family and taken their daughter?

Six months ago, they'd disappeared from the face of the earth. She'd gone looking for them. Spent the best part of a month searching, leaving Rose frantic at home and on the edge of a breakdown. But it was as if they had only ever existed within the frames of Aaron Black's video footage. Nat had been desperate to find the Dawn Children. She'd been desperate to make them pay for what they'd done. More than that, she'd been determined to ensure that Aaron Black hadn't died in vain.

Had the Dawn Children come back?

She hoped to God that it was a terrible coincidence. But deep down inside her, she already knew the truth.

5

HEATH STOOD ON the cliff edge, watching the dying embers of the day. The sun had almost disappeared over the edge of the horizon, submerging into the ocean's watery depths. Above him, stars were beginning to wake. Soon, it would be dark. And out here, the darkness was absolute. A breeze blew up from below to tickle his skin, teasing goose bumps to the surface of his arms. A despairing ache pulled at his insides. Last night's attack had gone as planned, but not as he'd hoped. He had taken the boy's life. Watched it drain from the hole in his neck like water from a bath. For a moment, Heath yearned for Jacob's guidance. It had been months since their leader had vanished. Months since they'd been forced to leave Burnt House Farm and find a new home. For a while, they'd travelled from place to place, living like scavengers off the land. Until Heath had stumbled upon the abandoned military base. Until he had taken charge.

Jacob was lost to them. They could only assume that he was dead, leaving the children vulnerable to the dangers of the outside world. It was why Heath had stepped up. There was no one else; no one strong enough or with a clear vision of what Jacob had planned. No one else who could lead the children into the New Dawn. But there was responsibility with leadership and it weighed on his shoulders constantly. Sometimes he yearned for the days when all he had to do was take orders and carry them out willingly. But those days were gone and now the burden of leadership was his alone.

He heaved his shoulders, watching the ocean churn far below.

"Heath?"

The voice startled him, but he kept his gaze firm on the rise and fall of the waves. A memory came to him. He was small, no older than three or four, sitting on the floor of a dirty living room, puke on the carpet and a bloody syringe balanced on a wrap of foil within easy reach. There was a dog with him. *His* dog. The dog's name was Scamp and he was lying on his side, fast asleep, paws making little jerking movements as Heath watched the animal's ribcage rise and fall, hypnotised by it in the same way he was now hypnotised by the sea below him.

"Heath?"

He flicked his gaze upwards, where stars were blinking awake in a sky that stretched as far as the eye could see. Morwenna came up beside him, her long hair whipping about in the breeze.

"I've been looking for you," she said, following his gaze. "Is everything okay?"

Heath glanced at her, noting her worried expression. He returned to staring at the horizon. "Everything is fine."

He could still feel her eyes upon him, analysing his body language. The ache in his chest grew heavier, dragging him an inch closer towards the cliff edge.

"How's the girl?"

Morwenna blew air through her nose. "A handful. But she'll learn." She looked at him again, searching his face. "Are you sure you're all right?"

"I said I'm fine." But then Morwenna was wrapping her arms around his waist and resting her head against his shoulder.

"It's because we killed the boy, isn't it? Because it goes against everything that Jacob taught us."

Heath lowered his head and whispered, "Children are innocent. It's adults who poison the world."

"Even so, you had no choice."

"Didn't I?" He tried to pull away from her, but Morwenna held fast.

"That boy was at an age where he'd already been poisoned. He would never have joined us; not after watching his father. . . But the girl is young enough to be saved. And she's strong. But do we have time to try? We're only a week away."

A gust of wind blew up from the sea, making Heath shiver.

"We didn't even try with him," he said. "Jacob would have, don't you think? I wonder if he would be disappointed in us?"

"What Jacob thinks doesn't matter anymore. He isn't here. And even if he was, he would have done exactly the same. That boy would have fought us. He would have put everything that we stand for at risk. If you want to blame someone for his death, blame his selfish father. What kind of father allows his children to die just to save himself?"

It seemed that in the minute they'd been talking, the last of the daylight had abandoned the sky. Stars glittered. The breeze grew stronger, the sea louder. A few miles down the coast, where the land curved sharply to the right, a lighthouse beam sliced through the darkness. Heath watched it, anger igniting in the pit of his stomach as he pictured the town that lay beyond, tucked away inside a cove. He snuffed it out. There would be time for anger. For retribution.

But this was not it.

"Anyway," Morwenna said, reaching up to stroke his cheek. "I came to find you because there's a problem with Luke. Alison says he won't eat and now he's stopped talking."

Heath turned his back on the horizon and stared at the two-metre chain-link fence and the shadowy buildings that huddled together beyond. "Where are they now?"

"Getting ready for bed." Morwenna slipped her hand into his and squeezed. "There's no room for weakness, Heath. Only the strong can bring in the New Dawn."

"Only the strong can bring salvation." It was Jacob's mantra.

Heath stared at Morwenna in the darkness and saw her eyes reflecting the burgeoning moonlight. Together they walked away from the cliff, ducking down to prevent their clothes from snagging as they climbed through a hole in the fence. Following a cement path, they made their way between rows of long, single-storey bunkers with curved roofs, until they came to the last one on the left. Entering the building, they were immediately plunged into shadows. Morwenna let go of Heath's hand and fumbled in her pocket. A spark of light flashed between them as she held up a cigarette lighter and reached towards a shelf of LED lanterns. Winding one up, she handed it to Heath, then lit another for herself.

"You go on," she said. "I'll check on the girl."

She kissed him, then turned to leave. Heath held on to her.

"Are we ready for what's coming, Morwenna? For what needs to be done? All these children, they're counting on me to save them. But I can't do that without your help."

Stepping closer, Morwenna kissed him again, longer this time. "You don't have to worry about me. I know what needs to be done.

And I have an idea that will guarantee our crossing."

"What is it?"

She smiled in the lantern light. "Not now. Later."

Then she was gone, darting along the corridor, glancing over her shoulder. Heath drew in a deep breath, felt the ache dragging at his chest again, then pushed open the second door on the right. It was a large room with bunk beds lining both sides. Lanterns sat on upturned boxes, casting a warm glow over a gaggle of children of varying ages, who should have all been clambering over each other and making a din. But they were silent now, listless and sullen. They'd been like that since Jacob had vanished, and nothing Heath had tried so far had been able to bring back their light.

Alison was stooped over the furthest bunk, tucking a young girl into bed. Noticing Heath, she kissed the girl on the cheek, then went over to join him.

"What's the problem?" he asked.

In the lantern light, Alison's thin frame was pale and gaunt, lank hair draping past her shoulders. She was a year or two older than Heath and Morwenna, but unlike them, Alison had always been sensitive in nature and better suited to taking care of the younger children rather than fighting on the front-line.

"It's Luke," she whispered.

Glancing over Alison's shoulder, Heath spied a young boy sitting on a lower bunk bed with his knees pulled up to his chin and his large, hollow eyes staring blankly at the wall.

"Morwenna said he isn't eating."

"Not for three days now. This morning, I had to practically force water down his throat. He's stopped talking, too. It's like he's given up."

"Alison, I'm cold!" one of the children complained behind her. "I need more blankets."

"There aren't any, so you'll just have to snuggle," she said, before turning back to Heath. "It's not normal for a boy Luke's age to behave like this. It's been months since he joined us. He should be used to this life by now."

Heath's eyes were still fixed on the boy. He remembered taking him from his home. Remembered encouraging Cal to knock the boy's father unconscious while the child watched from the stairs. *Cal.* He didn't want to think about him. Didn't want that name poisoning his mind like a cancer. If it hadn't been for Cal's betrayal, or Jacob's foolish, unwavering belief in him, they would still be at Burnt House Farm and not living like urchins off the land, without electricity or warmth, or enough food.

"That boy needs to toughen up," Heath said through clenched teeth. "This world is Hell and the New Dawn is at hand. He can't cross over if he's weak. He needs to learn that. Fast."

Alison shook her head. "He's too young to understand. All he knows is that he was taken away from his family and his father was killed."

"Punished," Heath corrected. Lantern light flickered in his dark eyes. "He was a rapist of children and he got what he deserved. We *saved* that boy. He should be grateful."

Alison's gaze dropped to the floor. "Even so, whatever's going on with him, it's nothing good. If he doesn't eat, he'll get sick. If he gets sick, he'll need a doctor."

"Then make him eat."

"It's not that easy. He doesn't want to be here, Heath. It's like he's broken." She glanced over her shoulder at the boy, who was far too thin and far too still for a child of his age. "What if we took him somewhere? We could drop him off at a hospital then disappear."

Heath glared at her. "So that he can tell everyone where we are? Tell everyone our names and what we look like? Have you lost your fucking mind?"

Alison stared at the ground again. "I don't think he would do that. I don't think he's well enough to—"

"Thinking and doing are two different things." Heath glared at the boy. He should have learned by now to follow the rules; that in this world, children like him were exploited and abused, then discarded, their bodies dumped in gutters. "We can't take him to a hospital. We can't take him anywhere without the risk of him exposing us. Then all the work that we've done—all the work Jacob has led us to do—will be for nothing."

"Then what do we do?" Fear had crept into Alison's voice. "We just let him starve to death? Let him lose his mind? Jacob would never agree to that. Jacob says children are sacred and we must do everything to protect them."

"Jacob abandoned us. I'm in charge now. And if that boy doesn't eat," he shoved a finger in Luke's direction, "if he can't follow the rules, then he's not one of us. And if he's not one of us, it means he's against us. Child or no child." He leaned in closer, feeling his breath bounce off Alison's skin. "The New Dawn is almost here. Are you with us or against us?"

He felt her muscles inching away from him. Sensed fear dripping from every pore. *Good*, he thought. *Know your place.*

"Of course I'm with you," Alison whispered. Behind her, Luke was still sitting on the bed, staring emptily into space, slowly disappearing into the shadows. The other children were sitting up, silently watching the adults. "I'll take care of it. I'll make him eat."

"See that you do," Heath said. "Or I'll take care of it myself."

He left the room, ignoring one of the children who called out goodnight to him. Shutting the door with one hand and holding up the lantern with the other, he stood in the corridor and stared into the darkness.

Would Jacob have said the same thing? Would he have been so heartless? Or would Jacob have sat with the boy and spoken gently to him? Nurtured and cared for him until he felt safe and sound? Until he felt like he belonged.

The dull ache in his chest pulled at him. Jacob was gone. The world was cold and cruel. Nurture and kindness were not weapons he could use. They let the world rip you to shreds and swallow you until there was nothing left. No, in a violent world, cruelty was the only means of survival.

Heath stared into the shadows. Then froze. He felt eyes watching him from the darkness. Spinning around, he held up the lantern. A middle-aged woman with a shock of red hair and a pale, haunted face stood beside a row of lockers, staring at him.

"What are you doing, Cynthia?" Heath said, feeling the ache in his chest start to burn.

The woman watched him. For a second, hate lit up her eyes. Then she glanced away, staring at her feet.

"Nothing," she whispered. "I was just coming to say goodnight to the children."

"Well, don't keep them long. There's work to do in the morning."

They stood in silence, shadows circling them. Then Cynthia said, "I heard there's a new girl."

"Nothing for you to worry about."

"But I hear she's in a cell. Shouldn't she be with the other children?"

Heath stared at her, eyes straining in the half-light. Fucking Cynthia. Always questioning him. Thinking she knew better because she was an adult. Thinking she had authority because Jacob had stuck his dick in her. Like she'd been the only one.

"Say goodnight to the children or leave them be," he spat.

He turned his back on her and continued down the corridor. Cynthia's voice made him freeze.

"Jacob would have put her with the others. He would have let their joy be her welcome and comfort."

Heath got going again. He could still feel the woman's disapproving eyes burning into his neck long after he'd entered his room and slipped into Morwenna's arms. He could still feel them as the two of them rutted on the bed, then collapsed in a tangled heap. And when he eventually fell asleep, he dreamed of Cynthia's eyes searing through his flesh to reveal a scared little boy curled up like a foetus inside.

Heath would show her what it meant to be strong and powerful. He would show the world what a mighty leader looked like. And when the New Dawn came—and it was just days away now—he would lead all his children into the light.

6

COVE HOLIDAY PARK sat at the very top of Porth an Jowl and boasted stunning, panoramic views of the ocean to the west and rolling green fields to the east. The site itself was made up of rows of static white caravans that looked like leftovers from a trailer park rather than the luxurious accommodation advertised in promotional brochures. But they were comfortable and clean enough if space and privacy weren't priorities.

Nat stalked between a row of caravans, a mop and bucket in her hands and a curled sneer on her lips. It was nine a.m. on Saturday morning and she was feeling irritable as hell. She'd been awake much of the night, thoughts churning her mind. The sleep she did get had been plagued by nightmares.

The Dawn Children were back. But now, instead of trying to find them, she was stuck here cleaning caravans.

With school still in session, most of the holidaymakers were either childless or older, their children all grown up. It was a small mercy, Nat supposed, as she glared at a white-haired couple who were heading out for the day. In a few weeks' time the park would be a deafening cacophony of tears and arguments and whining, with snotty kids running around her.

Heaving her shoulders, she made her way to the nearest caravan, set the bucket down, and hammered on the door. A moment later, the door opened, revealing a middle-aged man with thinning hair and a paunch. His congenial expression soured as he saw a girl with a freshly shaved scalp, black skinny jeans and a heavy-metal t-shirt, glaring at him.

"You want your room cleaned?" she barked.

"Um. . ." the man said, struggling to find his voice.

Nat huffed. Shifted her weight from one side to the other. "A yes or no would be helpful."

The man swallowed. Shook his head.

"Right answer." Nat stalked away, heading to the next caravan. Why did weekend jobs always suck? There was never anything cool like an artist's assistant. Even a job serving popcorn at a cinema would have been better than cleaning up other people's crap. As she stopped outside the next caravan, she heard Rose's sing-song voice in her mind: *Beggars can't be choosers!*

"Sure. Whatever, Rose." Blowing out a frustrated breath, she raised her hand to hammer on the caravan door.

"Natalie! Is that you? Where's your apron?"

A large, sweaty man in his early fifties was marching towards her. Dennis Penpol, son of local gossip Dottie Penpol. Proprietor of Cove Holiday Park and current pain in Nat's ass.

She watched him approach, unable to hide her disdain as he huffed and puffed, meaty arms swinging at his sides, his beady eyes fixed on her like she was something he'd just stepped in. Coming to a halt, he thrust his hands on his hips.

"Well? Where is it? It's not like I haven't told you a hundred times already," he said, his voice thick and raspy.

Nat shrugged. "It's in the wash."

"You were given two aprons. Don't you have the mental capacity to work out that you wash one, wear one? It's not rocket science, is it?" Dennis shook his head. Nat's grip on the bucket handle grew tighter. "And while we're on the subject of dress code, you can't be cleaning caravans dressed like you're about to sacrifice a baby on a full moon. Some nice blue jeans and a blouse will do, not this heavy metal chic, or whatever you youngsters call it these days. Get yourself over to the office right now and grab a spare apron from one of the lockers. At least that'll cover up whatever the hell *that* is."

He jabbed a stubby finger at Nat's chest. She stared down at the image on her t-shirt—a zombie with both hands held up, rotten middle fingers folded over to make horn signs—then back up at Dennis. Personally, she found his face more offensive. She resisted the urge to punch it. The only reason Nat had a job right now was because Rose had talked Dottie Penpol into persuading Dennis to employ her. No one else in the cove would give her a job; not even the idiots at The Shack beach bar, with most citing that Nat's appearance would intimidate the tourists, while others thought her social skills weren't exactly conducive to great customer service.

If she were to smack Dennis Penpol square in the face right now, Rose would never forgive her. Besides, as much as Nat hated every minute of working at the caravan park, it put money in her pocket, and that meant she could contribute to the household bills.

"Are you even listening to me, Natalie?" Dennis said, his red face growing a shade deeper.

Nat grunted. "Loud and clear."

"Good. Perhaps Rose has managed to drum some sense into you, after all. You're very lucky to have her, you know. Otherwise you'd have gone off the rails a long time ago."

Nat clenched her jaw. Perhaps she could get away with a quick slap of an open palm to the bridge of his nose.

"Tomorrow, you'll wear more sensible clothing," Dennis said. "Or I'll have to reconsider your employment."

Or perhaps a karate chop to the throat.

Nat grunted again, then strode past him, mop and bucket swinging violently in her hands. She heard him mutter something behind her, but she continued on, knowing that if she stopped right now not only would she be out of a job, but up on a murder charge. Stalking past more caravans, she reached the office; a one-storey portable cabin that had seen better days. She threw open the door, stomped inside, dropped the bucket and mop to the ground, then stood for a minute, quietly seething.

"Fucking prick. Stupid asshole."

People like Dennis Penpol had given Nat a hard time her whole life. Did he really think he was going to break her with a few harsh words? She cast an eye around the cramped room. Penpol's desk sat in one corner, a mess of paperwork and dirty cups covering its surface. An old, yellowed nude calendar hung on the wall, a topless woman with big hair staring provocatively at Nat. *Miss April 2008.* Probably the last time Dennis got laid. Wrinkling her nose, Nat crossed the room and pulled open one of three lockers. A row of identical aprons hung inside. She pulled one out, sneering as she examined the pink and lilac floral print.

Freeing the apron from the hanger and swearing under her breath, Nat pulled it over her head. A mirror hung on the wall and she stared at her reflection in horror. At least no one she cared about would see her in such nauseating garb. Not that there were many people she cared about. Her face burning, Nat stooped to pick up the mop and bucket. She froze, noticing the cup of coffee on the edge of the desk. She pressed her hand against the porcelain. Still warm. Smiling, she glanced over at the door, then leaned down and hawked a stringy globule of spit into the coffee.

"Choke on it, you dick."

There were more people outside now, heading for the shower block or out for the day. Nat ignored them all, keeping her eyes fixed on the ground ahead, feeling the weight of the apron around her neck, even though it weighed barely anything at all.

As she drew closer to her section of caravans, she saw a flash of blonde out the corner of her eye and heard someone laugh.

"Nice outfit."

Shoulder muscles tensing, Nat slowly looked up. She'd been expecting one of the other Saturday cleaners; air-headed sixteen-year-olds who worked for a pittance and whom she avoided like the plague. But it was a young woman, possibly eighteen or nineteen, maybe older, with wavy blonde hair and a curious face that was all sharp angles.

She stood in front of one of the caravans, wearing a faded *Panic! At The Disco* tour t-shirt, a pair of black denim shorts that cut off mid-thigh, and heavy black Dr Martens on her feet. She flashed a smile at Nat, who immediately glanced away.

"They really make you wear that?" the young woman said, smiling again. "Isn't that abuse or something?"

Nat stared down at the flowery aberration and felt her face burn hotter. She wanted nothing more than to be back at home and hiding under her bedsheets.

"I—" she began.

The young woman stepped forward. "Sorry. I was just walking by and saw your boss giving you a rough time. What a twat."

Nat stared at her again, but only for a moment. "Is there something you need? Because I need to clean."

"There is something, actually. I stupidly agreed to go on holiday with my dad and step-bitch when I should have stayed at home and enjoyed the silence. But they guilt-tripped me into it, said it would be good for me. So here I am and my god, I'm so fucking bored! Please enlighten me—what the hell do people our age do for fun around here?"

Nat glanced over her shoulder. She saw Dennis in the distance, his intimidating size bearing down on one of the other cleaners. Hopefully one of these days, he'd have a heart attack and die. Sooner rather than later.

She turned back to the blonde, young woman, whose eyes were an intense blue-grey fenced in by severe but expertly-applied slashes of eyeliner.

"Fun?" Nat snorted. "The most fun to have around here is plotting your grand escape."

"Great. Good to know. What about booze? If I'm stuck here, I may as well get obliterated."

"There's an off-license in town. Then there's The Shack. It's a beach bar, but I wouldn't waste your time. It's mostly full of assholes and tourists. No offence."

"At being called an asshole or a tourist?"

"Um, I didn't—"

The young woman smiled. "I'm kidding. What's your name?"

"Nat."

"I'm Rachel."

Nat stared down at her open hand. Slowly, she reached out and shook it.

"You from around here, Nat?"

"Not originally, but I live down there in Porth an Jowl."

Rachel dug her hands into her jeans pockets, then pulled them out and let them drop to her sides. "I'm sorry. Here I am complaining about being stuck here for a week and you actually have to live in this hell hole. No offence."

"None taken, believe me."

"How come all the towns have weird names around here, anyway?"

"It's the Cornish language. Porth an Jowl means—"

"Devil's Cove."

Nat stared at her. "You know?"

"Everyone knows that..." Rachel's smile faded. "But my parents aren't like those other freaks that come here to see where it all happened. The only reason we're in Porth an Whatever is because they're skinflints and the caravan park was cheap." Her smile returned, but this time it had a curious edge. "Were you here? When—"

"I don't want to talk about that," Nat said, her voice sharp and angry. For a second, she was no longer at the caravan park, but in her bedroom late at night, getting drunk and drawing terrible pictures of Aaron Black.

Rachel stared at the ground. "I'm sorry. I didn't mean to..." She looked up again and Nat felt guilt pinch her stomach harder.

"Forget it," she said. "I'd be curious, too. Anyway, I'd better get back to work."

"Wait. What time do you finish? My parents are off to St. Ives for the day, but I'd much rather grab some beers and hang out. You

71

in?"

"I—" Nat began. Five caravans over, Dennis had finished tearing strips off the young man and was now stalking his way back to the office. She watched him disappear, then glanced at Rachel. "I—I can't."

"Oh." Rachel's smile faded and it was like the sun being smothered by clouds.

"It's just that my fost—Rose, she's expecting me. There's this local festival coming up. Devil's Day? I'm supposed to be helping out with painting banners and making stuff."

"Devil's Day? That doesn't sound satanic at all. What's it about?"

Nat shrugged. "Some stupid celebration to do with a local legend. Honestly, it's boring. A bunch of annoying school kids parading through the street along with a shitty brass band, while everyone else gets drunk and throws up over the town square."

"Awesome," Rachel said, her sullenness quickly evaporated. "You're making banners? You like art?"

"It's okay, I guess. I mean, I paint all the time, so. . ."

Nat gasped as Rachel reached out and grasped her wrist.

"That's some pretty cool art right there," she said, exposing the forearm. Nat tensed but didn't resist as Rachel ran a finger along her skin. "I like this one. That's a cool dragon."

"Um . . . yeah. I designed it myself."

"You did? So you're a real artist? Impressive." Rachel let go of Nat's arm, and instead pinned her with a gaze. "You sure I can't tempt you? You could give me a tour and then we could get drunk and throw stuff at seagulls."

Nat hesitated. "Sorry. I promised."

"Bummer. In that case I'd better get ready for a riveting day out in St. Ives. At least it's not raining. That's something, right?"

Nat nodded. The burning in her cheeks had finally settled down to an embarrassing glow. Rachel was intense and seemed to know nothing about personal boundaries, but there was something about her that had piqued Nat's curiosity. She was from the outside, and she didn't seem intimidated by Nat in the slightest. Besides, it wasn't as if there was anyone else to hang out with, especially now her friendship with Jago had come to an end. She stared down at her feet, ignoring the floral glare of her apron.

"If you want, you can come along and help make banners for the festival. We'll be working on them today and tomorrow at the town hall. It's on Harbour Road. Which is . . . by the harbour. "

"We?"

"Just me and a bunch of annoying brats, so. . ."

Aware she was sounding too desperate, Nat shut up.

Rachel flashed another smile. "I guess I should go to St. Ives with my parents. After all, it's the first day of our holiday. But maybe tomorrow?"

"Cool."

"Yeah. Well, it was nice meeting you, Nat. Don't get shit on that apron."

With one last smile, Rachel turned and sauntered away.

Cheeks flushing, Nat watched her disappear, relieved that Rachel wasn't staying in her section of caravans. At least that would save her the embarrassment of having to clean in front of her. She stared down at the apron again and her bad mood returned.

"Fucking Dennis." She moved to the nearest caravan and hammered on the door. As she let herself inside, she peered over her shoulder and wondered if she would see Rachel tomorrow at the town hall. It would be nice to have someone else to talk to instead of a bunch of whiny kids, even for an hour. She just hoped that Rachel wasn't another so-called 'dark tourist', eager to hear all about the life and crimes of Grady Spencer, or his psychotic protégé, Cal Anderson. Because that would truly suck.

7

CARRIE SAT IN the waiting area, arms crossed, knees folded, foot tapping on the ground. On the plastic chair next to her, Melissa was sitting cross-legged and was currently conducting a wrestling match between two dolls. They'd been here for almost twenty minutes now, Carrie's shoulders slowly turning into knots and Melissa growing bored and restless, huffing and puffing as she played. Hanging out at the police station in Truro had not been part of their Saturday morning plan, but ever since Carrie had heard about the Church family murders and the abduction of Lindsay Church, her mind had been wandering into some very dark places. Places she'd vowed never to revisit.

At last, a door opened and a man in his early forties stepped out. Detective Constable Will Turner. He was handsome and smartly presented, wearing a charcoal coloured suit with a crisp, white shirt beneath. But around his eyes were the dark circles of someone who hadn't slept.

Carrie got to her feet. "I'll be one minute, sweet pea. Stay right here."

Melissa shrugged a shoulder and blew out another sigh.

"Carrie, how nice to see you," DC Turner said, meeting her halfway and extending a hand. "How are you?"

Now that she was up close, she saw just how tired he really looked. No doubt yesterday's murders and abduction had the force pulling long hours.

"I wanted to talk to you."

Turner glanced at a wall clock, then back at her. "About what?"

The expression on his face said that he already knew.

"It's those murders," Carrie said, shooting a glance at Melissa, then back at Turner. "The ones in Falmouth."

"Carrie, I know what you're going to—"

"Is it them? Are they responsible? Please, I need to know."

Melissa looked up, curious eyes flicking between the two. Turner nodded at Carrie to follow him, then made his way over to a coffee machine in the corner, pulled a coin from his trouser pocket and slipped it into the slot.

"Carrie. . . You know I can't tell you anything," he said, punching a button. A plastic cup dropped into the dispenser and watery, black coffee began to pour. "We're very early on in the investigation, and even if I did know something, I'm not at liberty to tell you. You know that."

Carrie watched the cup slowly filling. Turner asked if she wanted one. She shook her head. "They're saying on the TV that it's them. That it's the Dawn Children. What if they're right? What if they're back? I don't even know what to do with that."

Turner picked up the cup, a few excess drops landing on his finger, making him wince.

"The press don't know anything. They're putting two and two together and making five. You know what they're like—you've experienced it first-hand, so just take everything that you're hearing right now with a pinch of salt."

He sipped the coffee. Grimaced.

"So you won't even tell me that it's *not* them?"

"Look, I was working late last night, up at the crack of dawn this morning, I have a full day ahead of me. I don't know what else to tell you except to stop worrying and go home. Let us do our jobs."

Carrie stared at the floor. Why had she even come here? All she wanted was some reassurance, but Turner couldn't even give her that. Coming here had just made her feel a hundred times worse.

"We're doing everything we can to find out who's responsible," Turner said, his eyes softening. "Right now our priority is finding that little girl. Hopefully alive. But let us worry about it, okay? You have a family to take care of and I'm sure you already have enough on your plate." He paused, took another sip of the bitter coffee. "How's everything at home?"

Carrie shrugged. Looked away. "They've been better."

"And Cal? How's he doing?"

It was a simple, honest question, and yet to Carrie's ears it was pointed and accusatory. She glared at the floor. The truth was she didn't have the answer, and every time someone asked, she was reminded of how long it had been since she'd visited her son.

"Cal's not doing great. He's been transferred to a secure hospital in Bristol and he'll wait out the rest of his remand there. But you must already know that."

"Me? I'm just a lowly Detective Constable at the bottom of the chain, not some all-seeing Oracle."

Carrie hung her head, the weight of her troubles bearing down on her shoulders. "I just want it all over and done with. The trial . . . everything." She glanced over at Melissa, who was now busy swinging her legs and rolling her eyes. "We're all in limbo."

"Listen," Turner said, "I'm sorry that I can't tell you much, but what I can tell you is that you're one of the strongest people I've met. Certainly stronger than this coffee."

He smiled. Carrie, too.

"You're just saying that."

"I'm not. You forget I've been around for a while. I saw you deal with the shock of Cal coming home. I saw you deal with him disappearing again. I saw you go through hell with what he did to your family. But you're still standing. Still supporting him, when everyone else has turned their backs."

She looked down, biting her lip. If only Turner knew the truth.

"All I'm saying is to hang in there. The worst of it will be over soon. Then, one way or another, you'll know where you stand. You'll be able to get on with your life."

"God, I wish. That sounds like a dream." Carrie gazed up at Turner's weary face. Her smile faded. "Did you. . . Did you see the video? The one of Cal? The one, where he. . ."

Turner's face paled. He nodded. Looked away.

"Do you think Cal can come back from that? That he can be saved?"

Turner opened his mouth, shut it again. "I'm not professionally qualified to answer that question. I don't think it would be fair for me to say either way."

Carrie nodded. Crossed her arms. An image flashed in her mind: Cal being dragged away in handcuffs as she lay screaming on the ground.

"Go home, Carrie," Turner said softly. "Try to have a nice day. Concentrate on the here and now. There's a festival coming up, I hear. Are you involved?"

"Me? No. That little scamp over there is, though." She looked at him hopefully. "Are you going to be there?"

"I don't think so. Anyway. . ." He nodded at the door, indicating that the conversation was over.

"Thank you, Will. Sorry to take up your time."

"I'll be in touch if I hear anything I'm allowed to tell you. . ."

He touched her on the shoulder, winked at Melissa, then exited through the main doors, dumping his cup of coffee in a bin. Carrie watched him go, the anxiety in her chest growing worse. She turned back to Melissa.

"Come on, sweet pea. Let's go home."

8

LINDSAY CHURCH SAT on a makeshift bed in a tiny cell. There were no windows, the only light coming through the metal grid that made up the cell door. The door was locked, the square holes large enough to put her head through, but not large enough for her shoulders. From what she could make out, the room was bare except for the bed and a plastic bucket in the corner to go to the toilet in. At first, she had refused to use it. Then she'd wet herself. Now her clothes reeked of stale urine and her skin itched.

Lindsay longed for a hot shower, to change into her pyjamas and climb into her own bed, not this filthy mattress with springs poking through the surface. But she knew she would never see her own bed again.

Wherever they had taken her, it was deathly quiet, as if all the noise in the world had been muted by a TV remote control. To compensate, Lindsay's mind was creating its own sounds. Screams. Shrieks. The pitter-patter of her brother's blood raining down. With the sounds came images. Todd, kneeling on the floor. Her mother's contorted, terrified face. Those terrible red devil masks climbing out of a nightmare.

Lindsay sat on the edge of the bed, her limbs aching, her own stench making her nauseous. Why had they left her alive? What did they intend to do with her? Even though she was just ten years old, she already knew what bad people could do to children. She'd read horrifying stories on the internet when her parents had been downstairs. She'd watched YouTube videos of true crime accounts that had given her bad dreams. At school, scary tales of child abduction and Stranger Danger were always passing from clique to clique in the canteen and playground, the tales growing more graphic with each round. Lindsay had listened to every story with mounting fear. Now, she wondered if her own face would show up on the internet, the horrific story of what happened to her passed around the playground, nightmare fuel for generations of children to come.

In the darkness, she felt her chest growing tight and tears stinging her raw eyes. Through her shock and exhaustion, she felt something else. Hunger. She hadn't eaten since dinner two days ago, which had been so cruelly interrupted. Her stomach growled noisily as she tried to piece together the terrifying events.

She remembered a sackcloth sliding over her head, lying on the cold metal floor of a van, the rumble of the engine making her bones shake. She didn't know how long the journey had taken, or where she had ended up, but she remembered hands dragging her from the vehicle and throwing her over a shoulder. Then she was carried into the cell she now sat in and dumped on the bed, the metal door slamming shut with a thunderous clang.

She remembered kicking and screaming and wrapping her fingers around the cold metal bars and shaking the door so hard she thought the hinges would fly off. But they hadn't. After hours of screaming, her throat had grown painful and raw, so she'd started crying instead; long braying sobs that overflowed with grief and anger and horror, all wrapped up in one terrible sound.

Eventually, she had collapsed from exhaustion and fallen into a deep sleep. When she'd woken up, there had been a brief moment in which she'd forgotten where she was or what had happened to her family. But then it all came rushing back like a tidal wave, engulfing her body, drowning every cell. Now she was mostly numb. And hungry. Starving, in fact. If only she was at the seafront right now, munching on a greasy burger with extra ketchup.

From beyond the cell, she heard the metallic jangle of keys and the clunk of a lock turning. Somewhere out in the corridor, a door opened, the hinges squeaking, then dazzling daylight set the world alight. Lindsay winced, shielding her eyes. She scrabbled back on the bed, terror clawing at her insides.

A figure appeared in the light, stopping just outside the cell door.

Lindsay's spine pressed up against the cold, damp wall. She sat, blinking away red flecks.

"Hello, little one," a woman's voice said.

She was surprised by its kindness. Lindsay blinked some more and the figure came into focus.

"Did you sleep well?" the woman asked. "I brought you some food. You must be hungry."

The very mention of the word made Lindsay's stomach grumble loudly. She leaned forward a little, brushing her lank hair from her eyes. Now that her vision had adjusted to the light, she could see the woman clearly.

She was old. Older than her mother, with a shock of short, red hair and lines on her face. She was short and stocky-looking, like the wind couldn't knock her over. Except for her haunted, shadowy eyes, she reminded Lindsay a little bit of Santa's wife, Mrs Claus.

"My name is Cynthia," the woman said. "I'm very pleased to meet you. There's no need to be afraid. There's only love for you here, and food to fill your belly."

There was that word again, making Lindsay's stomach groan in protest. She leaned forward an inch, staring at the tray in the woman's hands. She couldn't quite see what it held, but she could smell oats. She hoped it wasn't porridge. She hated the stuff, even though her mum was always trying to make her eat it when it was cold. Her mother. . .

It was like a knife in the stomach. In the throat.

The woman called Cynthia stooped down. "I'm not allowed to open the door. Not yet. But I'm going to put this through the bars."

Setting the tray on the floor outside, she picked up a bowl and squeezed it through one of the door's metal squares. Lindsay leaned forward. There was no steam coming from the bowl, but the gunk inside definitely looked like porridge.

"I'm afraid it's cold," Cynthia said, still kneeling. "We don't have any heat. But I have plenty of sugar to make it sweet." She leaned closer, until her face peered through one of the squares, soft and friendly. "What's your name?"

Lindsay was silent, staring at the woman's face, then at the bowl. Cold porridge. She couldn't bear the thought of it. But right now, her stomach would gladly guzzle anything in its path.

"Don't be afraid, child. I'll make sure you're well looked after here. You won't be in this . . . room . . . forever. Why don't you tell me your name?"

Sitting on the edge of the bed now, Lindsay remained silent. The woman didn't seem like the others, who had broken into her home and slaughtered her family like animals. She seemed nice and kind, like the teachers at her school. Like her grandma. She cleared her throat, tried to speak, but instead a croak came out.

"You must be thirsty," Cynthia said, feeding a plastic cup through the door. "Have some water."

Lindsay licked her lips. She was more than thirsty. Her insides were a desert.

"Go on. Take it. I would never hurt you. I would never hurt any child."

Slowly, Lindsay inched forward, her eyes fixed on the cup. She put one foot on the ground, then the other. She crouched like a cat. On all fours, she crawled across the floor and reached for the cup.

"That's a good girl," Cynthia said, watching her gulp it down. "Drink up."

The water gushed down the back of Lindsay's throat. She felt her lungs singing. Her organs pulsing back to life. It had a funny taste but she drank it all. Setting the cup down on the floor, she eyed the bowl of cold, watery oats. It looked gross and disgusting, but she felt an urge to devour every last scrap.

A thought struck her: what if it was poisoned?

What if these people were playing tricks on her, trying to make her believe that they were kind?

Because they weren't kind. They had murdered her family right in front of her.

What if they were just playing with her right now, letting her think she was safe and sound, when in fact she was the next to die?

"Come on, now. I know it's not the best food in the world, but you need to eat, girl. And if you want to get out of this room, you're going to need all the strength you have."

Lindsay reached towards the bowl, then drew back. It was a trick. Cynthia was just being nice to get her to eat poison. She had another thought: what if the water she'd just swallowed had been poisoned, too? Lindsay suddenly felt the urge to throw up.

On the other side of the gate, Cynthia smiled. She held a finger to her lips, then glanced over her left shoulder, then her right, checking the corridor.

"I'll tell you what," she whispered. "I have something special. A treat for you."

Slipping her hand into an unseen pocket, she pulled something out. Lindsay watched the woman feed her hand through the door and unfurl her fingers.

She was holding a chocolate bar.

Lindsay's mouth watered. Her stomach roared like a lion. The wrapper was still sealed, which meant it couldn't be poisoned.

"Here," Cynthia said, waving the chocolate at her.

Before she could stop herself, Lindsay shot out a hand to take it. Cynthia pulled the chocolate back, just out of reach.

"You can have this," she said. "But you have to promise me that you won't tell anyone I was here. It'll be our little secret, just yours and mine. Do you promise?"

Lindsay nodded. She didn't care about poison anymore. All she cared about was the hunger that was eating her from the inside out.

"Good girl," Cynthia cooed. "One more thing—what's your name?"

Lindsay cleared her throat. No matter how hard she tried, she couldn't peel her eyes from the bright colours of the chocolate bar.

"Lindsay," she said, then gasped, surprised by her own voice, which was dry and cracked and sounded like an old woman's.

Cynthia nodded and smiled. "Well, Lindsay, it's very nice to meet you."

She leaned forward, holding out the chocolate bar once more. Lindsay snatched it from her, tore off the wrapper, and devoured half the bar in one large bite. Sugary, chocolatey goodness filled her mouth. Her taste buds crackled like lightning. She chewed and chewed, swallowing down every last delicious morsel, and just for a moment, she forgot the dank cell she was locked inside and the piss-stained clothes she was wearing.

Cynthia watched her, grinning and laughing. "Good girl. I can see you have lots of strength. Do you feel better now?"

Lindsay wiped her mouth with the back of a hand. She eyed the porridge, then looked at Cynthia, grateful for this kind woman, who had emerged from the darkness like an angel. Slowly, Lindsay nodded. But then she remembered her family and how kind her mother could be, when she wasn't in one of her moods, which had been more often than not lately. She remembered her father, who she guessed she loved but didn't see enough of him to know for sure either way. She remembered Todd, who could make her laugh or sometimes let her play video games with him, when he wasn't being a stupid, teenage dick.

Lindsay looked up at Cynthia's smiling face and burst into tears.

"I want to go home!" she sobbed.

Cynthia's smile faded and her eyes grew round and dewy. "Oh, there, there! Don't cry, child. I know it all seems scary and strange, but this is your home now."

Still crying, Lindsay looked around the darkened, cramped cell, at the plastic bucket in the corner. Her sobs grew louder.

"Oh, no, not this nasty old room!" Cynthia said, reaching a hand through the bars to pull strands of hair from Lindsay's face. "There's a whole other place for you to explore. One that doesn't have bars on the door. And it's filled with children. Children just like you. It's called the Dawn. All the children there want to be your friend, and you can play with them all day long, like they're your own family. Wouldn't you like that, Lindsay? Wouldn't you like to get out of this room? Wouldn't you like to play with the others?"

Lindsay stifled her sobs. She wiped her nose and eyes.

"I can make that happen," Cynthia said. "We just need to show everyone that you're good."

Lindsay stared at the woman. A roomful of children would be fun to play with, she thought. Especially if it meant she could get out of this dank cell. Slowly, she nodded.

Cynthia shut her eyes and smiled like she was in a dream. "Then all you have to do is stop your tears and eat your porridge, then I can tell the others how good you've been. When they can see that you're calm and that you're not going to kick up a fuss, they'll be only too pleased to have you join us. Does that sound fair?"

Lindsay stared at the porridge that was cold and congealing.

"Yes," she said. Slowly, she picked the bowl up. She pushed down the nausea bubbling in her throat and lifted the spoon to her mouth.

Cynthia watched her, clasping her hands together as if in prayer.

"Good girl," she said. "Another lamb brought into the fold. The Dawn will be plentiful and full of light."

Lindsay swallowed the gruel, screwing up her face as she tried to force it down. Cynthia watched her, smiling and cooing, as if

Lindsay was a baby.

She was halfway through the bowl when something strange happened. Lindsay looked up and saw Cynthia move away from her. Not just Cynthia, but the door and the walls. They all stretched out like bubble gum until they were a hundred miles from her. She blinked once. Twice. The room began to spin. Her limbs grew heavy.

"That's right, sweet girl," Cynthia said, but now she was only a voice flapping around Lindsay's head. "The New Dawn is beautiful like Heaven. And all the children will join hands and celebrate in their salvation, marching together over the horizon. Oh, if only dear Jacob was here to greet you! Poor, dear, Jacob! But we will walk to the Dawn together and his spirit will guide us. Oh yes, it will!"

Lindsay wasn't listening anymore. Tiny rainbow lights were sparkling in the darkness. Then they were exploding like fireworks. She gasped in wonder.

"A New Dawn!" Cynthia's voice was a heavenly chorus. Angels serenading her.

Lindsay lay back on the dark, damp ground of her cell and began to giggle. Then she was laughing and crying and screaming all at once.

9

THE TOWN HALL was an old building, almost as old as Porth an Jowl itself. It sat next to the police station, which had been closed for three years now, its boarded up windows a constant reminder that, thanks to budget cuts, the people of Devil's Cove had been abandoned by law and order. For what it was worth, the town hall had once been a hive of activity. Now it was mostly used for jumble sales and flea markets, and once a year, an arts and craft space for the Devil's Day preparations.

Presently, the main hall was humming with noise. Nat was on her knees at the centre of the room, a large dome of papier-mâché in front of her, a paintbrush in her hand that she flicked and swished with expertise.

All around her, groups of adolescent children worked on banners and chatted excitedly, while shooting occasional, curious glances in Nat's direction. As she worked, a face began to form: a bright red face with a wicked grin and reptilian yellow eyes, topped by two curved horns. The Devil in all his satanic glory.

Nat's creation would lead Devil's Day parade, so she was taking her time with the design, making it as detailed and as striking as possible. Some of the children were already casting frightened glances at the face, which made her smile.

The rest of her morning had gone as expected. There was only so much fun to be had changing holidaymakers' filthy sheets and cleaning their shit off toilet bowls. But she supposed she had met that girl, Rachel, who was infinitely cooler than anyone she'd met in ages. It was just a shame that Nat had made a complete fool of herself. But at least she'd been distracted from all those dark thoughts.

Sitting up for a moment, she stretched her spine and surveyed the children's work. It was okay, she supposed. Some of them even showed a little talent. She hadn't wanted to be in charge of the brats, though—that was Rose's doing. Apparently, she thought supervising the children would be good for Nat; melt some of that steely exterior she used as a shield.

A young boy with a shock of red hair looked up and saw Nat stretching. He smiled sweetly at her. She glared back. The boy returned to painting, his complexion a shade paler.

At the far end of the room, a group of older residents sat around a table, notebooks and pens in front of them. Rose was stationed at the end of the table, very much in charge of the meeting. Nat watched her closely. Her usual, jovial smiles were gone. Her soft, friendly gaze, now hiding something dark and disquieting.

It was the murders. Ever since she'd told Nat about them, she hadn't been herself. Nat wondered if Rose was worried that the Dawn Children had come back, or if Rose was worried that Nat was about to do something reckless. Like go after them, for example, or mess up her final exams.

The truth was that, so far, Nat hadn't done much at all. When she'd first heard about the murders, she'd been all fired up, ready to go tearing through the countryside, in search of the Dawn Children's hiding place. Then she'd reminded herself that she was an eighteen-year-old art student, whose only resources were the internet and a cutting sense of humour. And how was she going to scour the countryside when she couldn't even drive? For now, she'd decided to lay low, watch the news sites for any developments on the missing Church girl, and keep Rose happy by helping out with the festival.

She got painting again, using a thin brush to add shadows beneath the Devil's eyes. But now she was distracted, unable to stop thinking about the Dawn Children.

There had been too much trouble in Porth an Jowl this last year. If more was on the way, she needed to know about it.

An image flashed in her mind. Aaron Black's smug face. She shook it away, dipping the brush into the paint, then applying it to the papier-mâché, sharpening the devil's horns. Soon, she was lost in painting once more and the Devil's face was becoming frighteningly realistic.

"That's a bit scary looking, isn't it?"

Nat twisted around to see Rose leaning over her. She peered down at her work and shrugged a shoulder.

"It's the Devil," she said. "Did you want me to paint Santa Claus?"

"Still," Rose said, thrusting a hand on her hip. "It's supposed to be a fun day. That's going to give the kiddies bad dreams."

"Then my work here is done." Nat nodded towards the table. "How's the knitting circle?"

"Fine."

"Because you look scared to death over there. Are you worried?"

"About what?"

"The murders."

A little girl poked her head up and glanced in their direction, eyes growing round and frightened.

"Keep your damn voice down," Rose hissed. "And no, I'm not worried. I've got a lot on my plate getting this festival organised, that's all, and it's hard enough without you going on about all that unpleasant stuff."

"I mentioned it once. Take a pill or something."

Rose's gaze hardened as she glared at Nat's creation. "You better get back to your painting. And tone it down, for goodness sake. The last thing we need is for the town to be accused of satanism."

"Then maybe don't have a festival called Devil's Day?" Nat narrowed her eyes as she watched Rose stalk back to the table, then she muttered under her breath as she scrutinised her handiwork.

"Hope I'm not interrupting anything?"

Nat glanced up. Caught her breath. It was the girl from the caravan park. Rachel. Nat cleared her throat, brushed down her jeans and got to her feet.

"Um . . . Hey."

"Cool Devil," Rachel said, staring down at the papier-mâché head. "You're really talented. Maybe I should get you to design a tattoo for me."

Nat stared at her blankly.

"Is this a bad time? Because I was just in the area and you said to—"

"No, it's fine. I thought you were going to St Ives?"

"Yeah, we did that already." Rachel rolled her eyes. "So are you taking me for a tour or what?"

Nat glanced over her shoulder. Rose was watching her, then staring at Rachel, confusion narrowing her eyes.

"Sure," she said, glaring across the room. "It's boring as shit in here anyway."

*

Leaving the town hall, Nat and Rachel headed down Harbour Road, then took a left, emerging on the sea front. The day was warm, the breeze light and salty. The promenade was already full of people, tourists strolling up and down the pink concrete slabs, eating ice cream and taking pictures. Nat tensed. She hated crowds on the best of days. As they walked along Cove Road, then crossed over to the promenade, she rolled a cigarette and offered it to Rachel.

"No thanks. Those things will kill you."

Shrugging, Nat sparked the cigarette and brought it to her lips.

"Are you okay?" Rachel asked, glancing at her as they strolled. "You seem distracted."

Nat nodded then looked away. Down on the beach, The Shack had opened its doors to patrons, while holidaymakers had already set up deck chairs and laid out towels, despite the temperature still erring on the side of spring.

They walked on in silence for a while, weaving between the tourists.

"So you loved St Ives?" Nat said, smirking.

"Yeah, very charming. I mean, I get that Cornwall's pretty and all, but seriously what do people our age do for fun?"

"Get wasted. Then leave."

"Sorry, I'm a dick. This is your home and I'm insulting it. Again."

"Be my guest." Nat sucked on her cigarette. "How about you? Where do you come from?"

"London."

"Really? I was thinking about moving there."

"You should. You and me, we could hang out." Squinting in the bright sunlight, Rachel turned to stare at the sea. "Well, I guess it may be boring around here, but that is some view."

Nat followed her gaze, staring at the wide, green ocean. Her eyes moved up to the left cliff, where the Mermaid Hotel had once stood, then over to the right cliff, to Desperation Point and the old lighthouse that stood watching over the town. Unpleasant thoughts of Aaron Black crept out from the shadows. Forcing them back, she returned her attention to the left cliff and the archway of rock protruding into the sea.

"You see that?" she said pointing as they stopped by the railings. "That's the Devil's Gate."

"Creepy. Why is it called that?"

"You already know that Porth an Jowl translates from Cornish to mean the Devil's Cove—but it can also be translated as the Devil's Gate. Legend has it that the archway is a gateway to hell. Hundreds of years ago, the gate opened and the Devil came out. He rose up from the water to stalk through the streets, taking the town's children from their beds and leading them through the gate, straight down to Hell, where they burn to this day. People say that if you listen carefully at night, you can still hear the children crying for their mothers and fathers."

She glanced at Rachel, who laughed.

"That's fucked up. I like it."

"It's why we have Devil's Day once a year. The locals believe that the Devil's Day ceremony helps to ward off the devil, keeping the gate shut and the town's children safe from his clutches. It's superstitious bullshit, but I think it's kind of cool."

Nat finished her cigarette and stubbed it out on the sole of her boot, throwing the butt into a nearby bin. They got walking again.

"What does this Devil's Day ceremony involve?" Rachel asked. "Because I've seen The Wicker Man and I know how *that* ends."

Nat smiled. "Everyone in the town marches through the cove and down to the beach, where a sacrifice is offered to the Devil in exchange for him leaving the children alone for another year."

"Sacrifice? Oh God, they don't kill a chicken or something like that, do they? Because I don't want to see that!"

"We're not complete heathens, you know. The mayor makes an offering of cider to the Devil. Everyone in the town drinks a toast and then more barrels are cut open and rolled right into the sea. Which is a waste of good booze, if you ask me."

"I don't know. Cider's gross."

Nat smiled. But only for a second.

"Are you sure you're okay?" Rachel was staring at her again, making her feel uncomfortable. No one ever stared at her like that except for Rose. "When I walked into the hall earlier, you looked like you'd just heard some bad news or something."

Nat glanced away, watching a group of children playing badminton on the beach. It was nice to have someone to talk to. Someone who didn't treat her like a freak or take her for granted. But she didn't know Rachel. She didn't know how she would react if she told her what was really on her mind.

"Don't worry about it," she said at last. "There's some stuff going on right now, but you're on holiday and I don't want to ruin the obviously great time you're having."

Rachel shrugged. "Yeah, I'm having the time of my life."

"I should get back. Rose will be wondering where I've got to. And I have to make sure those miserable kids aren't messing everything up."

"Rose? Is that your mum?"

Nat tensed. She quickened her pace. "Yeah. I mean, sort of. Foster mum."

"Oh. How come you don't live with your own family?"

"It's . . . a long, unpleasant story."

They walked on in silence, Rachel shooting tiny glances while Nat pulled at the neck of her t-shirt. The scars beneath were beginning to itch, taunting her with bad memories.

"Sorry," Rachel said. "I have a bad habit of asking uncomfortable questions."

Nat shrugged. "It's fine. It's just no one ever asks me about it, that's all. But Rose, she gave me a roof over my head and she's been more of a mother to me than the shit head who gave birth to me ever was, that's for sure."

Rachel was quiet, walking beside her.

"You're lucky to have her," she said after a while. "My mum died when I was four. Slit her own wrists. I was the one who found her."

"God. . . I'm sorry."

"Yeah, well, Dad was so upset about it he remarried a year after her death." A sneer twisted Rachel's otherwise perfect lips. "Josephine. Talk about the archetypal wicked stepmother. You know, the only reason I'm on holiday with them is because Josephine thinks I can't be trusted home alone. I mean, Jesus, I'm eighteen years old. Old enough to vote, get married, and fuck!"

She flashed a grin at Nat, whose face flushed red. Stepping off the promenade, they crossed Cove Road and headed for the turning that led back to the town hall.

"Anyway, I'll be getting my own place soon, so Josephine can go fuck herself. Hey, when are you moving to London? We should share a place! Think of all the trouble we could get into."

She smiled at Nat again, who stuffed her hands inside her jeans pockets and avoided Rachel's gaze. The town hall was up ahead. Someone was walking towards it from the other side. A mother and child.

Nat stopped in her tracks.

"What is it?" Rachel asked. She followed Nat's gaze and her eyes grew wide. "Is that who I think it is?"

"It depends on who you think it is," Nat replied, hunching her shoulders, trying to make herself invisible.

"That's Carrie Whatshername! The mother. I recognise her face from the news."

They stood, watching Carrie mount the steps then disappear inside, Melissa's tiny hand grasped securely in hers.

"Shit."

"What's wrong?"

"Nothing. I don't . . . I don't really want to see her right now."

"Oh?" Rachel was staring, eyebrows raised.

"Long story."

"Everything's a long story with you."

Nat was still standing, rooted to the spot. She hadn't spoken to Carrie in months, somehow managing to avoid her—which was remarkable in a town this size, not to mention that Carrie was one of Rose's closest friends.

"So, are we going inside or what?" Rachel asked. She leaned back on her feet, her fingers drumming on her thighs.

Nat stared at the town hall steps. There was no way she was going in there while Carrie was inside. She hadn't been able to face her since handing Aaron Black's videotape over to the police. Guilt pressed down on her shoulders. She tried to shake it off, but it was stubborn and relentless, feeding off her like a vampire.

Now Aaron's smug face was staring at her again from the shadows. Oh God, Nat! They're coming! I'm up at Desperation Point. Tell the police to—

"I guess I should probably go?" Rachel said. She was frowning at Nat, who had drifted away, with no clue how long she'd been standing there, blankly staring at nothing.

An idea came to her. One that Rose would lose her mind over. She glanced at Rachel, wondering if she would be game.

"Do you want to get out of here?"

"With you?"

"Yeah."

"Sure. But what about your painting?"

"It can wait," Nat said. Her pulse was racing now, a heady mix of fear and excitement making her giddy. "How do you fancy a spot of dark tourism?"

Rachel's eyes glittered in the sunlight. "What's that?"

"You know, touring murder sites, places where people died, that kind of thing."

"You mean like Grady Spencer?"

Nat flinched. "Something like that. But not here."

"Where? Do they have beer?"

"I'm sure that can be arranged."

Rachel broke into a grin. "You're a sick, sick puppy. Count me in."

Returning her smile, Nat held out a hand. "After you."

They got going, hurrying past the town hall and on towards the high street, Nat glancing back over her shoulder every few seconds. She'd tell Rose that she'd lost track of time. She'd put in extra hours on the artwork tomorrow. And if Rose asked where she'd gone, Nat would tell her she'd been giving her new friend a tour of the land. Because if Rose discovered where they were actually going, Nat would never be allowed to leave the house again.

10

BY THE TIME Carrie and Melissa walked into the town hall, the day had grown hot and sticky. The coolness of the spacious, wood-panelled room should have brought welcome relief, but there were more townsfolk here than Carrie had expected—and they were all staring at her. For a brief moment, she considered turning around and going back home, but Melissa was already waving at a few of her school friends, who were busy painting banners in bright colours, and Rose had already seen them come in.

Forcing a smile, Carrie came to a halt at the centre of the hall; close enough for prying eyes to get a better look, but not close enough for keen ears to solicit any gossip-worthy information. She met a few of the stares as Rose waved. Some turned away, while others gave polite nods. Which was something, she supposed.

"Mummy, can I go and paint?"

"Of course you can, sweet pea."

Ruffling Melissa's hair, she watched her skip across the room towards her friends, then drop to her knees and pick up a paint-brush.

"Well, don't you look like a hot mess?" Rose said with a beaming smile. "I've got a jug of lemonade over there. Homemade and everything."

"Thanks. I think." Carrie ran fingers through her damp hair. Her gaze flicked to the group of adults sitting around the long galley table at the far end—older women mostly, because heaven forbid a man might take it upon himself to help out—who were busy stitching and darning costumes for the parade. They were all talking in low voices and not one of them was smiling.

"Everything all right, dear?" Rose asked,

Carrie stared at her. There was something hiding behind the woman's jovial smile. Concern? Worry?

"You hear the news?" Carrie asked, dropping her voice to a hushed whisper. "About the family that was murdered?"

"We all have," Rose said. "Nasty business."

They both glanced at the gaggle of children who were laughing and chatting away.

Carrie said, "They're talking about Cal on the TV. They think the murders are connected to . . . well, to that councillor and his missing son."

Rose shook her head. "But they don't have any proof, do they?"

"Similar circumstances, I guess. They brought up that video; the one that Nat found. They're suggesting those kids are responsible for killing that family." They both glanced at the children again. "Rose, I'm worried. They're still out there. They broke into my house, abducted me and took me to that farm. The same place where Cal. . ." She still couldn't say it out loud; after all these months, the words still got stuck in her throat. *The same place Cal murdered a man.* "What if they've come back? What if they're not done with me and my family?"

She could feel the tears stinging her eyes, could hear her voice growing loud and shrill, making the children look up.

Grasping Carrie's arm, Rose led her through the hall, past the table of staring townsfolk, through a door and into a tiny kitchen tucked away at the back.

"Melissa. . ." Carrie protested.

"She'll be fine. Now you sit down and take two minutes."

Rose pointed to a spindly looking table and chairs. While she filled an electric kettle and set about making tea, Carrie perched on the edge of a chair and sat, wringing her hands and glancing at the door behind.

Neither of them spoke until Rose set down two mugs of steaming tea on the table and positioned herself in the opposite chair.

"Go on, drink up," she said. "Tea will always calm you down even on the hottest of days."

Carrie did as she was told, picking up one of the mugs and taking a sip.

"The way I see it," Rose mused, "even if it is those same strange folk behind those killings, the police will find them soon. It's a terrible business and I'm praying for that poor girl they've taken— praying that she's still alive. But there's nothing you can do about it, Carrie. You have to live your life and goodness knows you have enough to deal with already." She paused, wrapping her fingers around her mug, but not lifting it to drink. "I know that sounds harsh. I know it probably doesn't help at all, but the trouble is that once you let those thoughts get inside your head, they're going to eat you up. You've been through so much this last year and it's not over yet. The trial's still to come. The divorce, too, if that's still happening."

"It is," Carrie said, a little too quickly. "I think."

"Well then, even more reason not to get yourself worked up about things beyond your control. Have you spoken to the police?"

"They can't tell me anything." She stared at the table, lines wrinkling her brow. "That video—Nat was working with Aaron Black, wasn't she? Helping him to find Cal and those people. Maybe she knows something and doesn't realise it. A clue about where they could be. If she could—"

"No." Rose's voice was stern and sharp, making Carrie flinch. "Natalie told the police everything she knew. They questioned her, over and over, until there was nothing left to tell. That girl's been through enough and she hasn't been the same since Mr Black was found dead, God rest his soul. She blames herself, you know. I don't know why or how, but she does. So the last thing she needs is for it all to be dragged up again. To be honest, it's the last thing I need, too. I swear, that girl is going to be the death of me!"

"Where is she, anyway?"

"She was here a minute ago. Went off with some new friend." The older woman heaved out a sad sigh. "I feel for you Carrie, I really do. No one in this town can understand how you must be feeling. Oh, there may be naysayers who think they've got it all figured out, but they don't. I'm begging you, for the sake of your sanity and for the sake of your family: let the police handle this. Try to focus on what's in front of you, not on what could be."

Leaning forward, Carrie pressed her face into her hands. She was quiet for a moment, trying to centre herself. "I'm tired, Rose. Sometimes I think I should just take Melissa and go. Somewhere miles away, where no one knows us. Somewhere we can start again."

"What about Dylan? He's Melissa's father. Doesn't he have a right to see his daughter?"

"I didn't say I'd do it. But even if I could just get out of this damn town. . . I don't know, move to Penzance or something, like Tess Pengelly."

"Except she's moving on, I hear. To Wiltshire."

"She is?" Carrie was surprised. It was hard to remember that she and Tess had once been friends. Harder still to remember that she'd once lived a normal life. She looked up, stared up at Rose's soft, kindly face. "Being here in the cove makes things so much harder. Everyone's always pointing fingers, whispering behind my back. With Cal in the hospital and the trial coming up, I feel like I'm going crazy."

Rose reached out and grasped Carrie's hands in her own, then gently lowered them to the table.

"Then take a step back," she said. "We don't know anything about that poor family in Falmouth, or who's responsible. True, the circumstances are similar, but let the police take care of it. Take a step back or you really will lose your mind."

Carrie slowly nodded, rubbed her eyes. She felt like she'd lost her mind months ago. "I just wish I could make sense of it all, you know? But if I'm honest, I'm starting to think I never will. If only Cal would say something. Just one sentence so I could understand."

"Carrie, love . . . as awful as it sounds, you may never know the truth. You know that, don't you?"

"Funnily enough, I do. Still doesn't stop me from hoping."

Rose let go of her hands and took a sip of tea. "How is the boy doing?"

"I . . . I don't know." Carrie dropped her gaze to the table. "I haven't been to visit."

"Since when?"

"A few weeks."

"Oh, Carrie..."

"I know, I know." There it was again. That stab of guilt puncturing her heart. "Everything's changed. Before, Cal was my little boy who was abducted by that son of a bitch, Grady Spencer. And yes, he did some terrible things. But then he tried to kill Melissa. He stabbed my mother in the chest. And when that video came out and he..."

Tears slipped from her eyes and splashed on the table.

Rose stared at her, mouth half open. "You haven't watched it, have you?"

"God, no! I could never... But Cal's solicitor has. He described it to me. My son stabbed Councillor Beaumont to death in front of a group of children. He was coerced into it by that man. The one that looked just like Grady Spencer. The one they believe was his son. And I know he made Cal do it. That whatever he whispered in his ear left him with no choice. But that doesn't change the fact that my son is a killer. I just can't get past it and I hate myself for it. That's not my little boy anymore. It's his body, but that's not him inside." She paused, the pain in her heart snatching her breath away, bringing tears to her eyes. "Cal is gone. He was gone the day I lost him at the beach."

They were both silent, staring into their mugs of tea. The children's chatter floated in from the hall, filling the silence.

At last, Rose looked up, her eyes wet and glistening. "I honestly don't know what to tell you except I'm here for you. We all are."

Carrie snorted. "Not everyone."

"Those that matter are. Screw everyone else!" Rose leaned forward. "You remember when Cal was, I don't know, maybe four or five? We went to the woods for a picnic—you, me, Cal and your mum—and when we got there, Cal saw that big old tree that grows right in the centre of Briar Wood, and he decided he was going to climb right to the top. Except he was so small he couldn't even reach the lowest branch. You remember that?"

Memories flooded Carrie's mind and she found herself smiling through her tears.

"He stamped his little feet and got all angry. Even kicked the trunk a few times. But he wouldn't give up."

"No, he wouldn't. He kept trying and trying, jumping up and stretching out his fingers to reach that branch, until he got so tired that he lay down and fell straight to sleep right there on the picnic blanket. He was always a stubborn little bugger, just like his mum." Rose leaned closer still, staring straight into Carrie's eyes. "That's Cal. That's your son. He's still inside there somewhere, Carrie. There's still hope for him. After everything he's been through, there has to be."

Memories of that day in the wood faded from Carrie's mind. "Hope? Rose, he's locked up in a mental institution awaiting trial for murder. His solicitor's confident that with enough evidence he can get the charge reduced to manslaughter due to diminished responsibility. But that doesn't mean Cal will be set free. It doesn't mean he should be, either. At best, he'll be locked away in the hospital. At worst, prison. And either way, he'll have to live for the rest of his life knowing that he killed a man. That he nearly killed his grandmother. How does he come back from that? Even if he does, it was me who handed him to the police. His own mother. He'll look at me every day and know that. Just like I do every time I look in the mirror."

"You did the right thing," Rose said gently. "You were protecting your family. Protecting him. He's still your son, Carrie. He needs you."

"And Melissa's my daughter. She saw him plunge that knife into her grandmother's chest. A knife that was meant for her. Even if Cal was released, how can I let him back into her life? Into her home?"

Rose stared at the table and heaved her shoulders. *She doesn't know*, Carrie thought. But who could blame her when there was no right answer?

"Start by letting the police take care of that terrible business in Falmouth," Rose said quietly. "Start by considering going to see your son. And right now, start by going back out there and helping me salvage some of these god-awful costumes. Honestly, they look like they were put together by a blind man with a blunt needle."

She looked up, flashed a smile at Carrie, who laughed in spite of herself.

"I can't promise I'll do any better," she said.

Rose shook her head. "Don't matter. Whatever it takes to keep you sane."

11

NAT AND RACHEL stepped out of the train station into bright sunshine and onto a leafy residential street. Passing under an old arched bridge, they made their way into town. Falmouth was five times the size of Porth an Jowl, boasting a creative arts university, large docks and marina, and even a castle. Like Porth an Jowl, the streets of the town were narrow and winding, but there were plenty more shops and boutiques and places of interest to keep the tourists busy and their wallets open.

Nat had a vague recollection of coming here as a child, during a brief spell in which her parents had attempted to ditch the drugs and try out stability. Needless to say it hadn't lasted long. But she vaguely remembered visiting Pendennis Castle.

In comparison to the great castles of the United Kingdom, Pendennis was modestly-sized, with only a few grand flourishes that overlooked the English channel, but a young Nat had been in awe of its stone walls and turrets. She had imagined herself as a knight, standing guard in the castle's keep, furtive eyes watching the ocean for signs of enemy ships.

"So this place looks dull as hell," Rachel said, puffing out her cheeks. Lost in thought, Nat had quite forgotten about her for a minute. "I thought you were taking me somewhere exciting."

"I am," Nat said.

They walked on, passing through familiar looking streets, where tourists sauntered by or milled in and out of shop doorways. Above their heads, the sky was vivid blue with only a smattering of clouds, an occasional airplane passing by to destinations unknown. As they walked, Rachel made sarcastic comments and huffed and puffed. She was beginning to irritate Nat. Rachel didn't know how lucky she really was—to have at least one parent who gave a shit about her enough to take her on holiday. And Cornwall wasn't all that bad, she thought, surprising herself. Not on days like this.

"Tell me about London," she said, as the street merged onto a crossroad. A narrow alley sloped downward on their left, where they saw a glimpse of the harbour.

Rachel screwed up her face. "It's okay. I mean, it's a lot more exciting than here and there's always something to do and the shops are amazing, of course."

"What about the galleries? Have you been to the National? Or the Tate Modern?"

"No, boring! Oops, sorry—that's more your thing than mine. But from what I hear, there are tons of galleries. You'd probably have an orgasm."

Nat turned away, her cheeks flushing.

"Anyway, it doesn't matter where you live if you're stuck living with parents who think they can control you." Rachel slowed down a little, her gaze wandering over the crowds. "You're lucky having someone like Rose. Someone who cares about you. Even if she isn't your real mum."

Nat supposed that she was, even if the scars covering her body were a daily reminder that Rose hadn't always been in her life. Even if Rose thought she knew everything about Nat that there was to know. Which she didn't. Pulling out her phone, she opened the map application and checked the directions. They were still another five minutes away. She looked up, suddenly noticing the dour faces of the other pedestrians. There was a mood in the Falmouth air today, and it had nothing to do with holidays. It was heavy and smothering, filling Nat's lungs with tar as she led Rachel away from the town centre and towards Pendennis Point.

The Church family's holiday home was located on Castle Drive. It was the last house on the end of a meandering strip of detached white buildings with large bay windows and palm trees in the garden. The road itself skirted the edge of the coastline and overlooked a rocky beach and the wide, blue ocean.

Nat had read as much as she could find about the murders of Donna and Paul Church and their son, Todd, but so far, details had been scant. Donna and Todd had been found stabbed to death in the dining room, while Paul Church had been mutilated and laid out on the front lawn. Ten-year-old Lindsay Church was still missing. Television news reports speculated a connection between the Church family murders and the murder of John Beaumont. The former councillor's five-year-old son, Luke, had also been abducted, his whereabouts still unknown despite an extensive police search. In the video footage captured by Aaron Black, Beaumont had begged for his son's life. If the Dawn Children had the boy, they now also had Lindsay.

"What the hell?" Rachel said, staring at the crime scene with round eyes. "This is what you brought me to see?"

"You said you wanted to see something interesting," Nat murmured. Her gaze flitted from the barrier of police tape still surrounding the property, to the uniformed officers standing outside, to the large white tent covering the front lawn. It had been over twenty-four hours since the bodies had been found, but the CSI team were still at work, their van parked ominously at the side of the road. A handful of residents were gathered on the pavement, whispering and pointing.

Why had the Dawn Children resurfaced now? These latest murders would only result in a heightened police presence and an escalated investigation. There had to be a reason for them to strike out so viciously.

Nat edged closer, until she stood near the whispering residents, earning herself a few wary looks. With the police standing guard in front of the barriers, this was the closest she was going to get. Frustrated, she moved to the side, trying to get a clearer view. What were you expecting? she asked herself. To be invited in for a guided tour?

"What happened?" Rachel said, her voice a whisper. Nat glanced at her, noting that a little colour had drained from her face.

"A family was murdered. One of the kids is missing. You didn't hear about it on the news?"

She looked at Nat, fine lines creasing her forehead. "I don't listen to the news, it's too depressing."

"Anyway, they think it could be connected to another murder and abduction from last year."

A detective was emerging from the house. She stopped to speak to one of the uniformed officers then glanced disapprovingly at the gathering crowd.

"What murder?" Rachel asked.

"You know all about Grady Spencer, right?"

Rachel shrugged a shoulder, shot a nervous glance at the police detective, who was still standing in the garden, surveying the crowd. Perhaps she wasn't as tough as she'd made out to be, Nat thought.

"I know what everyone else does. He murdered a bunch of kids. Kidnapped that boy—Carrie Whatshername's son—and tried to turn him into a killer." She turned back to Nat. "But I guess you know more, living next door to the murder house, right?"

Nat froze. Her mouth dropped open. "How do you know that?"

"You told me, didn't you?"

"No. I deliberately didn't tell you anything."

Rachel's gaze dropped to the ground. She was blushing. "Okay, fine. I spoke to one of the cleaners at the caravan park and asked about you. He told me you lived next door to Grady Spencer. That you were friends with the family of one of the kids he took. Noel or something."

"Noah," Nat corrected through clenched teeth. "Why were you asking questions about me?"

"Because I was curious. You're the most interesting person I've met in ages."

Rachel shot her another glance, a shy smile on her lips.

Anger bubbled in Nat's stomach. Perhaps Rachel really was just another thrill seeker, only getting close to Nat just to find out all the grisly details of Grady Spencer's horrific legacy. Or perhaps not.

She studied the young woman, noticing the glow of her cheeks, her downcast eyes, the way they flicked nervously up towards the crime scene.

She turned back to Nat. "I'm sorry. I didn't mean to pry. It's just that I never get to meet anyone cool."

"Not even in London?" Nat's shoulders softened. Suddenly, she wanted to tell Rachel everything. Sometimes it was easier to tell the truth to someone you barely knew. But now she regretted bringing Rachel to the crime scene. She was clearly uncomfortable being here—how would she react when she heard the whole story of Nat's involvement? Or that she was responsible for Aaron Black's death?

"It's true. I lived next door to Grady Spencer, but I had no idea about all the fucked up shit that was happening under his roof," Nat said, watching Rachel carefully. "He took Cal when he was just a kid and he broke him. Took away his humanity and tried to turn him into a killer. Noah was supposed to be Cal's first victim. But Noah's brother, Jago, he cut that bastard Grady Spencer's throat right open. The prick died. Cal escaped. But Noah was saved."

She paused, studying Rachel's expression for signs of horror, for a clue that she was about to turn and run. But Rachel nodded for her to continue.

"We thought it was over. Until Aaron Black came. He wanted to write a book about it all. Even hired me to be his assistant. He discovered the Dawn Children—some sort of cult involving missing children. He found out where they were living, but he got too cocky. He filmed them. He filmed Cal stabbing a man to death." Nat's voice stuck in her throat. She turned away, tears scratching her eyes. "But the Dawn Children caught Aaron. Chased him through Briar Wood, and then. . ."

And then they killed him. And it's my fault.

"I found his phone, up at Desperation Point. I saw what he'd filmed and I took it to the police. They went up to Burnt House Farm, but it was too late. The Dawn Children were gone. Aaron's body—what was left of it—washed up a few miles down the coast two weeks later."

A heavy, cloying weight pressed down on Nat's chest. She wiped her eyes and turned her attention to the big white house and the palm trees in front, fronds swaying in the breeze. The detective had left the scene, climbed inside her car, and was now pulling away from the kerb. A member of the Crime Scene Investigation team emerged from the tent, white disposable suit and face mask blinding in the sun.

"Jesus Christ, that sounds fucking intense," Rachel said at last, her voice a cracked whisper. "But I still don't understand what that's got to do with what's happening here."

"I think the Dawn Children killed these people and took their daughter. Just like they killed that councillor and took his son. It's what they do. I thought if I came here today, I might be able to learn something new."

"I don't understand."

"I've been looking for them," Nat said. "I've been trying for months. I even went up to Burnt House Farm, but it's like they vanished into thin air. Until now."

She'd hoped to see a smile on Rachel's face. Or at least surprise. But the young woman's expression was deadly serious.

"Are you trying to get yourself killed or something?"

Nat glared at her. "People are dead. A boy and a girl are missing. Cal's in an institution and his mum's life is in ruins. The Dawn Children may be kids, but they're dangerous. Whoever is leading them needs to be stopped. If the police can't do that, then I will."

"But you clean caravans for a living—what makes you think you can find them when the police can't?"

Nat flinched like she'd been slapped. This was not supposed to be happening. Rachel was supposed to be commending her on her bravery and ingenuity, not making her feel stupid, like a kid running around playing make believe.

"The police have limited time and resources," she said, avoiding Rachel's gaze. "I have all the time in the world. I won't stop. Not until I've found them. Not until I make them pay."

Rachel turned away, shaking her head. "Jesus. And here I was thinking you were smart."

They were both quiet for a moment, Nat seething and embarrassed as she watched the crime scene. Then she said, "Come on. Bringing you here was a big mistake."

Nat turned on her heels and started marching back the way they'd come, arms swinging, boots thumping on the tarmac.

"I'm sorry," Rachel said, catching her up. "I'm just a little freaked out."

"Forget it."

"Maybe we can hang out again tomorrow or something. Some place normal."

"Whatever."

They walked on in silence, all the way back to the station, Nat replaying the conversation they'd just had, over and over in her head. Had she said too much? Was Rachel overreacting or was she right? After all, Nat had only known the girl for two minutes and she'd already dragged her to a murder site and told her all about her hunt for a demented cult of killer children. *Oh God*, Nat thought. *What am I doing?*

At least Rachel was only here for a few more days. At least she could go back to London with a story to tell her cool friends. The story of how she met an eighteen-year-old caravan cleaner with an overactive imagination, whose only aspiration was to rot in the grave that was Porth an Jowl. At least there was that.

12

IT WAS JUST after seven, the evening still bright outside, the air sticky and warm. Carrie had put Melissa to bed and now she paced the living room, her phone pressed to her ear and her eyes flicking towards the empty drinks cabinet. Her heart raced. Her chest was tight and uncomfortable. Unreasonably jolly music played in her ear as she waited for her call to be put through.

A second later, the music was cut off and replaced by a woman's confident yet soothing voice. "Doctor Jensen speaking."

"Hello Doctor, it's Carrie Killigrew. Cal's mother. . ."

"Oh, Carrie," the doctor said, the softness of her voice like a sedative. "I was thinking to myself just this morning that we haven't spoken in a while. Everything okay?"

"Oh, you know. The same, I guess." She swallowed, her throat suddenly dry. "How is he?"

There was a pause before Dr Jensen spoke. Carrie continued to pace the room, the walls closing in on her as she moved.

"From one mother to another, I have to be honest with you, Carrie. I'm concerned. Cal is withdrawing more and more. He's refusing to eat."

Carrie froze on the spot, an invisible weight pressing down on her. "What do you mean? Nothing at all?"

"We got him to drink some water, but that's all. I'm worried he's shutting down. Yesterday, I could barely get him to look at me. Today, he wouldn't even turn around." Another pause. The silence crushed the air from Carrie's lungs. "Look, I'll be candid—I know things are hard for you right now, but Cal hasn't seen anyone from his family in weeks. Part of me has to wonder if that's why he fell apart and was transferred here.

"I think that if you visited him, that if he could see you, it might help him to come back from wherever it is he's disappearing to. I'm afraid that without any reason to stay tethered to the here and now, well . . . We're losing him, Carrie. Once he's gone, we may never get him back. I'm not saying this to frighten you, believe me. I'm saying it because I've seen it happen before."

Carrie was silent as she moved over to the mantelpiece and stared at the framed family photographs sitting on top. Cal as a baby, all soft and pink and wrapped up in a blanket. Cal as a toddler, sitting astride a plastic tractor in the backyard, a carefree smile lighting up his face. Nine-year-old Cal with Carrie, holding each other's hand and eating ice cream; the last photograph taken of them together.

In the short space of time that Cal had returned home last year, Carrie hadn't taken a single picture. Not one.

Dr Jensen whispered in her ear. "Are you still there?"

"Yes."

"Look, I know you're going through a lot," the doctor continued. "I know that coming to terms with your son being on trial for murder is an almost impossible task, never mind everything that came before—losing him, then finding him, only to lose him again—I know what I'm asking may seem a lot, but I really believe that seeing you, hearing your voice, might help to bring Cal back. It might be the only thing that does."

Carrie thought about seeing her son in that sterile place. Thought about seeing her mother slumped against the bedroom wall, the hilt of a butcher's knife protruding from her chest. Thought about sitting on the cliff top with Cal, watching the sky bruise purple and burn tangerine.

"I—" she began. "It's just that. . ."

What did she tell the doctor? That she couldn't bear to see her son locked up like an animal because she'd given him up to the police? Or that she couldn't bear to look into his eyes and see the killer he had become?

"Carrie?"

"Yes?" She cleared her throat. Straightened her spine.

"I probably shouldn't get your hopes up," Dr Jensen said softly. "But we've been running assessments in preparation for Cal's case, and while I'm no lawyer, I think we have enough evidence that could keep him here at the hospital instead of him serving time at a young offenders institute before being moved on to prison. The fact that Cal was found unfit to plead will go strongly in his favour, just as long as the defence can prove diminished responsibility."

Jensen paused again, and for a moment, Carrie wondered how the doctor managed to do her job, day in and day out, dealing not just with Cal but with all those other deeply troubled patients deemed unsafe to live among society.

"All I'm asking you to do, is to consider visiting your son. Don't you think it's worth trying?"

Carrie's gaze returned to the photographs on the mantelpiece. She thought about that day Rose had mentioned, a lifetime ago up at Briar Wood.

"Don't you?" Dr Jensen repeated.

But Carrie found she couldn't answer.

13

CYNTHIA CLOSED THE bunker door and followed the concrete path, the buildings to her left obscuring her presence from any prying eyes. It was a fine Thursday morning. The sky was pastel blue, the ocean below a sparkling green. Beads of perspiration were already forming on Cynthia's brow and her neck.

As the path turned, she glanced back over her shoulder at the bunker containing the holding cells. She was worried about Lindsay. She'd been locked up in that cell for a week now, without a change of clothes or soap and water to clean herself. The girl was eating what she was being given, but she was too subdued. Too quiet. Just now, she'd barely spoken a word the whole time Cynthia had been with her.

Perhaps they were dosing her too much. Cynthia had always been uncomfortable about administering the cocktail that Jacob had conceived, but it was necessary and joyous, he had once told her. A rite of passage so that the child could open her eyes to the New Dawn.

Who was Cynthia to question Jacob's teachings? He had saved her from a life of violence and a cruel, bitter world. He had made her his wife. And even now he was gone—dead, of course, because he would have never left her—she could still feel his presence. He shone inside the children like sunlight. He spoke to her in her dreams, promising to see her again in the New Dawn. Cynthia trembled with excitement at the thought of reuniting with her one true love.

Passing rows of green army barracks, she followed the path until she came to a stop outside the last building on the left. The coolness of the darkened hall welcomed her in. Brushing her fingers against the wall, she made her way along the corridor. Hearing the children, she slowed down; their voices always brought a smile to her face, even in troubled times.

Opening the door to what used to be the soldier's rec room, she stepped inside. It was a large space, once furnished with pool and tennis tables. Now all that remained were a few dog-eared chairs and peeling walls. The children were here, gathered in groups and dotted around the room, but they were not themselves. Some stood at the windows, staring at the bright day filtering in from outside, others sat around inventing games with a couple of old cardboard boxes. But they were all listless, as if the room had drained them of their youth and energy.

Alison was sitting with two young girls with dirty faces. Patting their heads, she got up and made her way to Cynthia.

"What is it?" she asked. Her gaunt face was all sharp angles, her eyes large and blank.

Cynthia shook her head as she stared at the children. "I'm concerned. They're not getting enough to eat. They need fruit and vegetables. They're desperate to go outside. It's sunny and warm, but they have to stay here in the dark. They're children of light, Alison. Children of the New Dawn."

Cynthia's heart grew heavy in her chest. When Jacob had been here, their angelic faces illuminated joy. Now, it was as if they had all become ghosts.

Alison shrugged. "It's a necessary evil. We're too close to the town. It would only take some nosey parker to look in the wrong direction and then it would all be over for us. Jacob said that no matter where we go, we will always be hunted because the world is Hell and filled with monsters. Monsters who want to tear our little angels apart, to strip the flesh from their bones and suck out the marrow."

"But we are their protectors, Alison. I am their mother and you are their sister. We could watch over them. Keep them on the cliff side, hidden by the buildings. Even if it's for five minutes. They'll lose their minds in here."

In the far corner of the room, Luke sat on the floor with his back pressed against the wall and his legs splayed out in front of him. His eyes were empty, staring at nothing.

Alison said, "He's not getting any better and Heath isn't happy. He says if Luke doesn't get stronger then he's not following the rules. If he's not following the rules then he's not one of us. If he's not one of us then he's against us."

Cynthia squeezed her arm. "Let me try."

Making her way over to the boy, she smiled at the nearby children, then sat down with a grunt. She wasn't getting any younger and her days of floor sitting were coming to an end.

"Hello, child," she said, giving Luke her warmest smile. "How are you feeling?"

It was as if Luke hadn't heard her. He remained motionless, his eyes glazed over, like a puppet whose strings had been cut.

"Don't you want to play with the other children?" Cynthia reached out a hand and ruffled his hair, but Luke remained, unblinking. "Or perhaps you'd like to hear a story. Why don't you tell me your favourite and I'll see if I know it?"

Nothing. Not even a flicker or involuntary flinch of a muscle. Cynthia glanced up at Alison, who shrugged her shoulders.

"You see?" Alison said, when Cynthia returned. "Heath is going to—"

Cynthia held up a hand. "Heath is not going to lay a hand on that boy. I'll take care of it. She glanced around the room, watching the children's slow movements, noting their downcast, hungry looks. "This isn't right. This is not what Jacob would have wanted."

Grief flooded her veins, drowning her heart. She yearned for Jacob's touch—not that he had touched her in years before he'd disappeared—and she yearned for his words of wisdom, for the kindness that he always wrapped around the children like a blanket. She hadn't always agreed with his ways of thinking when it came to the other women in their family, and the actions he'd started taking against the outside world had left her feeling glad that being Mother meant she never had to leave the confines of their home. But the children—they had been angels in Jacob's eyes and he'd treated them accordingly.

With Heath in charge now, those angels were becoming little soldiers.

"If Jacob was here, none of this would be happening," she said, shocked by the anger in her own voice.

But Jacob wasn't here, was he?

He'd left them alone and leaderless. He'd left Cynthia alone and unloved.

How had he died?

The only person who knew was Cal. He'd been the last person to see Jacob. But Cal had betrayed them all and now he was locked up away from the world, along with the knowledge of what had happened to Jacob, her one true saviour.

"We have Heath now," Alison replied in a monotone voice. "Heath will lead us into the light."

Cynthia frowned and decided to keep her doubts to herself.

Giving Luke one last glance, she left the room. Out in the corridor, she picked up her stride, until she was marching along like a soldier, heading for the meeting room. Stopping outside the door, she cocked her head and listened.

Heath was talking, addressing the others. Cynthia frowned. They had been making plans for weeks now, but she'd been kept out, not even permitted to enter the meeting room. That was something else Jacob would never have allowed. Because Cynthia was Mother —not Sister or Daughter.

"Punishing that family has kept them busy, but it's not enough," Heath said. "The New Dawn is two days away, and when the time comes, we don't want the police anywhere near."

Cynthia gasped. Her heart sang in her chest. *The New Dawn!*

Heath spoke again. "I thought I had it all planned out. How it would happen. What we needed to do to cross into the light. But now, thanks to Morwenna, the plan has changed. But we don't have much time. . ."

Cynthia threw open the door, revealing another cracked and peeling room, empty except for the desk at the centre, which the group of young people were presently crowded around. Heath stood on one side with Morwenna next to him. At least seven of the older teenagers made up the rest of the circle. They all glanced up as Cynthia entered.

"What are you doing?" Heath said, eyes flashing dangerously. "You know you're not to come in here."

Cynthia cleared her throat, held his gaze. "Lindsay is ready to come out of the cell. She's quiet, eating all her food. The fight's gone out of her."

"How would you know that?"

"Because I've been to see her. Someone had to."

A vein began to throb at the centre of Heath's forehead. He shot a glance at Morwenna, who shrugged.

Irritation burned in Cynthia's gut. She had always despised the young woman. Ever since the day Jacob had found her sleeping rough and had welcomed her into their family, Morwenna had been nothing but trouble. She'd seemed kind and grateful at first, but Cynthia had not fallen for her act—unlike Jacob. Like a Siren, Morwenna had tempted him away from Cynthia. He had stopped touching her. Then he'd stopped sleeping in the same bed, instead disappearing into his office for hours at a time with Morwenna. Now, here she was by Heath's side, doing it all over again. Men were fools, Cynthia thought, and Morwenna was cleverer than any one of the boys in this room. Which made her dangerous.

"Fine. I'll see the girl myself later," Heath said. "What about Luke?"

Cynthia still hovered in the doorway, an invisible barrier preventing her from getting closer. She stared at Heath, then at the others, whose eyes were all fixed on her, smirks on their lips, making her feel like a moth pinned to a display cushion. Perspiration trickled down her temple. Her hands dropped to her sides. Luke's catatonic expression flashed in her mind.

"The boy's fine," she said. "Getting stronger every day."

Heath's eyes were blank and unreadable. "Good. I'm happy to hear it. Because the New Dawn is upon us and every child must be ready to play their part."

"Oh, praise be!" Cynthia cried.

She *had* heard right. Laughter spilled from her throat as she clasped her hands together and stared up at the ceiling. Tears rained from her eyes.

She had been waiting for so long. Jacob had told her all those years ago, when he'd first saved her, and although she'd never known entirely what would happen, she knew the New Dawn would mean a new beginning. Freedom from all the cruelty in the world. And she had experienced so much cruelty.

"How will I know what to do?" she asked, vibrating with childish glee.

Heath shook his head. "No, Cynthia. You've misunderstood. Only the children will be saved. They are the ones who will be led into the light. They are the ones who will be set free from the tyranny of adults."

The joy drained from Cynthia's body. Confusion and fear poisoned her veins. "But it's my duty to go with them! Jacob told me. He *promised* me! He said the children will need their mother to guide them!"

"You've been a good mother to us, and we thank you for it. But in the New Dawn, there are no monsters. Children will be safe from harm. Which means we'll no longer need parenting. Jacob knew that. He told me himself."

"No. He would never. . . He promised me!"

"Are you calling me a liar, Cynthia?" Heath's voice was like a butcher's knife, cutting her down. "Because Jacob made it quite clear that if anything should happen to him, I would be in charge. Are you questioning his wisdom?"

Cynthia licked her lips. Around the table, eyes narrowed in disappointment and disgust.

"As I remember it, Jacob chose Cal to lead," she whispered.

Silence. Pressing down on her. Crushing the breath from her lungs.

Heath's face turned a violent shade of red. "Cal didn't follow the rules. Jacob warned him, time and time again, not to leave the farm, but Cal didn't listen. He led that writer straight to us and then our children's faces were all over the news. When we needed Cal the most, he chose his old family and left us to rot." Heath's voice grew louder with each word, until he was shouting. "Jacob is *dead* because of him! Now *I'm* the only one who can lead the children into the New Dawn! *I'm* the only one who can bring salvation! Me! Not you or anyone else! Are you with me, Cynthia? Or are you against us all?"

Cynthia's eyes dropped to the floor. She tried to speak but only managed a whisper. "I'm . . . of course, I'm with you. The children are my life."

Some of the colour left Heath's complexion. He was quiet for a moment. Then he nodded to the door. "So go and tend to them while they still need you."

Now it was as if Cynthia were invisible to him. He returned his attention to the table. One by one, the others followed; all except Morwenna, who watched her closely, a smile etched on her lips—a snake eyeing its prey.

Cynthia hovered from foot to foot. Her fingers jerked and twitched. Her stomach twisted in knots. Her heart smashed up and down in her chest, crashing like cymbals.

She left the room, plunging into the darkness of the corridor.

This is not how it's supposed to be! I'm not meant to be left behind! I am Mother of the Dawn!

She staggered along the corridor, nauseous and dizzy, swaying on her feet, until she reached the rec room. Alison and the children were still inside. They all turned towards her as she entered, all eyes filled with hope, except for Alison's, which remained apathetic and blank.

My babies! My beautiful children!

Over in the corner, Luke looked sick and ghostly, as if he were fading into thin air right before her eyes. It would only be a matter of time before Heath discovered Cynthia's lie, and then the child would also be denied passage into the New Dawn.

Alison was approaching. "What is it? Did you talk to him?"

"It's nothing," Cynthia managed to say at last. "Everything's going to be fine. I'll—I'll see if I can find something more to eat."

She stumbled from the room, leaving Alison with her mouth half open and the children staring, except for Luke, who hadn't even acknowledged her presence.

By the time Cynthia had reached the storeroom, her face was wet and her lungs were heaving and her heart felt like someone had set it on fire.

"Oh, Jacob!" she cried. "Oh, my children!"

She couldn't be left behind.

She would rather die than be tossed to the vultures in this terrifying, rancid world!

She couldn't allow Luke to suffer, either. He was a child of the Dawn. He had earned his place in the light just as much as Heath or Morwenna.

As Cynthia scoured the empty shelves and boxes, as she sobbed and shuddered, she vowed to set Luke free.

14

NAT STOOD INSIDE the caravan bedroom trying not to gag at the dirty underwear lying on the floor. She stripped the bed quickly and changed the sheets, making sure to flatten out the creases when she was done. She hated every second of her soul sucking job, but the perfectionist in her forced her to carry out her duties flawlessly.

Today, she was even wearing the vomit-inducing apron. *If only Rose could see me now*, she thought. But this morning, Rose had barely looked at her. She was still angry at Nat for taking off last Saturday, and for not answering her questions about the girl she'd run off with. Who was she? Where had she come from? What made her more important than Nat's commitments to the Devil's Day festival? All good questions. Not that she would ever admit that to Rose.

The truth was, Nat wasn't sure why she'd taken off like that. It was the sight of Carrie, she supposed. But it was more than that. Rachel turning up out of the blue had thrilled Nat. It had made her feel special. Even though now she felt like shit.

Because yet again, Nat had screwed up, exposing the freak she was within hours of meeting Rachel. What had she been thinking, taking her to the crime scene like that? Normal people didn't act that way. Normal people went for coffee or ice cream or lifted a couple of beers and went down to the beach. But Nat wasn't normal, was she? She was a freak and a loser. A killer.

She hadn't seen Rachel in days. Nat didn't even know which caravan she was staying in. If she did, she could go over and apologise. Not that she ever would. She'd only end up looking like a stalker as well as a psychopath. Besides, finding out which caravan Rachel was staying in would involve talking to the other cleaners, who all thought she was weird, or talking to Dennis Penpol, and she would rather drink her own puke than do that.

Picking up the dirty sheets, Nat shot a final, repulsed look at the used underwear on the floor, then stepped outside. As she dumped the bed linen into the basket of her cleaning trolley, she saw Dennis Penpol strolling past the caravan row. He stopped to leer at her. Satisfied that Nat was wearing her apron, he sloped off towards his office.

"You can fuck off, too," she growled.

Pushing the trolley along to the next caravan, she felt the weight in her chest grow heavier. Why did she always do this? Why did she take something good and tear it all apart? Why hadn't Rose thrown her out on the streets a long time ago? Everyone else had. Was Rose really that blind to the kind of person she had staying under her roof?

And now all this business with the murders. Everything was getting stirred up again. All those dark thoughts she'd been trying to lay to rest.

The Dawn Children.

Were they back? Or was Nat making connections that just weren't there? It was almost as if she wanted them to be responsible, and she wasn't for a minute stopping to consider that more people were dead and a little girl was missing. It was as if their lives didn't matter to her. All that mattered was getting revenge. All that mattered was making Aaron Black's death mean something.

But to whom? To the world? Or to herself? Because that was what it was really about. Wasn't it? It was about making herself feel better. It was about appeasing her guilt.

Meanwhile, she was hurting the one person who cared about her and freaking out potential friends.

Stopping outside the next caravan, Nat knocked on the door. When no one answered, she let herself in with a set of keys and headed into the bedroom. No dirty underwear on the floor. That was something, she supposed.

As she stripped the bed and replaced the sheets, she thought about Rose and her desire for Nat to leave the cove and do something with her life. She thought about Rachel living in London, daydreamed about them hanging out together, best friends exploring galleries and art cafes. It was a life that she could have. Maybe not with Rachel in it—she'd be surprised if Rachel ever wanted to see her again—but still, it was a life that could be hers. All she had to do was tell Rose and Rose would help her make it happen.

All she had to do was give up her obsession with the Dawn Children. All she had to do was forgive herself for Aaron's death.

Could she do that? Could she find it in herself to let it all go?

Finished with tucking in clean sheets, she stood back to admire her handiwork. There was something under the bed. More dirty underwear. Nat wrinkled her nose and heaved her shoulders.

She could try, she supposed. She could try for Rose. Even if she couldn't try for herself.

15

CARRIE SAT BEHIND the wheel, feeling hot and uncomfortable in her black trouser suit, as she drove along the A30, heading for Bristol. The mid-morning traffic was heavier than she'd expected, with vehicles of all shapes and sizes shooting along the dual carriageway. She didn't know why she'd dressed so smartly. It wasn't like she was going to a job interview or a business meeting.

It had been four days since her phone call to Doctor Jensen. Four days in which guilt had risen up to consume her. There had been no further developments in the Church family murder investigation. Lindsay Church had still not been found. Carrie had tried to do what Detective Constable Turner had advised—to get on with her life—but it was proving difficult. Like right now, for instance. She was on her way to visit her murderous son, who was locked away at a secure hospital in Bristol.

As she changed lanes, she glanced through the side window at the vast stretch of Bodmin Moor, barren peaks and crags rising up in the distance. The emptiness fed her anxiety, reminded her of how she felt sometimes in the cramped streets of Porth an Jowl with everyone staring and pointing fingers—isolated and alone. She checked the clock on the dashboard, then her arrival time on the

Satnav. The closer she was getting, the more her anxiety was spinning out of control.

Melissa was with Dylan until Saturday. She hadn't told either of them where she was going. Just last week, Melissa had said that if Cal came home, she would go to live with her dad. Who could blame her? She was still having nightmares, still traumatised by that night in her bedroom when she'd watched her brother stab her grandmother. All Carrie wanted was for Melissa to feel safe again. All she wanted was for Cal to be well. But it was as if she had to choose between the two. Like one would cancel out the other.

She thought about Cal coming home one day and re-joining the family. Wondered if that day would come. Or if it even should. She was still having trouble coming to terms with Cal's crimes. He'd taken a life. Almost two. And even though Carrie knew he was a victim himself, that Grady Spencer had destroyed him, she still couldn't separate the violence.

As for Dylan, she didn't even know what was happening. He'd been the one to suggest a trial separation, the one to say their marriage was impossible with Cal still around. But lately, since he and Carrie had been spending time apart, Dylan was behaving like he'd changed his mind. There were little signs—a warm smile, a lingering look, staying around for coffee after dropping Melissa home. The only trouble was Carrie didn't know if she felt the same. Melissa, Dylan, and Cal—they couldn't exist within the same circle. To have them all in her life, she would have to tear herself down the middle. Only give them half of her time. Would that mean she could only give them half of her love, too? She didn't think that was—

An urgent, angry, blast of a car horn ripped her from her thoughts. Carrie looked up, saw that she'd drifted halfway into the next lane, dangerously close to another vehicle. With a cry, she spun the wheel, quickly pulling away and back into the correct lane. The other car shot past, horn still blasting, an angry face screaming obscenities at the driver window.

Her heart crashed against her chest. Her hands trembled on the wheel. She'd almost died! What would have happened to her children then? What would have happened to Cal?

Seeing a sign for a service station, Carrie changed lanes, then took the next junction. She followed the road, slowing down, until she reached the service station, which was a mishmash of overpriced eateries, coffee shops, and fuel pumps. Parking the car, she let go of the wheel and buried her face in her hands.

What was she doing? Why was everything so damn hard? Tears came, splashing on her suit. How could she help Cal when she couldn't help herself? How could showing up at the hospital when she wasn't ready to see him do any good?

Pulling a tissue from her bag on the passenger seat, she dried her eyes, then glanced out the window. A family was leaving its car and heading towards one of the coffee shops. She watched the children skipping along next to their parents, happy and carefree. She'd had that once. Wondered if she would ever get it back again.

She'd call the hospital and apologise. Then she would go home. Maybe try again next week.

No. Whether you feel it or not, he's still your son. He needs you. Now more than any other time. And you need him.

Dumping the tissue, Carrie cleared her throat, checked her appearance in the rear-view mirror. "You can do this."

She started up the engine and continued her journey to Bristol.

*

By the time she arrived at the hospital, her heart was beating so wildly she thought she might faint. The guard at the security gate lifted the barrier and waved her through. Carrie parked the car in the visitors section and switched off the engine. She sat there for a minute, still and unsteady, trying to slow her breathing. She glanced up at the hospital building, clean and modern, its exterior masking the anguish that lay within.

Steeling herself, she pushed the door open and headed inside. At the reception desk, she signed in, then was shown to a room, where she emptied her pockets and put her belongings into a locker. Next came a body search. Then she waited, growing more and more anxious with the passing of each minute. Just when she thought she might turn around again and head back home, a burly nurse arrived to escort her to one of the visitor rooms.

He was waiting inside. Cal. Her son. Sitting at a table in an empty space devoid of sharp objects or anything else that could be used to cause harm.

The nurse stayed by the door. He was tall and muscular, his expression hard and cold. But Carrie had spoken to him before and knew that beneath the steely exterior he was sympathetic and kind.

Sitting down at the other end of the table, Carrie placed her hands on her lap and looked up at her son. His appearance shocked her. He was terribly thin. The skin of his face clung to his cheekbones. The hollows under his eyes were like two shallow graves. And those eyes, usually so deep and dark, had grown horribly dull.

"Oh, Cal... What have you done to yourself?"

But even as the words left her mouth, she knew that this was *her* doing. She'd abandoned him. Turned her back and left him alone for weeks.

"I'm sorry," she whispered, her voice cracking. "I'm so sorry."

Cal sat, motionless, disappearing inside his clothes, his head downcast and turned away from her.

"You need to eat, baby. You need to do what the doctors tell you and eat something. You need your strength or you won't get better."

She stared at him, mouth half open, tears brimming. Cal didn't even blink. It was like he was somewhere else.

It's the drugs, she thought. *They're pumping him with all sorts of medications, turning him into a zombie.*

No, it's because he's gone. Dr Jensen was right. My sweet boy is gone.

Carrie cleared her throat and tried again.

"Cal? Can you hear me? Can you just say hello?"

A thick globule of saliva slipped from the corner of his mouth and hung there precariously. Carrie recoiled, unable to tear her gaze away.

"Cal? Baby? I just wanted to tell you that—"

His fist shot out and slammed down hard on the table. Carrie flinched. At the door, the nurse sprang awake.

"Cal," he warned. "Watch yourself."

Slowly, Cal turned his head. The drool that was hanging from his mouth broke free. He looked up and stared at Carrie, his dead eyes coming back to life, glittering with hate, then growing darker by the second, until she felt like she was falling into a black hole.

"I'm sorry," she breathed. "I didn't mean to leave you. I was scared, but I'm here now."

Cal lowered his head. His fist, which was still curled on the table, quietly withdrew. The fury that had gripped him only seconds ago vanished. He looked at Carrie again and this time she saw two fathomless pools of sadness. A single tear escaped from one of them and sailed along the sharp contours of his face, before splashing on the table. Then he turned away and disappeared once more.

Carrie stared at him. *You did this. You gave him up and now he's never coming back.*

She looked at the nurse as she choked back more tears. He gave her a nod and a sympathetic sigh.

"Come on, Cal," he said gently. "Time to go."

Back in her car, Carrie sat behind the wheel and stared up at the hospital. She felt empty. Like there was nothing left to try. She couldn't fix this. Couldn't fix her son. Didn't know how. Or if he could ever be saved.

Let him go, a voice whispered in her ear. *Set him free.*

The tears she'd been fighting to keep inside escaped. She sobbed loudly, a flood of pain, guilt, and grief erupting from her body.

Let him go. You've done all you can.

But he was her son and she was his mother. She could never let him go.

Could she?

Her phone was ringing. Wiping her eyes and sucking in a steadying breath, Carrie pulled it from her bag and glanced at the screen, half-expecting it to be Dr Jensen calling to encourage her back inside. But it was a number she didn't recognise.

"Hello?" she said, trying to keep her voice calm.

"Carrie?"

The world turned upside down. A hundred memories came crashing through her mind like a train wreck.

"Kye? Is that you?"

"Yeah, it's me. I know this is out of the blue, but. . ."

Carrie was silent, shocked by the voice on the phone.

"It's been a long time," Kye said, sounding awkward. "How are you doing?"

The shock was fading, replaced by anger. "What do you want, Kye? This isn't a good time."

"I'm in town. In Porth an Jowl. I was wondering if we could meet up."

Memories danced behind her eyes. Sitting on a beach at night. Curled up in the back seat of a car, naked and sweaty, limbs wrapped around each other. Stepping out of a bathroom and showing him the blue strip of a pregnancy test kit.

"Please, Carrie. I need to talk to you. It's important."

She was silent, still reeling.

"How about eight tonight? At The Shack?"

Carrie clamped her jaw together, unable to speak. Instead, she listened to his breaths in her ear.

"Carrie? Are you still there?"

She stiffened. Glanced at her reflection in the rear-view mirror. Pushed away the memories and the grief. Pushed away Cal's angry dark eyes, full of hate.

"I'm here," she said. "What do you want to talk to me about?"

"It's better if we do it in person. Face-to-face. So, The Shack? Tonight?"

Carrie glanced out the window at the smooth, grey walls of the hospital.

"Fine," she said, her voice tight and clipped. "But it better be important."

"It is," he said. "See you at eight."

Then he was gone, leaving Carrie alone in silence and staring at her phone.

Dumping it in her bag, she pulled her seatbelt across and started the engine. What else was the week going to throw at her?

She stared up at the hospital again.

"I'm sorry, baby," she whispered.

Then she was driving out of the car park and starting the journey home.

16

SITTING IN THE dark, time had escaped her. She didn't know if hours, days, or merely minutes had passed. Lindsay felt strange, as if she were simultaneously sitting here on the bed in this dank cell and falling endlessly through space. Sometimes, she felt so hot that she thought her skin was blistering. Other times, it was if she felt nothing at all. And she was forgetting. Forgetting who she was. Forgetting her name. Forgetting the faces of her family. She was trying to remember them. Mum. Dad. Todd. But it was as if shadows had crept into her mind and were painting over her memories.

She'd been awake for a while now. Or maybe it was seconds. The ground beneath her feet felt cold and hard one minute, the next like sponge. Getting up, she shuffled over to the bucket in the corner, where she squatted and urinated. When she was done, she pulled up her shorts and reached out a hand, until she was touching the wall.

She began her daily routine: first walking the length of the wall, feeling the bricks against her fingertips, then turning right, hearing the dull thud of her fingers bouncing off the bars of the door, then turning right again, tracing the opposite wall, standing on the bed, walking along until she reached the far wall, then turning right again, stepping down, shuffling along until her foot kicked the bucket and sloshed some of its contents on the floor. Then the journey started again, over and over, around and around, until she grew dizzy or until she blacked out, whichever came first.

She was on her third cycle when she froze. Someone was unlocking the front door to the building. Moving unsteadily, Lindsay crawled onto the bed, pressed her back against the wall, and shielded her eyes. Bright light flooded the corridor outside, spilling into her cell. Was it Cynthia bringing her food again? She felt like she'd eaten only minutes ago. Or perhaps it had been days.

But it wasn't Cynthia. It was someone else.

Squinting through her fingers, Lindsay saw the outline of a man. Her heart thumped in her chest. She pressed her spine harder against the wall.

The man stood on the other side of the cell door, silently watching her. As Lindsay's vision began to adjust to the light, she saw that the man was in fact a boy. Maybe a year or two older than Todd. He was tall and lean, with short hair and intense, dark eyes that seemed to penetrate her skin.

"Don't be afraid," the boy said. "My name is Heath."

Every cell of Lindsay's body quivered. His voice—she recognised it instantly. Through the fog, she was suddenly back at the holiday home, watching a boy in a devil's mask open her brother's throat with a knife.

Heath leaned forward, wrapping his fingers around the door bars.

"I'm sorry for keeping you in here," he said. "Cynthia tells me you've been very well behaved. She thinks you're ready to join our family."

Images flashed in Lindsay's mind. Her brother's terrified face. The blade plunging into his neck. Blood spurting from the hole it made in a wide arc. Then her mind was growing blank again, her body growing numb and heavy. Lindsay fought to stay focused. She dragged nails across her shins. She pinched the skin on her calves.

"You killed my family," she croaked, barely recognising the voice coming out of her mouth.

Heath smiled, shook his head. "We freed you from their shackles. We're your family now. Children are the New Dawn and no one can hurt you anymore."

Lindsay stared at him. She didn't understand what he was saying. She didn't know what a New Dawn was and she didn't need to be set free from her family. No one was hurting her, except maybe Todd once in a while, when he'd pinch her for taking his things without asking.

She didn't like the way he was watching her. She didn't like the way he kept sniffing and rubbing at his nose.

"Are you ready?" Heath asked. "Are you ready to become a child of the Dawn?"

Lindsay scratched at her shins. She felt blood trickling down to her ankles. She hated this cell. She hated being swamped in darkness, the stench of her own filth burning her nostrils. She hated this feeling of falling. But she had a feeling that whatever lay on the other side of the door was far more dangerous.

"You're free to speak," Heath said, rubbing his nose again. "The Dawn Children are all equal. We are all each other. Together we will cleanse the world of all threats to children. Together we will bring in the New Dawn."

She watched him mutter something to himself, then glance over his shoulder as if someone was there. But Heath was alone. Where was Cynthia? She was much nicer, even if she hadn't let

Lindsay out of the cell.

Heath dug a hand into his pocket and pulled out a set of keys. They clinked together, singing of freedom.

"If you're ready to join us I can let you out," he said. "But first you must do one thing. You must say goodbye to the people you saw as your family. Because once you're out of this room, you can never speak their names. You can never think of them or shed tears for them. Because those people you call your family did not love you. You were their possession. A puppet they controlled. They told you what to do, what to wear, how to think. They poisoned your mind with lies so that you would never wake up and see the truth or question their authority. Those people are gone and you are born again. Do you accept the Dawn Children as your rightful family? As your brothers and sisters?"

Lindsay thought about it. If she stayed in this cell, she was going to die. She knew it with unfettered clarity. But if she stepped outside. . . She didn't understand half of the things this boy was saying to her. She didn't know who the Dawn Children were, except maybe kids like him. How did she know that she would be safe if she agreed to forget her family? Which she could never do. Not if she tried.

Heath was still watching her, his unnerving, predatory gaze making her skin crawl.

If she got out of this room, she could try to escape. If she could escape, she could go to the police.

Slowly, Lindsay pushed herself away from the wall and placed her feet on the floor. Her brother's terrified face flashed in her mind, begging for his life.

Lindsay nodded.

"I need to hear you say it. Do you accept the Dawn Children as your new family?"

Lindsay stared at him, unblinking. "Yes."

Heath slipped the key into the lock and twisted it to the left. The gate swung open on creaking hinges.

"Welcome Lindsay, daughter of the Dawn." Heath bowed dramatically, flourishing a hand, as if he were greeting royalty. When Lindsay didn't move, he glanced up and started laughing. "Well come on then, silly. You're acting like a big baby."

Lindsay stood in the centre of the cell, staring at the open door and the corridor beyond. Her legs were shaking and she was sure her heart was going to burst right through her chest, just like the alien in that stupid old film Todd had let her watch one evening, when their parents had been out.

Slowly, carefully, she forced one foot forward, then the other. She drew closer to the open door. To Heath, who laughed and clapped.

"That's it! You're one of us now."

He held out a hand as Lindsay reached the threshold. She stared at his outstretched fingers, felt them wrap around her own tiny hand.

"This way, my lady," he said, flashing her a smile, as if they were friends and she hadn't been locked up in a dark, filthy prison cell for god knows how long. As if he hadn't slaughtered her family right in front of her eyes.

Lindsay stepped out of the cell. Together, they walked along a long corridor, until they reached the front door. Heath told her to cover her eyes, which she did with her free hand. Heath opened the door and all the light in the world flooded in.

Lindsay gasped and squeezed her eyes shut. A cold breeze teased her skin and whipped her hair. She could smell salt and the sea.

She allowed herself to be led blindly along a path, its concrete hard and cold beneath her bare feet as she was pulled and turned and twisted, as the sound of ocean waves crashing on rocks roared in her ears. She wanted to open her eyes. To know where she'd been taken, but she was scared that if she dropped her hand right now the light would make her blind.

Then it went dark and quiet. The ground changed from rough to smooth. A door slammed behind her, making her jump. She was inside again, and for a moment, she was terrified that she was still inside that fetid cell and she'd finally lost her mind.

Lindsay lowered her hand. She was in another corridor, but this one had windows that let in squares of light high above her head. There were lockers. Coats hung on hooks. She heard voices. Heath pulled her along until they were standing outside yet another door. The voices were coming from the other side. Children's voices.

Heath stared down at her, his dilated pupils dark and glittering. "Are you ready to meet your new family?"

Lindsay nodded. Not because she wanted to, but because there was no way she was going back to that prison cell.

Still staring at her, Heath pushed open the door and a wall of noise rushed out. Lindsay sheepishly peered inside and saw children. Some were younger than her, others a year or two older. All were seated at rows of benches, eating cold food from tins. Some of them glanced up as Lindsay entered the room.

Heath was smiling now. "You see? We are all children here. Children of the New Dawn. All innocent and all strong."

Lindsay stared at the children's dirty faces and soiled clothes, hair sticking out along with their bones. Not one of them looked strong to her. If anything, they looked like those sad children she sometimes saw on TV or on posters at the bus stop; the ones that charities were always needing money for.

A girl was strolling over. She was tall and thin with long, straggly hair, and she was about the same age as Heath. Lindsay flinched as she leaned over her and smiled.

"I'm Alison," she said, her dull eyes huge and round. "I'm your big sister."

Lindsay stared at her. She didn't have a big sister and she didn't want one. She wanted her brother. She stepped back. A dark, empty chasm opened up inside her.

"You don't need to be afraid," Alison said, still smiling. "We're all family here. We all love you."

"Get her cleaned up and fed," Heath said. "She can sleep with you and the others tonight."

He let go of Lindsay's hand, who rubbed her fingers as she eyed the other children. Why were they all eating out of tins? Couldn't they afford a microwave? No wonder they were all thin as rakes.

"Come on," Alison said, taking Lindsay gently by the arm. "Let's get you some fresh clothes and something to eat. Then you can meet your new brothers and sisters."

But Lindsay wouldn't move. She was transfixed by the other children in the room. She wondered if their families had been taken away from them, too. She wondered if they had all been made orphans. Because that's what she was now, wasn't it? It didn't matter if Alison called these kids her brothers and sisters. Lindsay was all alone and no one from her old life knew where to find her.

"Where's Luke?" Heath said.

Lindsay stared up at him and it was like watching a storm roll in over a blue sky. His smile was gone, replaced by something else. Something much darker.

Alison hesitated, avoiding his gaze. She nodded uncertainly to the far corner. "He's over there with. . ." Her face turned the colour of sour milk. Lindsay followed her gaze towards the empty corner.

Heath's eyes flashed and he seemed to grow taller as he turned on Alison.

"Where is she?" he hissed. "Where is Cynthia?"

Frightened now, Lindsay returned her gaze to Heath. She thought it would be a good idea to keep watching him whenever he was around.

"Alison, I asked you a question. Where are Cynthia and Luke?"

"I don't know!" Alison whined. "They were here a few minutes ago, I swear to you!"

"Fuck!" Heath curled his hand into a fist and smashed it into the open door. The door slammed against the wall and bounced back. The room fell deathly silent, all eyes frozen on him, mouths hanging open.

Alison's grip on Lindsay's arm grew unbearably tight.

Then Heath was storming out of the room and screaming at the top of his lungs, calling people's names. Her breaths coming thin and fast, Lindsay stared at the space he'd left behind and she realised that she'd been transported from her tiny prison cell to a much bigger one.

17

THIS WAS THE end. The end of everything. Cynthia stood at the cliff edge, teetering in the wind. The sky was a maelstrom of burnt orange and blood red, the ocean seething and grey, smashing down onto rocks below. This world; it was full of poison. It had sought to make Cynthia sick since the day she was born. It had hurt her, manipulated her, forced her to do terrible things and have terrible things done to her. Jacob had saved her and then he had let her go. He had abandoned her and she had abandoned all hope. It was such a precious thing, hope. Precious and surprisingly fragile. Jacob had stolen hers. Reached into her heart and ripped it from her very soul.

Well, no more.

Cynthia inched closer to the edge. She was terrified, chilled to the bone. Could she do it? Could she keep her eyes shut all the way down? She didn't know where suicide would take her. She'd never believed in Heaven or Hell. But she had believed in Jacob and the New Dawn. It was gone. Nothing mattered. All Cynthia wanted was for the pain to leave her. All she wanted was to be in peace.

Movement caught her eye. A gull was hovering in the distance, wings spread wide as it cruised the winds. If only she could be like that bird now, free and unbound. She leaned forward, the wind snatching away her tears, making her eyes sting.

"Goodbye," she whimpered.

Commotion behind her. Panicked voices and footsteps. Chain-link fence clanging as bodies pushed through the hole.

Cynthia turned around. She heaved in cold, biting air. Her teeth chattered.

Heath, Morwenna, and a gaggle of teenagers were all gathered together in front of the fence, frightened and confused eyes fixed on hers. All except Heath's, which were dark and angry like the ocean below.

"What have you done?" he snarled. "Where's Luke?"

Cynthia trembled, the fingers of each hand clawing at her sides. "Don't come any closer!"

But Heath did come closer. His gaze flicked between Cynthia and the cliff edge, just inches behind. Cynthia started to cry. She didn't want to—tears were a sign of weakness—but so was leaping to her death.

"All I ever wanted was to go with you!" she sobbed. "It was all I ever dreamt of doing. Jacob promised me—he was Father and I was Mother, and we would go together, hand in hand, crossing into the Dawn with all our beautiful children!" She took a step back, dangerously close to the edge. "Why won't you let me go?"

Heath lowered his head but kept his gaze fixed on her. There was something violent and twisted lurking inside him. She'd always known it was there. Jacob, too. It was why he had used Heath to take care of all the obstacles that blocked their way, even those obstacles made of blood and bone. That was Heath's role—the Path Clearer. Bringer of Justice. But he was never meant to lead. He didn't have the discipline or the understanding. He wasn't capable of loving the children in the same way that Jacob had loved them. He was broken and brittle, a shard of glass, a serrated blade. How could he be Father when he still needed to be saved?

"Last chance, Cynthia," he said, stepping closer. "Where is Luke?"

"Get away from me!" she screamed.

Heath lunged forward. A hand pulled him back. Morwenna spoke soothing words in his ear. Gently stroked his face. Heath shook his head. His shoulders sagged. Then he took a step back.

Cynthia stared at Morwenna, her least favourite of them all.

"Listen," the young woman said, addressing her now. "I know we haven't always seen eye to eye, you and me, and I know things haven't been the same for you since Jacob was lost to us. But he was our father and losing him hurt us just as much as it hurt you."

Cynthia glared. Lies! All lies!

"Jacob paved the way for us all. He led us, kept us safe from harm. But Jacob could only take us so far—because Jacob is an adult. Just like you, Cynthia. Your work here is done. Now is the time of children. Now is the time for you to sit back and let us become who we were always meant to be." Morwenna paused, clasping her hands together as if in prayer. "Please, Cynthia. I'm begging you—what have you done with Luke? Because if you set him free, if you sent him into the world, all you've done is feed him to the wolves. A little boy alone out there is a target for monsters. Paedophiles, murderers, abusers that will hurt him then leave him for dead. Is that what you wanted? What kind of mother would do that to her child?"

Cynthia's gaze shifted nervously from Morwenna to Heath, to the other children. "No! I—I would never put a child in danger."

It was a trick. They were trying to confuse her. Trying to make her feel guilty. She was their mother. She would never hurt her children, not even Heath. But now she wondered if they were right. Had she set Luke into a world full of monsters? Jacob had always said that people were cruel. That, given a chance, anyone could hurt a child. Had she gone against everything that he had taught her? She slid a foot back, feeling the ground loosen beneath her shoe.

"Please!" Morwenna said, begging now. "Tell us where he is so we can save him!"

Cynthia shook her head violently. It was a trick. Luke was weak. Heath had made it clear—only the strong would be saved. If she told them where Luke was, that would be throwing him to the wolves. At least in the world of monsters, he could find a place to hide. Here, Heath would make sure no stone was left unturned.

Cynthia stuck out her chin, a smile on her lips. "Luke is already saved."

Morwenna's hands curled into fists. Beside her, Heath clenched his jaw, flashing his teeth.

"You will never feel the light of the New Dawn!" he screamed.

The Dawn Children rushed forward. They were all Cynthia's children. She had cared for each one of them. She had fed them, clothed them, healed them when they were sick and rocked them to sleep in their darkest hours.

Now, they were coming for her.

With a cry, Cynthia spun on her heels. The ocean swung into view. She leapt forwards. Then hands were upon her, gripping her arms, her back, her hair, pulling her away from the cliff edge, dragging her along the stony ground, back towards the compound.

"No!" she screamed. "No! No! No!"

She kicked and thrashed. Someone drove a foot into her stomach, knocking the air from her lungs. Then they were pulling her along again, wrenching her through the hole in the fence, sharp mesh scratching her skin.

"Adults cannot be trusted," Heath said. He and Morwenna followed behind, their eyes growing cold and blank.

18

LUKE'S FEET DRAGGED through the dust, kicking up stones, as he followed the dirt track that looped and coiled like a great snake. As he walked, his eyes stared blankly ahead. It had been a long time since he had been outside. A long time since he'd been trapped inside a dream. But now he was starting to wake up. He blinked. Once. Twice. The world pulled into focus.

It was evening, the sun setting in swathes of tangerine and plum, a cool breeze blowing up from the ocean to make his teeth chatter and his hair dance. He inhaled and air rushed into his lungs, cold and crisp, making him feel suddenly alive. A real boy, not a puppet.

The more he walked, the more he became aware of his surroundings. Moorland stretched out on both sides, speckled with yellow flowers and thorny spines. From somewhere to the left came the low roar of the ocean. It sounded like it was calling his name.

Luke stumbled on, not knowing where he was going, only that Cynthia had told him to follow the path, and that the path would take him somewhere safe. Away from the compound. Away from his brothers and sisters, even though he knew they weren't really his brothers and sisters.

Cynthia had set him free. He didn't know why. She had pushed him through the hole in the fence, had taken him roughly by the hand and led him along the perimeter, ducking down here and there, keeping silent, until they had reached the track.

"Go!" she had hissed. "Don't look back!"

She'd shoved him hard, sending him staggering along, almost tripping over his own feet. He'd been walking ever since, not looking back, only looking forward.

But something strange was happening to him.

The further Luke moved away from the compound, the more afraid he was becoming. And it wasn't because he was scared they would come after him. It was because he was afraid of what lay ahead.

The outside world was a cruel and dangerous place, filled with monsters who wanted to eat children alive, or worse. The outside world was a cup of poison. A knife with a sharp edge. The New Dawn was going to save them from it. He'd never known what that meant. He'd never known what any of it meant. But he knew what monsters were and he knew what they did to little children.

What if he was walking towards one now? Stumbling towards a wide, open mouth filled with razor sharp teeth? What if he was dragged, kicking and screaming, into an empty building, or into the woods, where he would be devoured, his meat stripped from his bones? The Dawn Children were his protection, Heath had told him. Luke had believed it for a while.

But now that he was waking up, he wasn't so sure.

The landscape was changing. Becoming softer, gentler. The track turned into a road. Hedgerows appeared alongside fields and trees. Up ahead, on the edge of the road, there was a house. Luke's father hadn't been a monster. He was sure of that. His father had been kind and caring and had always made him laugh. The day his parents had separated had been the worst day of his life. After that, his Mum sometimes cried or got angry. His Dad, too. But they never once tried to hurt him or eat him whole like Heath had said.

He could still remember the night the Dawn Children came. His memory was fuzzy at the edges and had gaps in it, but he could still recall standing on the stairs at home, watching in horror as his father was beaten unconscious with a hammer. He could still feel Heath's powerful hands snatching him up and throwing him over his shoulder, could still remember the smell of his father's blood in the back of that van.

Heath had tried to tell him he was remembering it wrong. Heath had tried to tell him that the Dawn Children had saved him from a world of monsters. But it hadn't felt like being saved, not for a second. It had felt like being eaten alive.

Above Luke's head, the last of the day was vanishing fast and the sky was growing dark. Exhaustion had crept up on him. His spindly legs ached and complained. He closed his eyes for a second and began to stagger. His mind was trying to send him back to the dream world again. But he had to stay awake. He had to get to safety.

Be careful of the monsters! Monsters are everywhere and they'll gobble you up!

His feet dragged along the ground. His breathing grew more laboured. The house was just ahead now, and further along the road even more homes. A whole village of them.

Luke shivered.

What if the Dawn Children were right and Cynthia was wrong? She was an adult. Adults could not be trusted.

Grinding to a halt, he glanced over his shoulder. The road was clear and still. He turned back to face the house, his empty stomach grumbling and churning. It was just a few metres ahead of him now, its front door opening right onto the road. The curtains were closed, but he could see light sneaking out through the cracks. He knew he should go in there, should knock on the door. But what if they were bad people? What if they threw him over a shoulder and dragged him into the basement?

What if he was never seen again?

Luke stared up at the house, tears brimming in his frightened eyes. Cynthia had told him to go to the village; that's where she said he would be safe. But now he wondered if he would be safer back at the compound, back with Alison and the other children. He could go to sleep again, even with his eyes wide open.

No. He had to keep going.

He didn't know where his dad was anymore, but he knew his mum was still out there. She would have been worried all this time. Scared that something had happened to her little boy.

Luke missed her. He missed his bedroom and his toys. He missed his reception class and his friends. And he'd missed his birthday, which he knew was in winter, and that meant he was five now, not four, because winter had come and gone a long time ago. Perhaps when he got home, there'd be a big birthday present waiting for him.

Luke pushed on, passing the house, heading for the village. Now there were more lights and there were people in the distance, walking their dogs. He liked dogs. Especially little ones with sandy-coloured fur and wagging tails. Sweat dampening his brow, Luke sped up.

Then came a rumbling sound from somewhere behind. Luke walked faster. He knew that sound. He'd recognised it instantly. It was the same sound that had filled his ears on the night he'd been taken. The roar of an engine belonging to a big, white van.

His little arms swung by his sides. His tiny muscles shrieked and complained. Tears sprang from his eyes and splashed down his face.

He didn't want to go back there! He wanted to see his mum! But now the van was pulling up beside him, its exhaust pipe spewing noxious fumes.

Luke froze. He glanced up at the van, saw the driver door open and Heath sitting behind the wheel.

His bottom lip trembled as Heath leaned forward.

"Hey there, little man," he said with a smile, then glanced along the road, clocking the dog walkers in the distance. "Where do you think you're going?"

Luke began to sob.

"I'm going home," he wailed and rubbed his eyes.

Still smiling, Heath extended a hand. "Then you're going in the wrong direction. Your home's back that way."

Luke shook his head. He turned around, saw the house that he'd passed by, contemplated running towards it while screaming at the top of his lungs.

But Heath was staring at him with a look that chilled his blood.

"Get in the van, Luke," he said. "Get in the van now."

Still sobbing, Luke did as he was told, slowly climbing inside and sitting next to Heath, who leaned across him and shut the door.

"Good boy," he said and wiped a tear from Luke's face, making him flinch.

He rolled the van forward, into the village, past the people and their dogs, past more houses and a church, until the village was disappearing in the rear-view mirror and they were driving through the countryside, the light almost gone.

In the passenger seat, Luke stared out at the darkness. The hairs on the back of his neck stood up. This was not the way back to the compound. He glanced over at Heath, whose eyes were fixed on the road. Maybe he had changed his mind. Maybe he was going to take Luke back home to his mother.

Heath turned, saw Luke staring from the shadows.

"Don't worry," he said. "We all have a role to play in the New Dawn. Even those who are too weak to cross over."

Then he was quiet, gazing ahead, one hand on the wheel and the other on the gear stick. Luke stared at the darkness again. He was worried. More worried than he'd ever felt in his short, young life.

19

THEY MET AT The Shack beach bar, which in hindsight had not been the best idea. It was busy with tourists catching an evening dinner and drinks, but there were locals here, too, filling the tables and sandy floorboards. And of course, they were staring. And whispering.

Carrie sat at a table in the corner, eyes flicking around the room as she attempted to focus on the surf rock music playing from the speakers. She'd only been here for twenty minutes but it already felt like a lifetime. She watched Kye at the bar, watched the way he smiled and chatted to those who knew him, some of the men clapping him on the shoulder and wondering what he was doing back here in the cove. The same question was on Carrie's mind.

Her first instinct had been to decline his invitation. Yet here she was and now he was coming back over with more drinks and a smile; one that didn't reach his eyes, she noted, which were haunted just like her own.

"Here," he said, setting a tall glass in front of her, then sitting down.

Carrie stared at the drink. It had been months since she'd touched a drop of alcohol but meeting up with a ghost from the past could never be done dry. She brought the glass to her lips, tasting the fizz of cola and the bitterness of vodka. She made a mental note not to down it as quickly as she'd done with the first.

Kye was staring at her. It had been almost seven years since she'd last seen him, but except for a few more weathered lines and a patch of premature grey in his beard, he looked much the same. He was handsome in a rugged kind of way; just like Dylan. But where Dylan had a steely countenance regardless of his mood, Kye's eyes were soft and deep, revealing some of the complexity beneath. He smiled at her, warm and disarming.

"He has your eyes," Carrie said at last, her voice barely audible over the din of the bar. An image of Cal sitting across from the table at the hospital flashed in her mind and guilt ripped through her.

Pain flickered across Kye's face and he glanced away. Someone called out his name. He raised a hand and smiled. When he turned back to Carrie, the smile was gone.

"Why are you here?" she asked him. "It's been years. So, why now?"

For a long time, he remained silent and staring. Then, taking a drink of beer, he set his glass down and said, "Dad's sick. Cancer."

"Oh... I'm sorry. How bad?"

"Stage four. They're treating him but it's not looking good. Anyway, it's not the only reason. I thought it was about time we talked."

Carrie leaned forward. It felt hot in the bar, like they had the heaters running despite the warm summer air. "It was about time six months ago. I gave up trying to call you."

"Well, that one you can't blame me for. If I'd found out sooner that . . . that he'd come home . . . I would have been here," Kye said, suddenly angry. "The only reason I knew he was alive in the first place was because my parents told me. What the hell, Carrie? You knew I was halfway around the world on a fucking oil rig. If you'd told me right away, I could have made it back in time before he. . ."

His voice cracked. He picked up his beer and swallowed half of it.

Carrie's gaze sank to the table. "Cal needed a couple of weeks to get used to being back. I had no idea what was going to happen. If I'd known I would have—"

"I was his father!" His eyes flashed in the dim lighting. On the next table, a middle-aged couple—strangers in this town—looked up from their meals. Kye ignored them. "I had a right to see my son. You should have told me as soon as he'd come back."

"Things were difficult. I was in shock. One minute Cal was dead, the next he was back." Carrie shook her head. The couple on the next table was still staring. All around the bar, faces were turning in her direction. "I can't stay in here."

She stood, the room closing in on her, Cal's hate-filled eyes burning into her mind. She pushed her way through the crowds, almost knocking someone's drink over as she headed towards the door. Somewhere ahead of her, a dog barked loudly from beneath a table. Throwing open the door, she rushed outside.

The world fell quiet. The air was cool on her skin, the sand soft beneath her sandals. It was dusk. Stars glimmered in the wide, darkening sky. Yellow lights twinkled from the town.

Carrie turned away from them. The last remnants of the sun lay on the horizon. The sea was calm, the gentle whisper of the tide soothing her chaotic mind. For months, she had struggled to come back to the beach. The place where her son had disappeared. Where, seven years ago, her life had been torn to pieces and thrown into the wind. The calmness she felt now surprised her. She walked a few paces, heading towards the ocean. The spot where the Mermaid Hotel had once stood on the left cliff was vast and open, the sky painting over its terrible legacy. On the right cliff, the old lighthouse kept watch over the town, its beam of light cutting through the sky. Behind it, Briar Wood shifted mysteriously in the shadows.

The door to The Shack opened and noise spilled out. Then it was quiet again. Until she heard the sand shifting as someone approached.

"I'm sorry," Carrie said, without turning around. "That's what you want to hear, isn't it? That's why you came."

She glanced over her shoulder to see Kye's tall, lithe figure cast in shadows. He was quiet, watching her. Returning her gaze to the sea, she watched the tide fold in on itself and break into white spools of foam.

"I should have called you. I should have let you know the moment he came back."

Kye came up behind her and she felt an old yet familiar crackle of energy surge between them. She didn't turn around, kept her eyes fixed on the flotsam and jetsam. Then Kye was beside her, eyes pointed in the same direction.

"I was never a good dad," he said. "I abandoned him. Went off to work on the rigs when he was so young."

Carrie glanced at him, saw his head hanging low. "We've all made mistakes. I made the worst one."

"What do you mean?"

"If I hadn't taken my eyes off him that day at the beach, none of this would have ever happened." She turned to him, desperation

164

choking her voice. "Do you blame me? Do you blame me like everyone else?"

Kye looked up, slowly shook his head.

"No, I don't. I blame the psychopath that took him. I blame the police for not looking close enough to home. I blame myself for leaving and abandoning our son. But I don't blame you. Maybe back then I did, but I was young and stupid. Mostly, I was just angry at myself."

He reached out a hand and brushed hair away from Carrie's face; an intimate gesture that she would have slapped away had it been anyone else. But she allowed him to do it, and for a second she was seventeen again, spending night after night down at the beach with him, the only place where they had privacy to talk.

"I'm sorry," she said. "I'm sorry for all of this." She turned around, fighting back tears as she stared up at the town. "This damn place! I can't breathe here. I feel like all the houses are falling on top of me. All I want is to leave."

"So, leave."

"How can I? I can't take Melissa away from her dad. She needs him. She needs regularity and routine. Besides, every penny I have is going to Cal's solicitor. I can't afford a day out in Truro, never mind moving to another town. I can't leave. I've lived here my whole sorry life. I'll probably die here, too."

She shook her head in frustration. Three nights ago, she'd sat down with a calculator and worked out that even if she sold Cove Crafts and re-mortgaged the house, she might just about break even. But there would be nothing left. Maybe that was the way it had to be. Sometimes you had to sacrifice yourself to save your children. Even if your children were stone cold killers.

Kye let out a long, trembling breath. "How is he? How is Cal?"

"Not good. He's stopped eating. His doctor thinks he's giving up. I went to see him today and it was like he was dying right in front of my eyes. I don't know what to think anymore. What to do. He's my son—our son—and I've loved him the same since he was growing in my belly. But he killed a man, Kye. He almost killed my mother."

"But you know that wasn't him, don't you?" Kye said. "It was Grady Spencer getting inside his head. It was that crazy cult, whoever they are, poisoning his mind and trying to control him. Our boy would never have done any of those terrible things. Our boy was always good and kind."

Carrie was losing the fight against her tears. "He was. But the Cal that came back isn't our boy anymore. Not in the same way."

A cool breeze blew up from the ocean, making her shiver. She wrapped her arms around her rib cage as she stared at Kye and a hundred memories danced behind her eyes. "How long are you staying for?"

He shrugged. "A couple of weeks, maybe longer. It depends on what happens with Dad."

"You're staying with them?"

"For now. You know they moved up to Padstow last year?"

"No, I didn't. So you came down to Porth an Jowl just to see me?"

Although the evening was growing darker by the minute, she thought she saw him blush.

"I wanted to give you something."

"You mean more than a piece of your mind?"

They both smiled.

"You should go and see him, Kye. Just call the hospital, explain who you are. It might help him."

"I. . . He hasn't seen me in years. Probably wouldn't recognise who I am."

"I'm sure he would."

"You don't know that."

"Maybe we could go together."

"Oh, sure. I can imagine your husband's face right now."

Carrie glared at him. "I told you. We're separated. Not that it has anything to do with going to see Cal."

Silence fell between them, the emptiness filled by the gentle crash of the surf and a chorus of sudden laughter floating out from The Shack.

Carrie glanced at Kye, noting his hanging head and sloping shoulders.

He has no intention of visiting Cal, she thought.

At any other time, she would have been angry with him. But how many weeks had she allowed to pass before going to see her son today? She stared at the tide, overwhelmed by sadness.

She understood how Kye felt. It would be easy for him to walk away. To leave his son in the hospital, medicated and surrounded by doctors, with who-knows-what chance of ever getting out. Cal had been dead to Kye for years. But Carrie had seen their son brought back from the dead. She had seen him return home, broken and traumatised, a shattered fragment of his former self. She had seen glimmers of hope that her son could be saved. And then she had seen that hope snuffed out.

Could she walk away from him? Turn her back on her son like everyone else?

Carrie blinked and brushed hair from her face. "What did you want to give me?"

Shifting his weight, Kye looked up at the town, then down at the sand. "You know how I used to send money for Cal at the end of each month? The money he used to buy that damn body board. . ."

Carrie put a hand on his forearm. "You don't blame me. I don't blame you, either."

Kye shrugged. "Well, after he was . . . gone . . . I kept saving the money. Each month, I put it away, thinking that if I kept doing it, maybe one day he'd come back. I know, it was stupid. But after a while, I was too scared to stop. It was like if I did, then he really would be gone." He paused. In the shadows, Carrie saw him wipe away a tear. "I've been saving money for him right up until now. There's a ton of it just sitting in an account, collecting interest. I want you to have it. Put it towards the court costs. I was a shitty dad. Let me do this for him. For both of you."

Carrie couldn't breathe. She'd been wrong.

It was Kye who was still clinging on to hope. *She* was the one who had let it go.

Kye turned, gently wrapping his arms around her waist.

"Stop," she whispered.

He leaned in, touching his head against hers. Tears glistened in the encroaching moonlight. "Sometimes I wonder what would have happened if we'd stayed together. Sometimes I wonder if Cal would still be Cal if I'd never left."

They stood for a moment, foreheads pressed together, breaths quickening and growing heavy. Carrie closed her eyes, lost in memories, enjoying the warmth emanating from his body. Then Dylan's face swam behind her eyes.

"We broke up for a reason," she said. "We were young. Stupid."

"And now we're older. Maybe a little wiser, too."

Carrie stared up at him, words catching in her throat.

"Take the money," Kye whispered. "It's a rock around my neck."

He leaned closer. His lips grazed hers. Carrie opened her mouth, letting him in. Then she pulled away.

"Don't!" she said, raising her voice. She turned back to him, tears running down her face. "It's grief, that's all! Grief makes you do stupid things."

Behind them, the door to The Shack swung open and people came spilling out. Carrie stepped back, watching the group of drunken locals—fishermen, no doubt—stumble across the sand, laughing raucously as they headed back to town.

Kye was still staring at her, his gaze dark and hopeless.

"Take the money," he said. "Please. Let me be a good dad."

Carrie stood, watching him, mind overwhelmed by conflicting thoughts.

"Come on," she said. "Let's get another drink and talk some more."

20

DAYLIGHT WAS GONE, the windows of the mess hall rectangles of blue-black. Lanterns lined each wall, making shadows dance and flicker as the children filed into the room. Each one was given a handful of tiny mushrooms, which they accepted gratefully, swallowing them down and grimacing at the bitter taste as they sat on the floor in a large circle. When the last of them was in position, Heath stepped into the centre.

He had eaten none of the mushrooms himself. He never did. He stood in silence, slowly turning, watching his subjects, waiting for the fungi's hallucinogenic properties to kick in. With some of the smaller children, it took just a couple of minutes. With the others, a little longer. But they would all soon succumb. It was their gateway to the New Dawn. Their way into the truth.

His truth—as it had been Jacob's truth before.

The problem with Jacob's truth was that it had been distorted by his adult mind, twisted with misguided views of the outside world. It was true that the world was cruel and full of monsters. But the reality was that nothing could be done to keep the children safe from harm.

Jacob believed that striking at the worst kind of monsters—paedophiles, rapists and murderers—would strike fear into evildoers' hearts, forcing them to leave the innocent unharmed. But there were too many of them. Cut off one head and another would grow in its place. Heath knew this with unfailing clarity. Which was why his truth was something more radical. His truth would set the world on fire. It would make it rain bone and blood.

The Children of the New Dawn would ascend to a new world filled with light. A world free of monsters.

He raised his hands like Jesus on the cross, staring into the soul of each captivated child. The Dawn Children stared in wonder and adoration.

"The New Dawn is upon us," he said, his voice bold and commanding. "In two days, we will emerge in a new world, where all those who hurt us shall kneel down in reverence. They will know our names! They will call us kings and queens! They will know the Children of the New Dawn!"

He continued spinning slowly, hands outstretched, lantern light making his skin sparkle and his silhouette dance and shimmer across the walls. The children gasped and laughed, their faces sharing the same mesmerised, drug-fuelled elation. Even the older teenagers were succumbing. Morwenna, too.

"For too long, the adults of this world have controlled you through violence and rape and abuse. They've tried to poison your minds. Punished you when you questioned. Chastised you if you spoke up. Well, no more! The New Dawn is upon us and they will burn in fire!"

The room erupted with excited chatter. Heath watched his subjects, eyes glazed, smiles frozen, electricity crackling around the circle, uniting them all. He held up his hands again. The children fell silent.

"Adults cannot be trusted. Even those who we thought cared for us. Adults we called Father and Mother." More silence. But now a few uncertain glances flickered in the light. "They tried to fool us. Tried to make us believe they were different. But they only sought to use us for their own gain. Father abandoned us, left us for the monsters. And now Mother—Mother has betrayed us."

He glanced at a teenage boy, no older than fourteen, who stood by the door. His name was Kit. He was young and confident. Years of abuse had sharpened his anger into a cruel blade. Kit gave a nod and left the room.

Heath continued his slow turn, staring at the swaying bodies before him, noticing the dilated pupils and half smiles. Some of the children were giggling.

Kit returned with two more boys. Cynthia was between them, hands tied behind her back, her face bruised and swollen. The circle opened up and she was thrown roughly inside. The children watched her trip over her own feet and land heavily on her stomach. The circle closed up again and the children all joined hands. An unbreakable chain.

Heath stared down at Cynthia. *So pathetic*, he thought. *Like a sick dog.* Leaning down, he helped her turn over and get onto her knees, where she swayed from side to side, seemingly half-conscious, her eyes glazed, barely registering what was about to happen.

But then Cynthia blinked and looked around the room. She was waking up.

Heath turned his palms towards the ceiling.

The children stood.

"In two days, we go into the light," he said.

Cynthia twisted her neck, searching the children's faces.

"Where's Luke?" she cried. "What have you done with him?"

"Soon we enter the New Dawn. We all must be ready. We all must play our part. Even those left behind."

He stared at Cynthia. The children stared at her, too.

"We loved you," he said. "You were our mother and you betrayed us for your own selfish means."

Cynthia screwed up her face. "Where is he? What did you do?"

"Our mother cast Luke out into the world of monsters!"

"No!" Cynthia shrieked. "You're lying! I would never hurt a child. I would never—"

"She pushed him out and left him to die! And why? Because she was jealous. Jealous that she has not been chosen to enter the New Dawn!"

"He's lying, children! It's not true!"

"Luke is dead." Teeth mashing, Heath jabbed a finger at Cynthia. Around the circle, horrified eyes glittered like dark pools. "For that, you must be punished."

Tears ran down Heath's face, the streaks glistening and sparkling. Cynthia had been a good mother to him. Together with Jacob, she had rescued him from a life of hell. She had cared for him as if he were her own. She had healed his wounds. Sung him to sleep. She had cradled him when he'd woken screaming from bad dreams. Which was why her betrayal hurt so much. Which was why what came next hurt even more.

He looked up and the circle opened again. Kit entered, a plastic cup carried gently in his hands. He handed it to Heath then retreated. The circle closed once more. Heath stared into the contents of the cup. A quiet voice in his mind pleaded with him to set Cynthia free. She can't go with you, it said, but she could stay here to live out the rest of her days.

Cynthia was weeping, her eyes puffy and red. She had betrayed the Dawn Children, but she had also saved them. She could not survive in this sick world alone. She had been rescued once, too. Better, then, to set her free.

Cynthia looked up at him, her swollen cheekbones changing her appearance. "You killed him," she moaned. "You killed Luke. That's why he isn't here."

Heath came closer, dropping his voice to a hush. "Everyone has a part to play, Cynthia. Everyone except you."

He raised the cup, turned full circle, addressing the children who were all now fully under his control.

"We set Mother free!" he cried. "We send her to Father! We thank them for leading us towards the New Dawn!"

He snatched up a handful of Cynthia's hair and wrenched her head back. Her face twisted into a grotesque mask as she hawked and spat in his face.

"Jacob would be ashamed of you!" she hissed.

Thick globules of saliva dripped off Heath's chin. He leaned in, eyes cold and dead. "Jacob was weak and pathetic. You were made for each other. Now you can rot together."

He pulled the roots of her hair again. Cynthia screamed.

Heath rammed the cup into her open mouth and poured the contents down her throat.

Cynthia choked and spat and shrieked.

Dropping the cup, Heath staggered back, excitement making him dizzy. The room grew deathly silent.

Cynthia dragged in a breath. Then another. She glanced desperately around the circle.

"My children! My beautiful boys and girls! Don't listen to him—he's lying to you! It's all a lie! This is—"

Cynthia doubled over. She glanced up at Heath in horror, then back at the children. Her face turned red, then a distressing shade of purple. She screamed in agony, fell on her side. Writhed and thrashed like a captured wild animal.

"It burns!" she wailed. "Oh God, it burns!"

Heath watched her convulse and spasm violently on the floor, spit and blood flying from her mouth.

She screamed again, a wretched sound of pure agony.

Then she was silent, body thrashing with the sound turned down, foam pouring from her mouth, eyes rolled back in her head. It went on like that for five more minutes, Heath and the children watching with frozen expressions.

At last, Cynthia's body grew still.

Heath stared into her open eyes, the whites now red. He leaned over her, hawked and spat.

He turned to the children, saw their expressionless faces. His gaze drifted back to Cynthia's lifeless body, at her dead, staring eyes. He thought he saw her smiling at him. Then Morwenna came into focus, nodding at him, bringing him back.

"This is our New Dawn," he said, hands clasped together in prayer. "In two days, we will be saved."

21

CARRIE WOKE WITH a jolt; someone was in her room. She blinked and rubbed her bleary eyes. The events of last night came rushing back. She'd been at The Shack with Kye. They'd become emotional. They'd walked back to her place for more drinks, and then. . .

Her head started throbbing at the base of her skull. She'd been sober for months and now here she was, her mouth as dry as sand and her body in the throes of a hangover. She rolled onto her side, hair springing up at awkward angles, eyelids sticky with sleep, body slick with sweat.

Kye was on his feet, naked and turned away from her, beads of perspiration sparkling between his shoulder blades, early morning light seeping through the window blinds and slicing across his back. She watched him for a second as he fumbled on the floor for his clothes, muscles shifting beneath his skin as he slipped his jeans over his legs.

"Leaving so soon?" Carrie said, a slight smile on her lips, a slighter sting in her chest.

Her voice startled him. He turned, eyes seeking her out before quickly looking away. Finished buttoning his jeans, he sat down on the edge of the bed and started pulling on his socks.

"Dad has an appointment at the hospital. I promised to take him."

"You're not even going to stay for a coffee?" She shut her mouth, hating the neediness in her voice. It wasn't even like she wanted him to stick around. Well, not for much longer than a coffee and a farewell.

Kye smiled, said nothing. He was like Dylan in that way; not much of a conversationalist. The thought of Dylan made the sting in her chest grow barbs.

Carrie pushed herself up on her elbows and checked the time on the bedside clock: 7:46 on a Friday morning. Thank goodness Melissa was with her grandparents or she'd be late for school. Not that Carrie would have entertained the thought of bringing Kye back home if Melissa had been here.

A car engine started up outside. Somewhere down the street a dog barked.

Kye pulled yesterday's T-shirt over his head and slipped on his shoes.

"So this is a surprise," Carrie said, smiling again. "I mean, the last person I expected to sleep with after the breakdown of my marriage is a ghost from the past." Even in the half-light, she saw Kye flinch. "Sorry. I make bad jokes when I'm feeling awkward."

"I remember."

She sat up, bringing her knees to her chest and wrapping her arms around her shins.

Now fully dressed, Kye stared at her. "You're feeling awkward?"

"Aren't you?"

"Maybe. A little, I suppose. But I had a nice time."

"Me too."

She searched for something else to say, but the throbbing at the base of her skull was working its way into her brain.

She hadn't gone into The Shack planning to sleep with Cal's father, but emotions had been running high and drinking had left her feeling vulnerable. The sex had been hurried and passionate, but she was still working out if she'd enjoyed it. It had been consensual, absolutely, and it had felt good, but at the same time there'd been an emptiness to it. An underlying sadness that felt too much like grief.

Was that what they had been doing? Grieving together?

Kye shifted on the bed, eyes flicking towards the clock.

"Look, this doesn't have to be awkward," Carrie said. "We're both adults. Both single. You are single, aren't you?"

"I'm not an asshole, Carrie."

"Well, then, we had a bunch of drinks, followed by a nice time. It doesn't have to be anything more than that."

She watched him closely as he nodded, thought she saw a flicker of something in his eyes. Kye stood, shot her another glance, then slipped a hand inside his jeans pocket.

"Here."

Carrie stared at the folded slip of paper in his hand, then back at his face. "What is it?"

"I meant what I said last night, about the money. I want you to have it." He unfolded the paper to reveal a cheque, which he held out towards her with a nervous hand.

Carrie's face grew hot. The throb in her head reached the back of her eyes. "We have sex and now you're giving me a cheque?" She stared at it in disbelief. "I feel so . . . wholesome."

"Oh. Yeah. I can see why that might look bad." He didn't lower his hand, though. "But it's not why I'm giving this to you and you

178

know it."

She stared at the cheque, too far away for her to see the exact sum, but she could make out several zeros. It would be so easy to reach out and pluck it from his hand. Suddenly the court fees wouldn't be keeping her up at night, her mind crunching numbers. Maybe there would even be some left over that she could use to get out of this town.

But then she would be indebted to Kye and she didn't know how she felt about that.

Besides, if she took the money and there was some left over, she really would have to do something about leaving Devil's Cove. Even if it was to move somewhere else nearby.

"You know, the last bank closed in town last year. What am I supposed to do with a cheque?"

Kye stared at it, then at Carrie, confusion rippling his brow like a puppy whose owner won't throw the ball.

"I'm sure the post office will accept it. Or, I don't know, take a bus to Truro," he said quietly.

His brow knitted together and in an instant, she could see Cal staring at her with those same sullen eyes. It hurt.

The cheque wavered in his hand.

Carrie stayed where she was.

Shrugging, Kye set it down on the bedside table. "If you don't want the money, fine. I was saving it for him, anyway."

Carrie's shoulders sagged. She brushed fingers through her knotted hair, suddenly aware that she must look a fright. But what did it matter? He'd seen her first thing in the morning before and last night was a one off. Besides, they'd both lost a son. Seeing each other looking a little rough was never going to change that.

Kye stood in the doorway, body half-turned to the outside world. "I should go."

"Are you coming to Devil's Day tomorrow?" It was the only thing she could think to say.

"I don't think so. Too many ghosts from the past. . ."

She winced. Ouch.

"Well, it was nice seeing you again, Carrie. I hope the money helps. Sorry that things got out of hand."

Sorry. It was a strange word to describe their night together. But she supposed she was sorry, too. Sorry for shutting Kye out when Cal had first come back home. Sorry that she hadn't asked him to stay all those years ago, even though she was certain they would never have stayed together, even if he had stuck around. But maybe, just maybe, Cal would have stuck around, too.

He turned to go, grasping the door handle.

"Kye, wait."

He looked at her, eyes sad and full of pain. There was so much grief in this room, choking the air, making them both sick.

"You were never a shitty dad. We were just young, that's all. We didn't know any better." Her voice suddenly cracked. "You should go and see him. At least think about it."

Kye nodded, but she couldn't tell if he meant it or if he was just agreeing so that he could leave. Then he was leaving, without saying another word, and she was watching him disappear. She listened to his feet on the stairs. Heard the front door open and close. Climbing out of bed, Carrie padded over to the window and opened the blinds.

"Oh, great," she moaned. Dottie Penpol was out in the street and making her way over to Kye. It was as if the woman had a sixth sense for scandal. Carrie watched them, feeling her heart sink into her stomach. Then Kye was making excuses and hurrying away. Dottie smiled to herself. Carrie shut the blinds before the woman could see her.

Throwing herself on the bed, she chastised herself for getting drunk and sleeping with her ex. Then she leaned over and picked up the cheque. Her eyes grew wide. Kye had amassed a small fortune over the years, as if banking the money was like banking his guilt. Carrie felt a rush of grief. She would make sure it all went to Cal. Every last penny.

Slipping the cheque inside the top bedside drawer, she reached for the TV remote and switched it on.

Regret about last night was already beginning to whisper in her mind. Devil's Cove was a small town. She'd been drinking with Cal's father at The Shack, where they'd been spotted by several locals, including fishermen friends of Dylan. And now the town's most accomplished gossip had just seen Carrie's dirty secret sneaking out the front door. It was only a matter of time before Dylan found out. Then it wouldn't matter they were in the middle of a trial separation.

Feeling wretched, Carrie switched on the news and turned up the volume. A terrible, cloying familiarity pressed down on her chest, making it hard to breathe.

On the screen, uniformed police officers were stationed along a perimeter of police tape, their expressions stony and unreadable. The camera pulled back to show a crime scene surrounded by trees. At first, Carrie thought it was Briar Wood, but then she looked closer and saw the vegetation was different.

The camera panned to show the white suits of a Crime Scene Investigation team standing by, then came to a rest on the serious face of the on-site reporter. A body had been found, he said, his voice empty of emotion. A child's body; and although the discovery was fresh and the body had yet to be identified, the reporter was speculating that the search for missing ten-year-old Lindsay Church had been brought to an abrupt and horrific end.

22

THE TINY BODY was laid out on the forest floor, the upper half concealed behind the thick trunk of a tree, leaving only the legs and feet exposed at awkward angles, one shoe on, the other nearby and flipped on its side. All around, birds sang joyful songs. Sunlight pierced the canopy and dappled the ground. A playful breeze rustled leaves on branches. The air felt wrong. Thick like tar and heavy with death.

DC Turner stood far back near the perimeter of police tape and barricade of uniformed officers, a growing crowd of camera crews and journalists making noise and hurling questions on the other side. They were waiting for more officers to be sent down, but resources had already been stretched long before the Church family murders and Lindsay's disappearance had brought them to breaking point. All eyes were peeled for overenthusiastic journalists or curious dog walkers tempted to break the perimeter. But it seemed that a murdered child, at least for now, earned obedience and respect.

Turner's gaze shifted from the police line to the Crime Scene Investigation team, who had set up camp just inside the perimeter and were patiently waiting for the crime scene photographer to finish her job. Then he found himself involuntarily turning his head to the left and his gaze wandering further, until it was resting on the body again. He was glad he could only see the feet. He'd seen murder victims before, back when he'd been stationed in London with the Metropolitan police, but this was his first murdered child. They seemed so out of place; those thin little legs poking out. The idyllic setting somehow made the crime even more heinous; if that was even possible.

Dressed in pristine white coveralls, the crime scene photographer was hunched over, ducking in and out from behind the tree as she snapped pictures of the body and the surrounding area. Turner looked away, certain he could hear the gentle click of the shutter despite the growing din of the press.

If only they knew, he thought. Because it wasn't Lindsay Church lying dead in the dirt, one shoe off and one shoe on. It was little Luke Beaumont, five-year-old son of John Beaumont, who had both been abducted one night in December. Now they shared something else in common.

The child's body had been found by an early morning dog walker, who had already been processed by CSI and was now on her way to the station in Penzance to give a statement. She'd told the first officer on the scene that she'd almost tripped over the boy's legs, that she'd thought they were fallen branches until she'd looked down and saw his blue eyes staring lifelessly up at her. Like two ice cubes melting on snow, she'd said. And there had been no blood. At least the boy had not been cut open. At least he'd been spared that.

Turner shivered in spite of the already warm day. Behind him, more journalists were joining the throng. It always amazed him how quickly the press found out about these things. It was like they had a sixth sense for murder.

And for failure.

Luke Beaumont had been missing for six months. The police had searched but found no trace of him or his abductors. The national press had accused them of being incompetent. Cornwall may have been rural and remote, but it wasn't exactly huge, they'd said, as if there weren't a thousand places you could hide a body in a county made up of fields and woodland and ocean on three sides. As if over twenty of Cornwall's police stations hadn't been shut down in the last few years alone.

All those tiny bodies unearthed at Grady Spencer's house hadn't helped the situation, either. Or the video footage of Cal Anderson murdering John Beaumont in front of a cult of children; a cult that the police still knew nothing about.

Except they're still out there, Turner thought, his eyes wandering back to the body.

Who were they? What did they want?

How were they connected to Grady Spencer?

These were questions that neither he nor his colleagues could answer. Perhaps the press was right to cry incompetence. Children were dead and missing. At least the local newspapers had been more sympathetic.

The photographer had finished preserving the scene on film. She emerged from behind the tree, her white suit so alien against the earthy colours, like the abominable snowman had made a wrong turn and lost its way. Turner watched her approach the rest of the CSI team, heard the jostling of media bodies, their voices growing loud with excitement. He supposed they were just trying to do their job, just like he and his colleagues were trying to do theirs.

The rest of the CSI team got to work, tool kits and notebooks in hand as they advanced along the plastic walkways that had been laid down to prevent contamination of the crime scene.

Turner looked away, saw Detective Sergeant Hughes walking towards him, a similar, grim expression souring her face. She didn't speak as she stood beside him, only nodded. Like Turner, she was doing her best to avoid those tiny legs sticking out from behind the tree, toes pointed skyward.

We failed him, Turner thought.

It was a heart-breaking, unbearable confession, but one he believed was true. Which was why it was more important than ever not to sink into despair.

Six months after Luke Beaumont's disappearance, his body had turned up freshly deceased, which meant that the people who had taken him—the same people that both Cal Anderson and Grady Spencer had been connected to—were out there somewhere. Possibly even nearby.

What's more, they'd dumped the child's body out in the open, in a place well known for dog walking.

It was almost as if they'd wanted him to be found.

He glanced over at the gaggle of press.

"Look at them," he said, suddenly needing to shift the blame. "Like hyenas fighting over a lion's spoils."

"They just want to know what everyone else does—what the hell is going on here?" DS Hughes said, the first words she'd spoken to him that morning. "Well, I'll tell you what's going on here. We're about to be fed to the wolves. Those delightful chaps have more or less announced on morning television that it's Lindsay Church lying dead over there. Wait until they find out it's Luke Beaumont. He's half the age of Lindsay, which means twice as much outrage and appointing of blame. Three guesses who's getting it in the neck."

Yet again, Turner's gaze wandered back over to the tiny body. The medical examiner was on his way but running late. The sooner he got here and did his job, the sooner the poor Beaumont boy could be taken away. At least the press couldn't see him from where they were being contained.

"What are you thinking, Will?" Hughes said.

"That I'm glad I'm not the one who has to inform the poor boy's mother."

Hughes chewed the inside of her cheek. "They'll need a stiff drink after."

Another surge of noise.

The detectives both turned to see that the medical examiner had finally arrived, red faced and flustered as he signed in with a uniformed officer.

"About bloody time," DS Hughes muttered. "Stay here and keep watch. Make sure none of our press friends break the line."

She nodded at him, flicked her eyes back to the body, then marched over to the doctor, who was old and tired-looking and who waved his hands manically in the air as he attempted to defend his tardiness. Hughes was having none of it. She directed him over to the CSI base camp to suit up, then shot a glance over at Turner, rolling her eyes.

Turner let out a sigh, fought the urge to seek out little Luke Beaumont. His body would soon be gone, stretchered away in a black bag too large for his tiny frame.

Good, he thought.

Not that it would make a difference. He would be seeing those spindly legs and feet in his dreams tonight, one shoe on, one shoe kicked off on the ground.

The medical examiner was making his way over to the body now.

On the other side of the cordon, two paramedics waited silently with a stretcher. Turner pictured it rumbling along the bumpy ground, body bag on top, Luke Beaumont's teeth chattering inside.

He pictured the child on a cold metal slab. Imagined the sharp blade of a scalpel slicing through his chest.

His phone vibrated in his jacket pocket. Absentmindedly, he pulled it out and checked the screen. Carrie Killigrew was calling him. No doubt she'd seen the initial news report on TV.

She'd tried to warn him, hadn't she?

She'd been petrified that the Dawn Children were back and he'd brushed her off.

How did he tell her that she was right? That the murders of Luke Beaumont and the Church family, and the abduction of Lindsay Church were all connected? Because they had to be—the timing was too much of a coincidence.

He stared at the phone screen. More questions he couldn't answer.

He waited for the call to ring off, then slipped his phone back inside his jacket pocket.

There was one person who could answer all these questions and more. One person who knew everything the police did not. But those answers were forever trapped behind a wall of silence, inside a broken mind.

Turner cleared his throat and tried to clear his mind.

Something was happening.

Something bad.

He could feel it all around him, pressing down.

For now, he returned his gaze to the tiny body lying half behind the tree. It was the least he could do.

23

NAT SAT AT her bedroom desk, poring over art history textbooks and scribbling notes on a pad, while screechy guitar music played from laptop speakers. She'd been studying for two hours now, deep into it, enjoying the flow. Something had changed in her. More and more, she'd started to contemplate moving to London. It wasn't like she hadn't daydreamed about it before, but ever since Aaron had died, she'd wiped the idea from her mind. But now, it was creeping back in.

Why was she turning her back on the potential to live an artist's life in London? Was it solely because she felt responsible for Aaron Black's death? Or was it more than that? Her whole life, she'd been told she was no good, a deviant, a mistake. She'd been told it so many times that it was as if her body had absorbed the words, processing it into DNA, until every cell believed it was true. But something had changed.

It was Rose. Nat had hurt her feelings time and time again. She'd acted up, lashed out, taken from Rose, then pushed her away. But Rose had kept coming back. Even after Nat's disappearing act last Saturday, Rose had returned to her usual, cheery self. Yes, it had taken her a few days this time, but now it was like it had never happened.

Nat had never much liked herself. But Rose did. And if Rose believed in her, surely Nat could at least try to believe in herself. That was the change. The idea that perhaps Nat was worth something. That London could be more than just a daydream. She just had to get this final exam out of the way.

Through the music, Nat thought she heard the doorbell ring. A moment later, she heard Rose calling her name.

"Natalie! You've got a visitor!"

Nat sat up, switched the music off. She must have misheard.

"What's that?" she called.

"I said you've got a visitor. Get yourself down here!"

Nat stared at the door, frowning. She didn't get visitors. She didn't know anyone in Porth an Jowl who would call on her. Unless it was Jago, but he'd said that he'd never—

"Are you deaf, girl?"

"Coming!"

Still wondering who it could be, she left the room and headed downstairs. Reaching the bottom step, she froze. Rachel was standing by the front door, arms crossed awkwardly over her stomach. She raised a hand, then looked away. Nat was silent, gaze flicking from Rachel to Rose then back again.

"I'll leave you two chatterboxes to it," Rose said, when the silence became excruciating. Arching an eyebrow at Rachel, she disappeared into the kitchen and shut the door.

When they were alone, Rachel let out a long breath and glanced around. "Wow, you do really have a thing for floral print, *Natalie.*"

"What are you doing here?" Nat said, the words coming out more hostile than she'd intended.

Rachel lowered her head, then looked up. "Just wanted to say hi. And to say sorry about—"

Nat stepped forward and opened the front door, escorting Rachel outside. Closing the door behind them, she shrugged. "Rose doesn't know where we went and I don't want her finding out."

Rachel nodded. "As I was saying . . . sorry for disappearing on you. That crime scene freaked me out and, well, maybe I'm not as tough as I make out to be. Not as tough as you, anyway." She blew out more air, shook her head. "Sorry if I made you feel like a freak. I'm not very good at making friends and I'm always saying the wrong thing. If I hurt your feelings, then—"

"You didn't. I'm fine." Apologies usually made Nat feel uncomfortable, but this one seemed to be having the opposite effect, which made her nervous.

They were both quiet, shifting their weight from one foot to the other.

"How's your holiday going?" Nat asked. "Been anywhere nice?"

Rachel rolled her eyes. "Yeah. Lots of pissy teashops and boring old gardens. Exactly my idea of a good time!"

Nat smiled. "Sounds thrilling."

"How about you? It's Devil's Day tomorrow, isn't it?"

"That's right. Is your family coming?" she clamped her jaw shut, wincing at the hope in her voice.

Rachel shook her head. "The folks are going to Padstow for the day."

"Oh."

"But I'm sticking around." She flashed a smile at Nat, who smiled back and ran a hand over her shaved head. "In fact, I was wondering if maybe we could hang out together. Festivals are no fun when you have no friends. Besides, I'm only here for another day, then we're going back to London. I'd like to hang out with you some more."

Nat drummed her fingers nervously against her thigh. She liked Rachel. She did. Would even consider becoming friends with her. But that would mean letting her guard down. Opening the gates and letting her in. And she still felt awkward about the other day. Still wondered if Rachel thought she was a sideshow freak.

She wouldn't be here if she did. Maybe she actually likes you.

"Don't take too long to decide," Rachel said, smirking.

Nat pursed her lips. "Um . . . Sure. Whatever. We could hang out."

"Great! That's really great."

"So, the parade starts at eleven tomorrow. Why don't you meet me here fifteen minutes before? We can watch the parade together, then you can come down to the town hall with me, Rose, and a bunch of old ladies."

"What's at the town hall?"

"Several giant barrels of cider and four hundred empty cups needing to be filled."

"For the toast you told me about? The offering?"

"That's right. And that's the deal—we hang out, you work. Take it or leave it."

Rachel flashed another smile. "Well, lucky for you, I happen to love hanging out with old ladies, so count me in."

They both laughed. Rachel turned, her eye catching the plot of earth where Grady Spencer's house had once stood. Her smile faded. Nat followed her gaze. She could almost feel the energy there, pulsing in nauseating waves. The sooner the town council decided what to do with it, the better.

"You want to come inside? Hang out for a bit?"

"I can't," Rachel said. "But I'm looking forward to tomorrow. It'll be the highlight of this whole boring holiday."

Winking at Nat, she turned and headed down the garden path and out through the gate. Then she was off, sauntering along Grenville Road and turning up the hill.

Cheeks flushing, Nat watched her go.

"You see," she told herself. "Maybe you're not so bad after all."

24

SATURDAY MORNING CAME around, bringing good weather to Porth an Jowl. Nat stood at the end of Grenville Row, nervous energy crackling through her limbs. She peered up at the crest of Cove Road and saw the tops of people's heads bobbing up and down amid a sea of dazzling colours—the Devil's Day parade taking shape. Down the hill on Nat's right, crowds were gathering—mostly neighbours, with the bulk of tourists and visitors from nearby locales already waiting in town.

Pulling out her phone, Nat checked the time: 11:12 a.m.

The parade was running late. Rachel, too. She should have been here thirty minutes ago. So why hadn't she turned up?

The performers were still milling about. A woman was barking instructions over a megaphone, her voice straining with frustration as she attempted to get the performers into their places. "Children behind the marching band! No, Oak class, *then* Birch! *Where* are the dancers?"

She was interrupted by the accidental crash of cymbals, followed by a chorus of laughter.

Yesterday, Rachel had shown up at Nat's house of her own volition. She'd asked Nat to hang out with her, practically begged her to let her help with the parade. And now she was a no show.

Nat heaved her shoulders, ignored the voice whispering in her ear. *It's the same old story—you let someone get close and then they disappear. You're a freak, Tremaine. Why else would you take someone you just met to a crime scene? Why else would you be obsessing about a murderous cult when just about everyone else your age is down on the beach and drinking beers and getting laid in the dunes?*

More neighbours were coming out of their houses and lining the fringes of Cove Road. Nat checked her phone again. Stuffed it back inside her jeans pocket and stared at the ground. She was a freak. Rachel had even called her one, too. At the time, she'd thought Rachel had been paying her a compliment. That the two of them were aligned. But Nat had got it all wrong yet again.

Here was more proof: she'd texted Jago this morning, trying to persuade him to come to the festival—a desperate attempt to reignite their friendship. So far, Jago had yet to reply. Nat cast an eye over the empty, fenced off ground to her left. She couldn't blame him, she supposed. Why would he return to the place that had almost destroyed his family? And yet his name still tasted bitter on Nat's tongue. Because if Jago hadn't rejected her in the first place, she wouldn't have gone chasing after Rachel like a needy puppy, desperate to please her. Desperate to be liked.

You're a freak. No good. Stop trying to convince yourself that you're anything else.

"Hey!"

She glanced up, heart leaping into the throat. Then sinking into her stomach.

"What are you doing, girl?" Rose called out, swinging her arms as she descended the hill. The day was already warm and her face was shiny, beetroot red. "Why are you standing on your own like a lonely lemon?"

Nat shrugged. Turned away as Rose stopped in front of her.

"Well, we're just about ready to get going. Once those bloody kids work out which way front is. Don't they teach them anything in school these days?" Rose winked. Then frowned. "What's wrong? You've got a face on you like a wet weekend."

"I'm fine."

Nat leaned out, staring past Rose and up the hill. Perhaps Rachel had overslept. Or she was in the middle of an argument with her parents, who no doubt wanted her to spend another day with them on another boring excursion rather than hang out with a new friend. The holiday park was just over the crest. It would take Nat just a few minutes to find out the truth.

"Be back in a sec," she muttered as she started forward.

Rose held onto her arm. "Where do you think you're going?"

Nat didn't answer. Only glared as she attempted to shrug her off. When Rose showed no sign of letting her go, Nat blew air through her nose. "Rachel's supposed to be here. I'm just going to find out where she is."

"No, you're not," Rose said. "The parade is about to start."

"So? I'll be two minutes."

"No. Absolutely not. You're staying right here whether you like it or not!"

Nat glared at her, surprised by Rose's sudden anger. She shrugged her off and rubbed her arm.

"Jesus, what's your problem?"

"I'll tell you my problem, Natalie Tremaine! You've put blood, sweat, and tears into this festival. Spent hours of your time creating all these wonderful designs and helping all those little kids to finish their own. And now you're going to turn your back on it all, just because you've gone all doe-eyed over some girl you've known for two bloody seconds!"

Nat stared at her, mouth hanging open.

"Oh, I'm not a bloody idiot!" Rose said throwing her hands in the air. "I've known forever that boys aren't your cup of tea and it don't make no difference to me, neither. But what *does* make a difference is the lack of respect you have for yourself."

Nat could feel her cheeks burning, her heart pounding in her chest. "No, you're wrong. It's because—"

"You're always putting yourself down, you are. Always making a joke of things. Always saying everything is terrible, like the world is at an end. And yet you filled those kids with smiles and laughter. You created all those bright colours and you made me proud. All those nasty thoughts you have about yourself just ain't true—you're a good person, Nat! A good person with a gentle heart—and for once, just once—I want you to stand here with me and watch all the good you've done come to life. Because you deserve it. No matter how bad you think you are, you deserve it."

Her face was crimson now. There was a lump in her throat, rendering her mute and unable to defend herself. Tears were coming, welling up from the depths. Everything Rose had said was a lie. Nat was not a good person. She did not deserve to stand here, feeling proud of herself for a job well done. She was a freak and a loser, and she didn't care about anything or anyone, least of all herself. Why was Rose even trying to convince her otherwise?

Nat glanced up the hill, heard the band starting up. She thought about making a run for it.

"Please," Rose said, gently now. She leaned in closer and ran a hand over the back of Nat's head. Nat flinched, but didn't shrug her off. "You've done me proud, girl. It breaks my heart to see you so beaten down, never giving yourself a break. When are you going to learn that what happened to Aaron Black isn't your fault? You didn't kill him."

Here they came. The tears—welling in her eyes, blinding her, spilling down her face. Nat shook her head. Took a step back. Why was this happening now? In broad daylight, with the parade about to begin and all the neighbours out in force?

Stop fucking crying! Stop it now!

But they wouldn't stop. There were years and years of grief buried inside her. Now, it was all coming up in one go.

"It is my fault!" she said, her voice breaking. "You don't even know what you're talking about!"

"I may not know what happened that night," Rose said, her voice soft and soothing, making everything worse. "But neither do you. Whatever happened between the two of you—whatever words were said—you're not responsible for his death. Those people from that video are. The police know it. I know it. The only one who doesn't seem to know it is you."

At the top of the hill, the marching band started up, filling the air with a swooping traditional Cornish ditty.

Nat shook her head, freeing more tears. She wanted to tell Rose. To tell her the truth about what happened that night. The truth that had been festering inside her like an infected wound, spreading poison through her veins, killing her slowly.

"What is it?" Rose urged, her face taut with worry. "What is it you're not telling me?"

"He called me!" Nat cried. "The night he died, Aaron called asking for my help. I didn't pick up, Rose! I sat there, angry at him and getting drunk. They killed him, but it's my fault! He's dead because I didn't pick up!"

Her face was wet and stinging. Nat furiously rubbed her cheeks with the back of her hand, then flashed a glare at her neighbours, who were pretending they hadn't seen or heard. Then she was sobbing uncontrollably.

Rose grabbed Nat by the shoulders and stared up at her. "Look at me! You'll never know if answering that call would have made any difference. You need to let it go. If you don't, it will eat you from the inside out."

Nat stared back, felt her legs trembling, the fight extinguished as she wept. She was a child again, lost and terrified of everything in the world. Rose pulled her close, wrapping arms around her back. Nat melted into her embrace. But only for a minute. She was letting her guard down. Making herself vulnerable. Showing weakness.

Shaking Rose off, she turned away and wiped her face.

It was as if Rose had sensed it was enough. She dropped her hands to her sides and cleared her throat, then glanced up at the crest of the hill.

"They're coming," she said. "Now, stand here with me and watch all your great work come to life."

Nat watched. A giant red devil was appearing over the crest of the hill, reptilian yellow eyes flashing in the sunlight. It was at least fifteen feet tall, with sharp, curved horns pointing up to the heavens and a maniacal grin that leered over the town of Porth an Jowl. Its papier-mâché body swayed from left to right as the six people carrying it struggled to keep it balanced. And then the devil was descending the hill, followed by a gaggle of schoolchildren in fancy dress, carrying bright banners ablaze with an explosion of colours; banners that Nat had designed. The colours seem to dance in the sunlight, swirling and spinning in a kaleidoscope. Behind them, the marching band continued to play, cymbals crashing, xylophones chiming, flutes and clarinets rising and swooping through the air. More people followed behind, all dressed in red devil masks and garishly-coloured rags, all skipping and dancing in wild rhythms.

Nat watched the procession draw closer. Saw the devil loom over her like a titan. Next to her, Rose reached out and squeezed her hand. Nat squeezed back, tears like diamonds on her skin, pride rising and soaring along with the music.

25

THE HIGH STREET was filled with hundreds of people, all swarming the pavements and jostling behind the metal barriers that had been erected on both sides of the road. Music, barely audible above the din of the crowd, played from speakers attached to streetlamps. Most of the shops were closed, their staff joining the gathering throngs in anticipation of the Devil's Day parade.

Carrie stood at the edge of the square, arms clamped around her rib cage, a mild headache pulsing at the top of her skull. It was a hot day, but the sheer amount of bodies was turning the air to treacle. She glanced up, nervously eyeing Dylan, who was standing next to her along with his parents, Joy and Gary, who were commenting on the growing crowd—a huge improvement on last year's turnout and hopefully a good omen for the town's profit margins this summer. Carrie hoped so, too. But Kye's cheque would greatly lighten the burden.

She was still unsure how she felt about him turning up out of the blue and handing it to her after years of silence. She was even more unsure how she felt about having slept with him. She knew that the two elements were disconnected—the only trouble was no one had told her conscience. It wasn't that she regretted sleeping with Kye— she was a grown adult, who was currently separated and exploring her options—but she was afraid of how Dylan would find out. And he *would* find out, sooner or later. She was surprised that the news hadn't already reached him; after all, twenty-four hours in Devil's Cove could sometimes last a lifetime.

Shifting her weight, she turned her back on Dylan and stared down the length of the high street to watch the excited faces of the crowd. There were locals here, but most of the visitors were either tourists or came from nearby towns. It was good to see the streets of Porth an Jowl buzzing with excitement, which was infinitely better than the emptiness that pervaded the town during winter, made worse by all the terrible events of the last year. Perhaps this summer would bring the change that the town so desperately needed.

"Hey." She felt Dylan's lips brush her ear in that intimate way reserved for couples. Startled, Carrie pulled away. "Everything okay?"

"Sure," she said, her skin prickling as she winced at her non-committal tone. "I didn't sleep well, that's all."

"The heat keeping you up?"

"Something like that." She turned away, sure that her cheeks were glowing and poker-hot. "It's those murders in Falmouth. I've been worrying."

"About what?"

She stole another glance at his concerned face, then at Gary and Joy, who, to her relief, were deep in conversation of their own. She could only imagine what they had to say about her behind closed doors. The separation had sparked all manner of gossip around the town. Gary was a private man; Joy, popular among the women. Carrie was sure everyone had something to say to them about their son's disaster of a marriage and train wreck of a wife.

"About what?" Dylan repeated.

Carrie shrugged. About the fact that the police still hadn't released the identity of the child found dead in the woods. About the fact that DC Turner had yet to return her calls. About the fact that she'd had a terrible, cloying feeling in her stomach since turning on the news yesterday morning. Which could be guilt, she supposed. But she wasn't convinced.

"Forget it. It's just flashbacks, that's all."

"Well, I think this is good for us all being here together today, don't you?" Dylan said. "I mean, for Melissa's sake. It's been a difficult year for everyone, especially her. She's so young, probably doesn't understand even half of what's going on. It will be good for her to see her mum and dad getting on so well."

Carrie smiled, avoiding his hopeful gaze. "I guess."

She only hoped that Melissa seeing her parents together like this didn't give the wrong impression. Expelling a deep breath, she glanced across the road. Dottie Penpol was on the other side of the barrier, hands twitching in the air as she chatted to Mabel Stevens, who ran the post office, and Jack Dawkins, proprietor of Porth an Jowl Wine Shop. Carrie groaned. The three biggest gossips in town conspiring together, with Dottie no doubt filling them in on every juicy detail of who she'd seen leaving Carrie's house early yesterday morning.

Her mind wandered back to the cheque, wondering if she should just cash it in and get out of this town before the rest of her life finally imploded.

She felt a hand on her arm, gently squeezing her.

"Are you sure you're okay?" Dylan said, closer now, the vein in the centre of his forehead gently pulsing. "You seem . . . I don't know

. . . distracted or something."

"I'm fine."

"Actually, I thought we could talk later. Tonight maybe. About us."

Carrie shot a glare at the gossiping trio across the street. Dylan was going to find out about her encounter with Kye one way or another. She could either tell him herself, then watch the hope die from his eyes and any chance of a working relationship, parent to parent, die with it, or she could sit back and let Porth an Jowl's Gossip Brigade do the work for her. She didn't know which would be worse. Either way, the end result would still be the same. She and Dylan would not only be over, but their co-parenting would be reduced to monosyllabic greetings on handover days and snide comments made behind each other's back.

"Carrie?"

"Hmm?"

"Did you hear what I just said?"

Their marriage was over. She knew it now. If she was honest, she'd known it for months. But what else was she supposed to do? Stay with him for the sake of Melissa? Smile and laugh in all the right places, attend dinner dates and family gatherings, pretending every-thing was okay when she was dying inside? How could that be better for Melissa? Or for Dylan? Or for herself?

Shoulders heaving, Carrie stared up at Dylan's deep, brown eyes. How could he not know that it was over? How could he bear the uncertainty or the hope? The right thing to do was to tell him face-to-face. To save him the indignity of finding out through a bitter chain of embellished whispers.

But not now. Not here. He deserved more than that.

Marching band music suddenly soared over the din of the crowd.

"They're here!" Joy exclaimed.

Relief pouring through Carrie's body, she turned towards the junction where Cove Road met the high street. The music grew louder. The crowds bristled with excitement. Then gasps rang out from the throngs as a huge, lumbering, red devil emerged straight out of a monster movie. Cheers and applause ran up and down the street. The devil towered above them, yellow eyes glinting, white, pointed teeth flashing.

Carrie shot a glance at Dylan, who had turned away from her, the sting of disappointment still lingering on his face.

"Look at that!" Joy cried, clasping her hands together. "What a fright!"

Beside her, Gary nodded appreciatively. The devil rounded the corner, turning onto the high street. The rest of the parade followed, rounds of schoolchildren waving brightly-coloured banners in the air, the marching band blowing trumpets and banging drums, and dancers dressed as smiling demons all spinning and twirling.

Carrie felt nothing but sorrow. Her heart grew heavy in her chest. Her breathing, thin and shallow. Her relationship with Dylan was over. She didn't know why the grief was hitting her now. After all the trauma they'd experienced this year, all the pain, and betrayal, the end had been a long time coming. She stared at him, watching a smile light up his face as he pointed at the parade.

"There she is!"

Carrie followed his gaze, searching the painted faces and brightly-coloured costumes of the schoolchildren. There were butterflies and ladybirds, pirates and parrots, and two children dressed as Cornish pasties. Melissa was dressed as a pirate, a patch over one eye as she and her partner held up a fluttering banner with a skull and crossbones. She glanced up as Dylan called her name. A smile, bright and joyful spread across her face. She freed one of her hands from the banner, making it wobble, and waved in her family's direction. Carrie and Dylan both waved back, followed by Joy and Gary.

"What a smile!" Joy laughed. "Butter wouldn't melt!"

"That's my sweet pea," Carrie whispered. She owed it to her daughter to work things out with Dylan. Not to get back together. Not to lie. But to find some amicable middle ground so that Melissa always felt safe and loved.

Someone was watching her.

She felt eyes on the back of her neck. Prickles on her skin.

Carrie turned around in time to see a young woman disappearing into the crowd. She only saw a glimpse of her face, but she was struck by an uneasy feeling of familiarity. She stared at the empty space that the young woman had occupied just moments ago, then scanned the crowd.

"Mummy! Mummy, watch me!" Waving her hand wildly, Melissa almost dropped her end of the banner, earning a cutting glare from her partner.

Carrie smiled and waved back, a sudden and inexplicable dread chilling her to the bone.

26

CHAPERONED BY ALISON and Kit, Lindsay carefully made her way along the wide stone causeway that led from the sandy beach to the tiny island in the distance; a slab of rock with a small village sitting at the base of a sloping, tree-covered hill. Protruding from the top was an impressive-looking castle. St Michael's Mount. Lindsay had visited it before, a few years ago on one of the annual family holidays. She thought the Mount itself was cool, but the castle interior was stuffy and boring, filled with old things that held no interest for a young child.

What were they doing here now?

They had travelled from the compound in a battered old car, Kit driving, even though she didn't think he was old enough, Alison in the back seat with Lindsay lying across her lap and Alison's firm hand making sure she stayed there. They'd driven for what seemed like a long time, parked the car on a stretch of gravel overlooking the long strip of beach, then Alison had made Lindsay put on a wig of thick, dark hair. Getting out of the car, they'd made their way through the dunes, Kit and Alison dressed in dark clothes, their heavy boots kicking sand over sunbathers.

Now they were walking along the causeway. The last time that Lindsay had visited St Michael's Mount, the tide had been in and they'd had to take a boat along with a bunch of other sightseers. Although she'd enjoyed the brief journey across the bay, she'd been looking forward to walking the causeway, which could only be crossed at low tide. In other circumstances, she would have been enjoying herself right now, dodging the slimy knots of seaweed and picking up shells that littered the walkway. But something was wrong.

She had a feeling that she'd witnessed something terrible. Not what had happened to her family. Something else. Something new. Her memories were foggy at best. She remembered being filed into a room with the others, eating something from the palm of her hand, and then the rest was a haze of scary images that seemed better suited to a bad dream. She remembered screaming. Remembered a terrifying shape convulsing on the floor. Nothing else. It was as if her mind had pulled a steel shutter down, protecting her from the truth.

All she knew was that Cynthia hadn't been around yesterday; the only person to show Lindsay any kindness since she'd been taken. And now she was here, walking towards St Michael's Mount with Alison and Kit.

They weren't the only ones to have left the compound, either. Everyone had; splitting up into groups, some departing on foot, while others clambered inside a big white van.

Lindsay, Kit, and Alison were the last to leave. And now here they were, marching across the causeway, Lindsay wedged between her captors as they passed tourists dressed in bright colours, some heading back to the beach, while others journeyed on towards the Mount.

The day was already hot and clammy, the sun bright in a cloudless sky, the ocean green and inviting.

The wig was making Lindsay's scalp itch. She reached up and slipped a finger beneath it. Alison slapped her hand away, gripped her arm tightly, sending rivulets of pain up to her shoulder.

They walked on, Lindsay's legs heavy beneath her. As they passed the other people, some of the adults glanced at her, a few raising their eyebrows. She wondered if they'd recognised her. If her face had been shown on the television like those other missing children she sometimes saw on the news.

She thought about screaming. About making a run for it.

But she knew what was in Kit's pocket.

She knew that if she screamed, he would take it out and cut her open.

So, Lindsay walked, until her legs trembled and her scalp burned. The causeway was coming to an end, opening onto a stony beach and a cement walkway. They followed it along, mingling with the sightseers, more and more of them shooting curious glances at Lindsay.

The walkway narrowed into an alley, then they were entering the village. It was small, a cluster of old stone cottages. Lindsay looked around, remembering that people lived in those houses and wondering if they ever got fed up with holidaymakers crawling over their home.

She wondered what would happen if she ran to one of the cottages now and asked to use their phone. She could call the police, tell them yes, she really was Lindsay Church, the little girl that had gone missing while holidaying with her family. Then she noticed Kit was staring at her. Turning away, she fixed her gaze on the sloping hill in the near distance and the castle protruding from the top like a crown.

The crowd was thicker here. People were ambling like snails, snapping photographs of the landscape and each other. Lindsay risked a glance up at Alison, then back at Kit, saw their clenched jaws and alert expressions. She had thought Alison was kind. She'd called herself Lindsay's sister. But Alison was just as bad as the others.

They walked on, cutting through the crowds, moving past the houses, passing hedgerows and lawns, the narrowing walkway making it difficult to stay together. Alison tightened her grip on Lindsay's arm as Kit scooted in front, his hand still clutching the blade inside his pocket.

They pushed through a gate and stopped at the centre of a crossroad. The path led to a gift shop on their right and a small lawn up ahead, where a few people sat enjoying the sunshine. On their left, the path continued on to the castle.

A group of women on the lawn looked up and stared at the trio. One of them whispered something, then they were all staring at Lindsay.

Why had she been brought here?

In a brief moment of hope, Lindsay wondered if it was to set her free. She couldn't think of any other reason. But if it was true, why take her all the way to the Mount? Why not leave her at the beach, or on the outskirts of town?

No. They were here for something else. Something bad.

"Come on," Kit said. The three of them headed left, Lindsay's arm throbbing in Alison's grip. They walked along the path, through another gate with a notice saying something about tickets. And then they were grinding to a halt.

Two middle-aged women were up ahead, dressed in casual uniform and standing next to a booth. Lindsay watched them smile as they checked the tickets of a middle-aged couple and waved them through.

She could hear Alison's breath quickening beside her, felt her fingernails digging into her flesh. She saw Kit slip the knife from his pocket and press it against his thigh. They moved forward as one, until they reached the two women.

The one on the left, a woman with kind eyes and greying hair flashed a smile at Lindsay. The smiled quickly faded as she turned to Kit.

"Do you have your tickets?" she asked. Lindsay felt the other woman staring at her, saw her eyes widen with recognition.

"This is my ticket," Kit said. He held up the knife, keeping it close to his chest. "Now move."

Both women stared at each other, then at the knife, faces pale as winter.

"I said fucking *move*!"

The women did as they were told, shooting panicked glances at each other, then at Lindsay.

Knife still in front of him, Kit moved forward.

Alison followed with Lindsay in tow.

As they hurried along the path, Lindsay glanced over her shoulder and saw one of the women staring in horror and the other running for help. The path twisted and she almost tripped over her feet.

"Come on!" Alison snapped, wrenching her arm.

Lindsay turned back, saw palm trees at her sides and a set of big stone steps up ahead. Tourists were moving out of their way, some making disgruntled comments, others whispering in concern. Someone must have seen Kit's knife because a shriek rang out on Lindsay's right.

Every cell in her body told her to run. If she could free herself from Alison's grasp, then she could disappear in the crowd, or hide in one of the houses with the door locked. With all these people around, surely Kit and Alison couldn't hurt her.

They had reached the steps; large, ancient slabs with iron railings on both sides that rose sharply up the hill. Leafy trees and tall bushes closed in on them as they began to climb.

Lindsay tilted her head, staring upwards. Her legs ached. Her lungs were on fire. There was no way she was going to make it up those steps, all the way to the top.

If she ran now, there was a chance that Kit and Alison would catch her. But perhaps the ticket lady who had gone for help had managed to call the police. If Lindsay waited, Kit and Alison would get arrested and then she would be safe.

Or perhaps one of the tourists would be brave enough to stop Kit and Alison in their tracks and set Lindsay free.

"Get going!" Kit growled.

He shoved her, his palm flat against her back.

Lindsay pitched forward, stumbled and grabbed the railing. Onlookers muttered disapprovingly, but no one intervened.

Alison grabbed Lindsay's arm again. She smiled. "Come on, you can do it."

The three got going again, taking the large steps one at a time, climbing higher and higher.

Soon, the steps turned into a smooth path that spiralled, around and around, until the trees fell away and were replaced by open, rocky ground.

The castle loomed over them like a giant.

Lindsay still had no idea why she'd been brought here. Only that it was for nothing good. Her leg muscles screaming, she climbed even higher, praying that the police would get here before it was too late.

27

THE PARADE HAD reached the town centre, where throngs of people lined the pavements, all jostling for space behind the barriers. Excited tourists snapped pictures of the lumbering, giant devil. Children *oohed* and *ahhed*. A few of the youngest started crying and buried their faces into their parents' shoulders. Excited cheers and gasps travelled through the crowds as the parade continued along the street, the red devil stalking through the town, its ominous shadow creeping across the buildings. The band played on. The children swung their banners in time to the music and a horde of red-faced demons danced hypnotically at the rear.

Nat's tears had almost dried. The ache in her chest was slowly dissipating. Rose had been right: to see her artwork proudly on display had left her bursting with pride. She'd already heard several people commenting on the designs, admiring the colours and the patterns, and pointing out their favourites. It was the first time she'd dared to have her work displayed in public and now she wondered why she hadn't done it before.

She felt different. Less empty, somehow. Even the crowds that would have normally had her running to the safety of her room seemed less claustrophobic. It was funny, Nat thought, as she and Rose picked their way between the bodies, how even the slightest change of heart could transform the entire world.

"I'm off," Rose called out above the din, then waved at a neighbour standing across the street. "It'll take another twenty minutes for the parade to get to the beach, and those drinks aren't going to pour themselves."

Nat nodded, moved to go with her.

Rose shook her head, a smile etched on her lips. "Why don't you go and find that friend of yours?"

"But the drinks. . ."

"I'll be fine for five minutes. Just make sure you bring her straight to the town hall. It's all hands on deck."

Nat's face was heating up again. "No, it's fine. I'm coming with you."

"Go. Before I change my mind." Rose waved her away again. "Just do me a favour and don't fall in love. These holiday romances always end in tears."

"Oh, shut up!" Nat cried, her face now almost purple. "We're friends, that's all."

"And I'm the Queen of England."

Flashing Nat one last smile, Rose disappeared into the crowd. Fuming, Nat watched her leave, then headed in the opposite direction, pushing her way through the bodies, back towards Cove Road. The crowd parted and she saw Carrie and Dylan standing on the other side of the parade, smiling at the passing children. Neither smile reached their eyes, Nat noted.

A minute later, she was making her way up Cove Road, the steep gradient punishing her calves as the town dropped away behind her and the din of the parade grew muffled and distant. Halfway up, she broke into a sweat. The day was growing hotter by the second, as if Devil's Day had opened up the gates of Hell instead of sealing them shut. Nat paused to catch her breath and stared down at the town. It was nice to see Porth an Jowl so alive, she thought. The streets filled with vibrancy and excitement instead of hopelessness and despair. She wondered if the mood would last beyond today.

On the move again, she passed Carrie's street, then her own. Finally, she reached the top.

The sound of an approaching vehicle made her turn around. A police van was climbing the hill, its engine growling as it strained against the gradient.

Nat watched it drive past, saw a cluster of uniformed officers filling the back of the van. Now on flat ground, the vehicle sped up, shooting past the holiday park, then the school, its siren piercing the calm with a high-pitched wail.

Nat watched the van disappear into the distance, wondering what was so urgent that the police officers keeping the festival safe had been called away.

A knot of anxiety twisted her stomach. It reached up, sinking tendrils into her chest. She tried to shake it off, then crossed the road, heading for the caravan park.

28

THE PROCESSION WAS moving slowly along the street, the crowds following along on both sides, feet shuffling, bodies bumping into each other, a deafening chorus of voices fighting with the music of the marching band. The tune had changed to another Cornish ditty, one that moved along at a brisk pace, punctuated by cymbal claps. At the back of the parade, the troupe of dancing devils skipped and swooped, red ribbons trailing their twisting bodies. Carrie watched the dancers, a creeping unease moving through her. Ever since she'd glimpsed the woman in the crowd, she'd been unable to shake the feeling that something was wrong.

You're imagining things, she thought. Guilt and paranoia were playing tricks on her mind.

She replayed the events of Thursday night. It was strange to think Cal's father had ever been here. Like a ghost he'd materialised from nowhere then faded into the ether. Except he'd left behind the cheque.

Her thoughts turned to Cal. She imagined him locked in his room at the hospital, his body limp and his mind numbed by sedatives and anti-psychotics. She wondered what he would make of the Devil's Day festival. Would the crowds delight or terrify him? Would all the colours and noises make him laugh or quiver?

A wave of shame came crashing down on Carrie. Her son was disappearing—from the world, from himself—and here she was, watching a parade like he didn't even exist.

A chorus of gasps rang out from the crowd. Carrie glanced up, pulse racing, eyes alert. The gasps quickly turned to claps and cheers as two performers on giant stilts waded through the crowd. Carrie watched them, her neck craned as she took in their scaly costumes, cloven hooves, and demonic, painted faces that snarled and snapped at the onlookers. She turned back to the parade, watching Melissa idly swing her banner and chat to her schoolmate, boredom clearly setting in. Then Carrie was searching the crowd again.

What was she looking for? Danger? Trouble? Something that wasn't there? She wasn't sure.

A hand grasped her arm. She spun around.

"It's just me," Dylan said with a sting in his eyes as Carrie shrugged him off. "You're jumpy today."

There it was again: the pinch of guilt in her chest. The worry on his face. Carrie nodded, mustering a weak smile. On her right, the troupe of devil dancers rushed together then pulled apart, red ribbons swirling over their heads. Among the crowds, more devil masks were appearing, vicious, yellow eyes seeming to point in Carrie's direction.

Jack Dawkins emerged from the throng, waving at Joy and Gary. He had the glint in his eye of someone about to deliver front page news.

Dylan moved to the left, blocking Carrie's view. "Has something happened? You've barely said a word since we got here. You're not exactly giving Melissa your undivided attention, either."

"Yes, I am. And I'm fine."

219

"Okay... Well, you didn't answer my question—about meeting up to talk tonight."

"Tonight's not good."

"Why not?"

"Just leave it, will you? Jesus, don't you think I have enough going on right now? And don't give me that wounded puppy look— you were the one who wanted to call it a day. You don't get to act all hurt, like it was all my idea!"

She turned her back on him, hot and irritable, wanting nothing more than to be left alone. She was an adult, a consenting one at that. Which meant she could do what she damn well pleased. Thursday night had been nothing more than momentary relief from all the trouble weighing her down. A distraction. Nothing more. She hadn't intended to hurt anyone or cause more trouble, but now it was out of her hands, spreading from person to person like wildfire. And the trouble with fire was that once it caught hold, it burned everything to the ground.

Carrie glanced over her shoulder. Dylan had moved away and was now standing alone, watching Melissa with determination.

She felt eyes, watching her again. Looking up, she saw Joy, Gary, and Jack Dawkins staring in her direction, their expressions stony and grave. She turned away, thought she saw the young woman again, melting into the crowd. A memory triggered in her mind. She was standing in her hallway late at night, a young man and woman peeling from the shadows, rushing at her with knives.

"Mummy! Mummy, you're not watching me!"

Melissa was trying to get her attention, waving the banner manically above her head, much to the annoyance of her young partner. Her throat running dry, Carrie waved back.

The woman in the crowd was gone. If she was ever there in the first place.

Ghosts, Carrie thought. *You're chasing ghosts.*

Anxiety pressed down on her chest. The throngs surged and heaved around her as they followed the parade. The marching band's tune came to an end and they immediately started another. It was dark and mysterious, horns blowing a spiky melody that made Carrie's skin crawl. A cold sweat broke out at the back of her neck. A wall of faces and bodies closed in on all sides.

This was not how the parade was supposed to go. She was supposed to stand and smile and wave at her daughter like a dutiful mother, quietly following along, down to the beach, where she would join everyone in a toast to ward off the devil and close his gate for another year. Then she was meant to open up Cove Crafts for the rest of the afternoon, to take advantage of the festival-goers' good moods and open wallets.

Right now, Carrie wanted nothing more than to push her way through the swelling sea of bodies, leaving Dylan behind and Melissa in his care. She wanted to run and run and not look back, until she was far from this town and its pointing fingers. Until she'd outrun the devil himself.

But Carrie was fenced in with no hope of escape, the feeling that something bad was about to happen growing worse by the minute.

29

THEY'D MADE IT to the top. Not the top of the Mount, but the top of the castle. Lindsay stood on the roof with Alison and Kit close by, the wig she'd been made to wear now discarded on the ground. Her skin was slick with sweat, her lungs burned, and every inch of her ached with pain. But the view made up for it all.

She could see for miles. The ocean was like coloured glass, rippling with shades of green and blue. Yachts drifted across the bay, sails fluttering in the breeze. The beach glittered in the distance, stretching out for miles, while at the edges of the coastline, tiny towns clustered together, sunbeams bouncing off tiny windows. Lindsay was in awe, her fear momentarily forgotten.

Until she turned to see Kit standing at the very edge of the rooftop, leaning over the tooth-shaped battlements.

The knife was still in his hand, the blade sharp and serrated. Alison stood at the centre of the roof, tears streaking her face. But she wasn't sad. She was laughing to herself. That, more than anything else, filled Lindsay with terror.

"Why. . .Why are we here?" she asked, her voice still dry and cracked.

Alison pressed her hands together, as if in prayer, and smiled through her tears. "Because it's finally here. The New Dawn!"

She stretched out her arms, her palms pointing skyward, making a cross. "Oh, it's a happy, joyous day! The day we free ourselves from the shackles of this world and step into the light!"

Lindsay trembled. She had no idea what Alison was talking about. All she knew was that she wanted to go home.

But what was home without a family?

She wondered where that left her. Wondered who she would live with now if she ever got free. Beneath her terror came a tidal wave of grief. She pictured her mother, her father, Todd. If only they were here now. If only they could see what she could see. Maybe they were in heaven, right at this moment, looking down at her. But Lindsay didn't know if heaven even existed. Her dad said no. Her mum said yes. Lindsay had always thought it was a weird idea. Why go somewhere else when you could stay here with your toys and your friends and the people who loved you?

Was that what Alison meant? That they were leaving to go to a new place?

Lindsay gazed at her, a small, terrified part in her brain beginning to understand.

"Someone's coming," Kit said, shoulders tensing. He was still leaning over the battlements, staring downward.

Lindsay's heart leapt into her throat. She moved closer, until she was dangerously close to him. Standing on tiptoes, she peered over the wall and was hit by a wave of dizziness. Far below, she saw the rocky ground and the tops of trees, and even further down, the tiny roofs of the village.

The police were coming. She could see their black and white uniforms as they swarmed up the path like ants, clearing tourists out of the way and sending them back down the hill.

Hope made Lindsay's stomach flip and turn. She was going to be rescued.

Kit turned to her, the knife blade glinting in his hand. "Get away from the wall! All the way back!"

Lindsay did as she was told, scuttling away from the edge, until she stood at the centre. Behind her was the heavy wooden door they'd used to access the roof. Alison stood in between, her smile gone, her eyes sparking with excitement.

She glanced at Kit. "Are you ready?"

The boy smiled.

The silence was pierced by an ear-splitting screech of feedback, followed by a woman's voice, thin and distorted, as she spoke through a megaphone.

"This is Detective Sergeant Hughes. Lindsay Church are you up there?"

Lindsay's pulse raced.

Yes! she thought. *I am!*

But she dared not say it out loud because Kit had a finger to his lips and the knife pointed towards her throat. The police detective said something else, but Lindsay wasn't listening. Her eyes were fixed on the blade, then slowly shifting over her shoulder to stare at the door.

She could escape. Dash past Alison and run down the steps, straight into the arms of the police. She weighed up her chances. Her legs were in pain, the muscles still reeling from the long walk up. She was a child, easily overpowered. And she didn't have the knife.

"I need to know if Lindsay Church is alive and well," Detective Sergeant Hughes called out, the crackle and pop of the megaphone startling birds from trees. "Lindsay, answer if you can hear me."

Lindsay bolted forward, arms outstretched, running straight at the door.

Alison lunged, grabbing her by the arm.

Lindsay swung her foot and kicked Alison hard in the shin. The young woman shrieked. Her face twisted with fury. She lashed out, slapping Lindsay hard in the face, knocking her to the ground.

Pain shot up Lindsay's spine. Alison bent down and grabbed handfuls of her hair. Lindsay's scalp burned. She screamed as Alison dragged her across the rooftop towards Kit.

In one swift movement, Kit sprang up onto the battlements, switched the knife from his left hand to his right, then reached down and grabbed Lindsay's arm. Before Lindsay could gasp for breath, she was hoisted into the air and set down on the wall.

Alison came next, scrambling onto the battlements. Then all three were teetering on the edge.

Lindsay couldn't breathe. Her heart thrashed wildly. There was nothing between her and the open air. No safety net to catch her if she fell. Only the hard ground far, far below. She would be killed on impact. Her bones and brains raining down over the Mount.

Kit and Alison held Lindsay's hands in cast iron grips. They stood, a string of paper dolls swaying in the wind. One breath and they would all blow over. One slip and they would all be dead.

Terrified, Lindsay stared down at the cluster of police officers. They were tiny, like plastic figurines.

Alison drew in a deep breath and screamed at the top of her lungs, "We are the Children of the New Dawn! Now is our time! Our time to cross into the light!"

Below, the officers were moving around, forming panicked patterns and shapes.

"We are the Children of the new Dawn! We free ourselves from the shackles of the adult world!"

Trembling uncontrollably, Lindsay glanced up at Alison, then at Kit. Ecstatic smiles and joyful tears plastered their faces. In that moment, Lindsay knew why she'd been brought here, all the way to the top of St Michael's Mount.

She'd been brought here to die.

30

THE FIRST THING Nat noticed as she entered the caravan park was the quiet. It was eerie, like someone had turned down the volume of the world. There were no radios playing, no chattering voices of holidaying guests, no drone of vacuum cleaners as staff tidied caravan interiors. Nothing. Only the distant murmur of the marching band floating up from the town far below, the melody coming and going as the ocean breeze dipped and soared.

Nat slowed and looked around, the sky a magnificent blue above her head, the hairs on the back of her neck standing up despite the heat.

Something was wrong.

She stepped cautiously into the park, reaching the centre lawn, the grass beneath her boots dry and crisp. The surrounding caravans were pristine and brilliant white, the sun dazzling against their exteriors. A deckchair lay on its side, as if someone had jumped up in a hurry. A bright red sandal lay beside it. At the edge of a lawn, just outside caravan number six, a pile of dirty towels lay half in, half out of an abandoned laundry basket. Nat stared at the towels, then at the upturned chair, her scalp itching in the midday sun.

She was being paranoid. The Devil's Day festival was in full swing. The park's guests would be down below, watching the parade.

But where were the cleaners? Dennis Penpol had refused to give them all the day off. The only reason Nat had ducked out of her shift today was because Rose had convinced Dennis that she was needed for the parade. Penpol hadn't like it but giving Nat the day off had been infinitely safer than facing the wrath of Rose Trewartha.

Nat glanced over her shoulder. Where was Dennis? He'd let everyone know how ridiculous he thought Devil's Day was, even though it was the reason the caravan park was currently fully booked.

More importantly, where was Rachel?

Nat didn't know which caravan she was staying in. She couldn't recall Rachel saying and she hadn't asked. Her gaze still lingering on the lone red sandal, Nat exited the lawn and headed towards Dennis Penpol's office.

The door was ajar. She knocked, waited a second, then pushed it open. It was cool inside. An electric fan on the desk whirred noisily, making papers in a filing tray flutter up and down. Dennis wasn't here. No one was.

Nat scanned the room, noting the pile of aprons spilling out of the locker and the mess of files on the floor next to the desk. The fan had probably blown them over. So why did the sight of them make Nat's stomach churn with unease?

Crossing the room, she stooped to pick up the files, dumped them on the desk, and placed a paperweight on top. Behind her on the wall, the loathsome centrefold calendar flapped in the fan's breeze, teasing flashes of naked flesh.

Sitting in Penpol's chair, Nat switched on the computer and scanned through the week's guest list and allotted caravan numbers. There were fifteen permanent caravans in total, with space at the back for a limited number of guests to park their own. Nat tried to remember Rachel's surname, but wasn't sure if she'd even given it. In fact, now that she thought about it, she didn't know much about Rachel at all. She didn't even have a phone number for the girl.

A strange sensation crawled over the back of her head. She stared at the screen, her chest growing inexplicably tight.

The only thing she knew about Rachel was that she was on holiday with her parents. Nat scanned the guest list again, looking for caravans containing three guests. There were two in total: caravan number eight, booked under the name Whitby, and caravan number fourteen, booked under the name White.

Getting up, Nat crossed the room and headed for the door. A row of keys hung on the wall. She grabbed a bunch on her way out.

Just in case, she thought. But just in case of what?

As she stepped outside, the heat of the day hit her in waves. It was even quieter now, the music from the festival fading to a whisper. Nat strode past the central lawn and headed to Row C. Stopping outside of caravan number eight, she rapped her knuckles on the door and waited. Seconds passed. She knocked again, then moved to one of the windows and stood on the tips of her toes, trying to peer inside. The caravan was empty, the interior cast in long shadows.

Nat moved on towards Row E, the stillness of the holiday park coiling around her. Anxiety was growing like a tumour inside her chest. She couldn't explain it. She had no reason to be worried. And yet, it was as if her body knew some terrible secret and was hiding it from her brain.

Turning on to Row E, she walked three paces, then slid to a halt. There was something on the grass ahead. Long, dark streaks that glistened in the sun. And there was a smell, sharp and coppery, burning Nat's nostrils. She stared at the wet stains on the grass, inching closer. She hurried past them, veins turning to ice as she reached caravan fourteen.

There was blood on the door. A partial handprint smeared on the edge.

"Rachel?" She hammered her fist on the door. She stared at the stains on the ground. "Rachel! It's Nat. Are you in there?"

She leaned to the left, trying to see through the window. The blinds were down. Remembering the keys, she pulled them from her pocket and took a second to find the correct one for caravan fourteen. She slipped the key into the hole. Heard the sharp snap of the lock releasing.

Nat froze.

She had no idea what lay on the other side of the door. It could be something terrible. Something dangerous. Something so horrific that its image would be burned into her brain, forever scarring it.

Or Rachel could be lying on the other side, with only seconds remaining to save her life. Seconds that Nat was wasting.

Sucking in a trembling breath she opened the door and stepped inside. Her breath caught in her throat. Broken plates and shards of glass were strewn across the kitchenette. At the far end of the caravan, a mattress had been upended and clothes tossed to the floor.

It wasn't until Nat had taken it all in that she saw the blood. It spattered the kitchen counter and pooled on the linoleum, thick red swashes leading up to the door.

Drag marks.

Nat stumbled back, a hand clamped over her mouth. She tripped over the threshold and fell onto the grass outside. She lay there for a second, her stomach cramping, her lungs gasping for air. She turned her head to the left, saw thick streaks of blood glistening on flattened green blades.

Scrambling to her feet, she stood rigid, heart thrashing in her chest, throat drying and constricting. She followed the drag marks with her eyes, seeing them curve and twist, then disappear around the side of the caravan.

"Rachel. . ." she gasped, then staggered forwards, following the bloody trail.

She rounded the corner of the caravan. The smell hit her, bitter and acrid, making her gag and her eyes water. The drag marks were turning again, vanishing behind the rear of the caravan.

Despite the heat of the day, Nat shivered uncontrollably. Her mind shrieked at her to turn and run, but it was if her legs had a mind of their own.

Nat stepped behind the caravan.

She was unprepared for what lay there. Her brain tried to make sense of it, but got scrambled, making the world spin and her vision flash yellow then red.

She stumbled backwards, keys slipping from her hands, spine colliding with the adjacent caravan.

The bodies were piled on top of each other, like a game of human pickup sticks. Arms and legs stuck out at unnatural angles from blood-soaked torsos. Dead eyes were open and staring.

She didn't know how many people there were, but among the corpses she saw flashes of floral print cleaning aprons and recognised the faces of an elderly couple who'd tipped her generously on her last shift. Now they lay on top of each other, drenched in their own blood, with more bodies pressing down on them.

On top of the pile, splayed on his back, throat slit wide open and smiling at the sky, was Dennis Penpol.

Nat retreated, sliding along the caravan, feet tripping over themselves, hands splayed out against the warm metal. She turned and vomited. Then she staggered between the rows of caravans, choked wails and cries spluttering from her throat, vision blinded by acid tears.

They were dead. All of them.

Stabbed and slashed and cut and hacked. All stacked on top of each other in a pyre ready for burning. She didn't know if Rachel was among them. But Nat's colleagues were.

As she cleared the caravans, she realised that if Rose hadn't managed to get her the day off, she would have been on that pile, too.

Nat ran harder, racing past the car park, which was filled with the guest's vehicles, tyres slashed and ripped open. She reached the entrance gate of the holiday park, flung herself through it, and fell to her knees.

She vomited again, hot bile splashing on the dusty ground. Then she was staggering to her feet and running onto the road.

What did she do? Where did she go?

The police had left just minutes ago, called elsewhere. But there had to be others down there watching over the festival.

Digging into her pocket, Nat pulled out her phone, dropped it, picked it up again, then dialled 999. She waited for the line to connect. When it didn't, she glanced at the screen. The signal bar was empty.

Which was ridiculous. Because she was standing fifteen metres away from the only mobile mast in town.

Spinning on her heels, Nat stared down the road at Cove Primary School. Her eyes widened. The mobile mast, which was attached to the school roof, had been twisted and mangled beyond repair. She stared at it, open-mouthed, barely comprehending what she was seeing. Then she turned back to the cove.

Something terrible was happening.

She didn't know when it had started. But she knew that it wouldn't end until everyone was dead.

A face flashed in her mind. A name rang in her ears, over and over: *Rose. Rose. Rose.*

She was down there, with no idea of what was happening. Nat needed to find her. She needed to get Rose to safety.

Legs unsteady beneath her, she started forward, hurrying over the crest of the hill. Then Nat was running towards Porth an Jowl. Running towards Rose.

31

AS ROSE MADE her way through the throngs, she couldn't help feeling a swell of pride for Nat. Oh, she may have been moody, bad tempered, sometimes even spiteful, but under her spiky exterior was a scared child still trying to make sense of the terrible things that her parents had done to her. Rose had tried her best over the years to smooth it all over—not to cover it up, though, because you couldn't heal wounds if you didn't know what had caused them—and somewhere along the way, she'd fallen in love in the way a good parent falls in love with her child. Nat wasn't her own, she knew that. But some days, she forgot. She'd loved all the children she'd fostered over the years, but Nat was the one she could happily call her daughter.

If only the girl could see that. If only she could take a moment from beating herself up to notice all the love surrounding her like a blanket.

The crowd was getting heavier, making it hard for Rose to squeeze through. People had turned out in droves this year and she wondered if it was because of all the bad things that had happened. Grady Spencer. All his poor little victims. Cal. People were always curious about morbid things—the grislier the better—and Porth an Jowl had had more than its fair share to gawk at. Despite their reason for coming, Rose was glad for the crowds. More people meant more money for the town. And a good day made for a good memory to help smooth over all the bad.

As Rose reached the end of the high street and turned on to Harbour Road, the crowd thinned and the marching band's music grew a fraction softer. The town hall was just ahead. As she reached the steps, a voice rang out behind her.

"Rose? Yoo-hoo! Is that you?"

A familiar face was hurrying in her direction. Rose heaved her shoulders. "Hello, Dottie. How are you, then? Enjoying the festival so far?"

Dottie moved surprisingly fast for a woman of her age. Rose wondered if all that gossip she liked to spread acted like rocket fuel.

"Oh yes, yes, it's lovely, very nice," Dottie said breathlessly. "But have you heard about Carrie?"

Rose tried not to roll her eyes. "No, but something tells me I'm about to be enlightened."

"Well," Dottie said, ignoring the remark. "I was coming back from town yesterday morning after collecting the paper, and who do you think I saw leaving her house?"

Rose puffed out her cheeks and shook her head.

"I wouldn't have believed it if I hadn't seen it with my own eyes—but I saw, of all people, Kye Anderson—Cal's father! It was very early in the morning, mind you. Not visiting hours, so I would imagine he probably stayed the night." She arched her eyebrows and smiled conspiratorially. "What do you make of that? I mean, I know Carrie and poor Dylan were having problems but clearly, it's worse than everyone thinks. Clearly, Carrie has no intention of trying to make amends!"

"Well," Rose said, "I expect that whatever Carrie and Kye were up to, it's nobody's business except their own."

"Oh, of course, I agree, absolutely! I'm not one for gossip, but you know, I just thought it was unusual. I didn't even know that Kye was back in town."

"Well, now you do and I suppose so will everyone else. Excuse me, Dottie, but unless you want to help me pour out four hundred cups of cider, I really must be on my way."

Dottie's smile collapsed into a frustrated sulk. "Oh, I'd love to stay, but I promised to meet my son."

"Give him my best regards." With a forced smile and a wave, Rose turned her back and marched up the steps of the town hall. Opening the main door, she stepped inside and was welcomed by a cool drop in temperature.

"Stupid woman," she muttered. But she wasn't sure if she was talking about Dottie or Carrie.

She'd been hoping that Carrie and Dylan's separation was a temporary measure—despite Carrie's insistence that it wasn't. But Kye Anderson? What was he doing back here? And why was Carrie so eagerly jumping into bed with him?

Shaking her head, Rose crossed the foyer and entered the main hall.

She stopped still. Someone was here.

Rose stared at the young woman standing by the galley tables, where barrels of cider sat next to trays filled with hundreds of paper cups.

"What are you doing?"

Startled, the young woman looked up. "Oh... Um, hi... I was waiting for Nat?"

Rose stared at her. "It's Rachel, isn't it?" She took a few steps into the room, eyeing the girl as she drew closer. She was holding something behind her back. Something she didn't want Rose to see. "Nat was expecting you half an hour ago. You were supposed to meet her at the top of town."

She moved closer. Rachel turned, her hands still clutched behind her back.

"Oh? Nat asked me to help out with the drinks today. I guess I must've got mixed up."

Rose was by the tables now. The girl was definitely hiding something. She could tell by her flustered voice, the way she kept angling herself so Rose couldn't see what was behind her back.

"Nat's gone off looking for you. Might as well wait here—she'll be back soon enough." She nodded at the girl. "What's that you've got there?"

Rachel shook her head, then smiled. Rose's withering stare wiped it from her face. Biting her lip, Rachel slowly lowered her hands. "Busted."

Rose arched an eyebrow at the cup of cider the girl was clutching. "I hope you're eighteen? I won't be accused of serving drinks to underage tourists."

Rachel stared at the floor. "I'm really sorry. I was waiting around for Nat and . . . never leave a bored teenager alone with a vat of booze."

"Well, don't you dare take another drop. It's bad luck to drink the toast before time."

Rose raised an eyebrow. No doubt kids these days thought the Devil's Day ceremony was a silly old tradition filled with superstitious nonsense. But evil had shown its ugly face in this town one too many times. If raising a glass and wishing good cheer brought about some good, then Rose was happy to pour out a thousand glasses and drink every superstitious last drop. She marched up to the first barrel of cider, located the tap near the bottom and slipped a paper cup beneath it. Sparkling, yellow cider poured out, filling the cup.

"Don't just stand there, girl. Make yourself useful and get pouring. Nat will be back soon, and a few of the women should be here any second to help. We've only got twenty minutes to fill that lot up." Rose nodded to the stacks of cups on the tables.

Rachel stepped forward. "Sorry. Sure. Thanks."

Rose shook her head, set down the filled cup and reached for another. Rachel moved over to the adjacent barrel.

"Um, it's Rose, isn't it?"

"That's right."

"Where did you say Nat went to?"

"I believe she's gone off to the caravan park. That's where you're staying, isn't it?"

"She's gone there now?"

Rose stared at the girl's empty hands. "That's right. But she'll be back. Are those cups filling themselves?"

There was something strange in the girl's expression that Rose couldn't read. Was it worry? Fear?

"You alright, girl?" she asked.

Rachel nodded, picked up a cup and started filling it.

Rose flashed her another look. She could see why Nat liked the girl. She was weird and awkward, just like Nat.

They worked in silence, filling the table with cups of glistening cider. The front doors opened and voices rushed in. A group of women entered, chatting and laughing. They fell silent as they saw the stranger pouring drinks next to Rose.

"Less gawking and more pouring, ladies," Rose said, "If we don't get these drinks out in time, old Mayor Prowse will have a fit."

"At least he'll be sober for once," one of the women said and they all laughed. They got to work, pouring drinks and setting them on trays, shooting curious glances at the awkward teenage girl who avoided their stares and smiled uncomfortably.

Minutes passed. Rose found herself staring at the door, then at Rachel, then at the women.

Where was Nat?

An uneasy feeling was unsettling her stomach, like she'd swallowed a bird and now it was trying to find a way out. She turned back to Rachel, whose smile had faded, replaced by steely concentration as she poured cup after cup of cider, almost filling the second table of trays by herself.

Rose reached for another cup. The fluttering in her stomach continued to grow.

32

TWISTED IMAGES TORTURED Nat's mind, over and over, like a scene from a horror film stuck on repeat. *A pile of corpses. Puncture wounds and blood-soaked clothes. Slashed throats and dead, staring eyes.* She had seen more than her fair share of horrors in her life, but nothing that she'd experienced could come close to what lay festering in the sun behind caravan number fourteen.

Now, as Nat desperately ran, feet kicking up dust on the tarmac, she was afraid that the images would never leave her. Like blood, they might fade and turn rusty with time, but they would always be there, catching her off-guard at unexpected moments and snatching her breath away in the middle of the night.

She knew who had slaughtered these people.

It was the Dawn Children. They were responsible.

The Church family murders had been a warmup act. Now they were here in Devil's Cove and the main show was only just getting started.

Pelting down the hill, she saw Grenville Row coming up on her right. An idea came to her. She didn't know what the Dawn Children were planning, but she knew that Devil's Day was part of it. There were hundreds of people in town, all completely unaware of the horror she'd found in the caravan park.

Nat veered right, racing past the fenced off site where Grady Spencer's house had once stood, then throwing open her garden gate and running up the path.

Seconds later, she was inside her kitchen and leaning over the sink, drinking mouthfuls of icy tap water and dousing her face. Droplets dripped from her chin as she moved over to the knife block and pulled out the knife with the biggest blade. Then she was on the move again, racing back through the hall and grabbing the telephone from the wall. She punched 999 on the keypad and waited for the line to connect.

The emergency operator spoke in her ear. Nat asked for the police, then she was on hold again, the seconds dripping by like melting tar as she tried and failed to steady her breathing.

"Come on!" she hissed. The police operator answered and the panic Nat had been fighting to contain came flooding out in a tsunami. "They're dead! They're all dead! You have to come!"

The operator's voice was soft and steady. "Try to remain calm. I need you to say that again."

"They're here! The Dawn Children are here in Porth an Jowl! People are dead at the caravan park. Please, you need to send someone now!"

Hanging up the phone, Nat ran to the front door and threw it open. Then she was outside, hurrying through the garden and back onto Cove Road. She ran, down and down, past row after row of stone cottages, feet stumbling, almost tripping, until she reached the town.

The high street was empty. The shops all closed. The town square silent and still. The Devil's Day parade had already made it down to the promenade.

Nat raced along the pavement, footfalls echoing eerily all around. Reaching the end of the street, she slid to a halt.

What did she do?

Did she head back and take the shortcut to the promenade through the town square? Or did she head for the town hall?

Movement glimmered at the corner of her eye. She glanced over her shoulder to see two uniformed officers emerging from the square. They were moving quickly, heading in the direction of Cove Road.

Relief surged through Nat's body. The phone call had worked. Porth an Jowl might be saved. She waited for more officers to emerge from the square.

No one else came.

Waving her hands, Nat called out to the officers. But they were already gone, disappearing from sight as they turned onto Cove Road. She knew she should chase after them, tell them that two police officers were not enough. But she needed to find Rose.

Nat crossed the street and entered Harbour Road. Pounding up the steps of the town hall, she barged inside. Then slid to a halt.

The hall was empty, the tables cleared. Which meant Rose and her team were already down at the promenade, handing out drinks for the toast.

It would be hard to find her, harder still to get her out before the Dawn Children struck. And they were going to strike at any moment. Nat felt it in the air, sick and cloying, an impending sense of doom that made her want to curl up under a table and cover her face with her hands.

She spun around, sick and terrified. Her gaze snagged on a door at the back of the hall. She ran towards it, foolishly hoping to find

Rose inside.

The kitchen was empty, except for two large plastic containers that had fallen out of the waste bin and lay on the centre of the floor, a few drops of glistening liquid drying on the tiles.

Nat stared at the bottles, a cold sweat dripping down her neck. Leaving the kitchen, she hurried back through the hall. Her legs were begging for respite. Her lungs were hot and prickly. But Nat kept moving. She couldn't stop to rest. If she did, Rose was good as dead.

A fresh wave of adrenaline surged through her limbs, Nat flew from the hall and down the steps, out into brilliant sunshine. She raced towards the seafront and the hundreds of people gathering on the promenade, all unaware that Death had come to Porth an Jowl.

33

DETECTIVE CONSTABLE TURNER stood staring up at the castle battlements, pulse hammering in his ears. He flashed a look at DS Hughes, who returned his troubled gaze as she reached for her police radio.

"I'm calling the hostage negotiation team," she said.

Turner returned his attention to the three figures teetering on the edge way above him, little Lindsay Church clamped between the two adults.

"This isn't a hostage situation," he muttered to himself. "This is something else."

He'd returned to his empty home late last night, after one of the darkest, most upsetting days of his career. He'd sat in an armchair, drinking rum in silence, Luke Beaumont's tiny legs sticking out from behind a tree in his mind, a lurking, twisting dread in the pit of his stomach.

Something was coming. Something big.

All the fragmented pieces were fusing together and finally starting to make sense: the abduction of Noah Pengelly; the return of Cal Anderson; Grady Spencer's house of horrors; the murder of Councillor Beaumont—captured on video by author Aaron Black, also now dead; the Church family murders; the killing of Luke

Beaumont, his body purposefully left to be found.

And now this—Lindsay Church had reappeared. And she was not alone.

Everything was connected in an unnerving, sinister chain, one event unfolding to reveal another, like unfurling petals of a poisonous flower.

Turner stared at the bodies above him. Was this it? The main event?

Or was this just another petal?

Hughes was busy on the radio, the uniformed officers all standing by, bodies tense and ready to spring to action on her command.

How long would it take for the hostage negotiation team to arrive? For Armed Response? The murders of the Church family and Luke Beaumont were already using up valuable police resources. And now officers securing the Devil's Day festival had been pulled out to attend what looked like a hostage situation, even though Turner's gut was telling him it was anything but.

It was as if all of these events had been purposefully timed to stretch an already depleted force thin, to scatter it across the county like a handful of chicken bones.

Done on the radio, Hughes turned back to him. "They're on the way. We need to keep the area secure until they arrive."

The fluttering in Turner's gut turned to panic. "They're going to be too late."

The sudden certainty was like a kick to the groin, white-hot and excruciating.

Above their heads, the woman was shouting again, her voice echoing across the bay. "We are the Dawn Children! Children of the light! Our father tried to protect us from a world of monsters. But he was taken from us. Now we will show the monsters that this is our time! Now we will take back all that is innocent and light. Now the monsters will fall and we will have Our Salvation!"

"What the hell is she talking about?" Hughes said.

The Dawn Children raised their arms, lifting the Church girl's hands above her head.

Turner didn't wait for further instructions.

He bolted forwards, through the open castle door and across a large hall, his footfalls echoing around him. Outside, DS Hughes screamed at him to come back. He knew he was breaking protocol. He knew it was his job on the line. But seeing the lifeless body of Luke Beaumont had broken something inside him. If Lindsay Church died too, he knew he would never recover.

Turner ran, eyes darting from side to side as he searched for a way up. Finding a set of stairs, he raced up to the next floor, barely aware of the grand furnishings and tapestries, all blurring into one.

He threw open another door. Then another.

He was outside again, racing through a tiered garden at the rear of the Mount. An elderly gardener was bent over, digging up weeds. He glanced up as Turner thundered towards him.

"Which way to the roof!" Turner yelled.

The startled gardener pointed wordlessly upwards and to the right. Turner skidded to a halt, almost tripping over his feet, found another door and raced inside.

More halls. More doors.

He wrenched each one open, sweat pouring down his back, lungs burning in his chest, room after room revealing nothing more than dusted antiquities. Until he came to the last door. Then more steps reaching up, hemmed in by narrow walls. He took them silently, his hands tracing the brickwork, until he reached the door at the top.

Perspiration ran into his eyes. He wiped them with the back of his hand, tried to steady his breathing as he pressed his ear to the door. Light poured in through the sides, along with the whisper of a sea breeze and the woman's hollow voice still ringing in the air.

Slowly, carefully, Turner gripped the brass ring handle and pulled.

The door swung open an inch. Daylight rushed in, burning away shadows. Holding his breath, he pulled the door open wider and peered out.

He could see them. Fifty feet away. Still standing on the battlements. Hands linked. Their backs turned. The young woman on the right, the boy on the left. Lindsay Church trapped in between.

There was something in the boy's hand, glinting in the sunlight. A knife.

Turner swallowed. Shut his eyes for a second.

What was he doing?

He was breaking every rule. Every code of practice. All it would take was for one of them to turn and see him and then Lindsay Church was dead. But if he stood and did nothing, she was dead anyway.

Because the Dawn Children were about to jump.

Turner opened the door a fraction wider, letting in more light.

Sounds of approaching footsteps made him turn around. Two uniformed officers were heading straight for him.

He shot up a hand, pressed a finger to his lips. They nodded, eyes round, pupils dilated.

Turner stepped outside.

He moved like a cat, his keen eyes fixed on the trio. The breeze was gathering momentum, making their hair flutter.

He came closer. One more step. Then another.

The air was thick and hard to swallow.

The Dawn Children were silent, their hands still gripping Lindsay's, leaving her balancing on tiptoes.

Turner was halfway across the rooftop. Close enough to hear Lindsay's frightened sobs. He risked a glance behind him and saw the uniform officers at the top of the stairs. He held up a hand, telling them to stay there.

Then he turned back to the Dawn Children and slid another step forward.

He was closer now. But still not close enough.

He took another step. Then another. Sweat running into his eyes. Blood rushing in his ears.

Closer. Closer.

Arms reaching out. Hands splaying.

Fingertips almost touching the back of Lindsay's t-shirt.

The boy turned. Glanced over his shoulder.

Turner froze.

He watched the boy's eyes widen with surprise. Heard his breath, sharp and shocked.

Now the woman was turning around, recoiling in horror at Turner's presence.

Turner lunged forwards, springing through the air, desperately reaching for Lindsay.

The woman jumped. The boy, too. Catapulting Lindsay into the air.

Then the three were falling.

Turner screamed. His fingers shot out.

Grabbed the back of Lindsay's t-shirt.

He lurched forward, chest slamming down on the wall, the air bursting from his lungs.

The Dawn Children fell. Swung. Still holding onto Lindsay, Turner was pulled forward. Skin tore from his chest as he was dragged across the battlements.

The weight was too much. He was falling with them.

The Dawn Children slammed into each other.

The boy lost his grip on Lindsay. He fell, arms swinging wildly, legs kicking, young eyes filled with terror.

Hands grabbed Turner's legs. An arm wrapped around his chest. The officers held onto him as he watched the boy plummet, then smash into the ground, blood and bone spraying over the police officers below.

Shrieks of horror rang up. Lindsay screamed. The woman was still holding onto her wrist, refusing to let go.

Turner's grip was slipping on her t-shirt. He reached down with his other hand and grasped her upper arm.

"Pull back!" He hissed between clenched teeth.

The officers dug their feet into the ground and heaved. The woman kicked and thrashed. She glared at Turner, who was growing weaker by the second. Not in terror, he realised. But in anger.

The officers heaved again, lifting them up an inch.

"No!" the woman hissed. "This is our New Dawn! We have to go into the light!"

The officers heaved again. Turner felt his feet touch the ground. Felt adrenaline surge through his veins. He wrapped an arm around

Lindsay's chest.

An ear-splitting scream tore from the woman's throat. She thrashed her body again, dragging the officers forward, then down.

Far below, the young man's broken body was afloat in a sea of red.

"We are the Children of the Dawn! Our Salvation is here! This is our—"

Lindsay brought her foot up and smashed it down into the young woman's face. She gasped. Then she was falling. Tumbling and flipping, screaming all the way down. There was a sickening, far away crunch. Then silence.

Turner and the officers dragged Lindsay over the battlements and they fell to the ground, where they lay in a tangled pile, panting and heaving.

Lindsay was alive. Turner had saved her.

He wrapped his arms around her trembling body and held her close.

"It's okay. You're safe. We've got you."

It was a terrible lie and he knew it. Because Lindsay's family was gone and she was alone. Nothing in her life would ever be okay again.

As more officers arrived, followed by Detective Sergeant Hughes, Turner couldn't shake the feeling that today wasn't over yet. That Lindsay Church and poor Luke Beaumont were only the sideshows. A distraction. Little petals of a poisoned flower.

That flower was about to bloom. Suddenly he realised where.

But it was much too late.

34

THE PARADE HAD made it down to the promenade, the lumbering, giant devil leading the way and the swarming throng of spectators following alongside. The marching band played on, xylophones tinkling, cymbals crashing, drums beating, the musicians sweating in their bright uniforms. Two volunteers dressed as mermaids danced by, spraying fine mists of cool water over them, bringing temporary relief from the soaring temperature.

The performing school children were also suffering from the heat, growing irritable and sluggish. Two little pirates had abandoned their banner completely, leaving it on the roadside for a pair of teenagers to snatch it up and swoop it around. Even the demonic dancers had started to tire. Lucky then, that the parade was coming to its end.

The giant red devil came to a standstill in the centre of Cove Road, his wicked, grinning face staring out at the calm, blue ocean. The Devil's Gate protruded from the left cliff in a wide, rocky arch that plunged into the water. On the beach, three timber slipways had been constructed near the shore and spaced equally apart. Resting on top of each one was a wooden keg filled with cider.

This was the pinnacle of the Devil's Day festival. The moment an offering was made.

Rose and her gaggle of volunteers worked through the crowds, handing out cups of cider from trays. People accepted them eagerly. A few even tried to drink straight away, until a cutting glare from Rose quickly changed their minds.

Carrie stood at the far end of the promenade, the designated meeting place for parents to collect their children from the parade. Dylan, Joy, and Gary stood together next to her. No one was speaking. Dylan watched the crowds, a mixture of confusion and hurt in his eyes. Gary stared at the ground, while Joy had made it her duty to flash disapproving looks at her daughter-in-law. She hadn't said anything to Dylan yet, but Carrie sensed the woman was struggling to keep what she now knew to herself.

Feeling hemmed in, Carrie turned away from the Killigrews and stared at the other waiting parents. They offered her no solace, either blanking her completely or shooting her down with withering glares. She was a pariah. The mother of a killer. Somehow, she was just as responsible as Grady Spencer for turning her son into a psychopath. It was easier to blame the parents, Carrie supposed, than to accept that a child was capable of murder. To do so would be to question their own children.

But it wasn't Joy Killigrew's accusatory glares or the other parents' cold shoulders that were bothering Carrie right now.

It was that young woman's face. The one she'd glimpsed in the crowd. The one who had been watching her.

She searched the multitude of bodies on the promenade with her eyes and scanned the rows of stalls selling sweets and soft toys and cheap keyrings. A white beer tent bulged with drinkers quaffing from plastic pint glasses. Halfway along the promenade a small funfair captivated young children with a spinning carousel of brightly coloured horses, a coconut shy, and a red and white striped helter-skelter with a spiral slide. Stilt walkers picked their way through the throngs, some dressed as clowns, others as fantastical creatures. Near the promenade railings, a troupe of jugglers tossed burning torches in the air, sparking cries of delights from their audience.

Weaving between them all were Rose and her volunteers.

Carrie turned away from the crowds and looked down at the beach, where Mayor Prowse and a group of town councillors were gathering by the wooden slipways. Beyond them, the sea was calm, patiently waiting for the ceremony to begin.

This was where it had all gone wrong. Seven years ago, when Carrie had taken her eyes off Cal for just a minute. A small slip in concentration that had led to a lifetime of hell with no end in sight. Not for the first time, Carrie wondered what life would be like now if she hadn't looked away.

"Well, hello Killigrews!" The voice was warm and familiar, easing Carrie away from darkness. Rose smiled and slipped her a secretive wink as she held up a tray of cups. "How are we all doing?"

Joy clasped a hand to her chest. "Oh, what a show! The children looked marvellous, don't you think?"

"Didn't they? That big bugger over there's quite impressive, too!" Rose laughed as she nodded at the giant devil, who was starting to wilt in the heat. "That was my Natalie, you know. She designed it all by herself!"

The Killigrews all smiled and commented on Nat's talent.

"How are you, love?" Rose said. She stared at Carrie, a frown rippling the space between her eyebrows.

"Hot and sweaty." Why was Rose staring at her like that? Like she was disappointed? "Did you see Melissa?"

"Oh, yes! The little bird looked like she was having the time of her life!" Rose glanced up at Dylan. Then back at Carrie. "Well, grab a drink because the ceremony is starting in five minutes. After the year you've had, I'd advise drinking every last drop!"

Dylan leaned forward, taking a cup. "I'll drink to that," he said, then lifted it to his lips.

"What are you doing?" Joy snapped, grabbing him by the wrist and lowering it back down.

"Bloody hell, Mum! Next you'll have me throwing salt over my shoulder and dancing naked on a full moon."

Joy wrinkled her face. "No one ever needs to see that."

Taking two cups from Rose's tray, she handed one to Gary and shot him a warning glance. He shrugged and stared wistfully at the beer tent.

"Carrie? You having one?" Rose held up the tray.

Carrie stared at the cups of sparkling cider. Memories of Thursday night swamped her mind and churned her stomach. "No, I think I'll stick to water."

"Everyone needs to drink to make the offering work," Joy said, her voice suddenly sharp. "Even those who think they're beyond reproach."

Dylan frowned. "Wow, Mum. Be nice. If Carrie doesn't want to drink, she shouldn't have to."

"Why not? From what I hear, Carrie does lots of things she shouldn't."

Carrie opened her mouth, then shut it again.

"What's that supposed to mean?" Dylan said.

Joy glanced at Gary, who stared at the ground. "Nothing. I'm sorry. The heat must be getting to me."

Rose cleared her throat and flashed a smile. "Well, here's to happier times ahead. Now, I best get the rest of these handed out or Mayor Prowse will have my guts for garters." She turned to leave, then frowned again. "By the way, you haven't seen Natalie, have you?"

The four of them shook their heads.

"Well, if you do, tell her to get her backside down to the beach."

Giving Carrie one last concerned look, Rose slipped away into the crowd.

She knows, Carrie thought, clenching her jaw. She was going to kill Dottie Penpol. Joy Killigrew, too. She glared at her mother-in-law, who had turned her back and was pretending to watch the fun fair. Carrie and Joy had never been close, but they'd always been amicable. Even in those early days, when Carrie and Dylan had first got together, Joy had been kind and welcoming, and she hadn't shied away from Carrie's grief. There had been a handful of times when talking about her lost son had reduced Carrie to tears. Joy had handed her tissues and fussed over her, making her tea and cake. Which had been more than her own mother had done.

To see Joy turn so cold and prickly hurt more than she'd anticipated. But Joy was a mother. And mothers would kill to protect their children.

"Mummy!"

Melissa ran towards Carrie, her pirate costume dishevelled and her eyepatch twisted around to the side of her head.

Behind her, a tired and sweaty gaggle of mermaids, robots, and butterflies, were being herded towards waiting parents by their teacher, Miss Rhodda. Seeing Melissa with her family, Miss Rhodda waved a hand and did her best to avoid making eye contact with

Carrie.

"Did you see me, Mummy?" Melissa asked as she wrapped her arms around Carrie's thighs. "Did you see me in the parade?"

Carrie crouched down and hugged her. "Of course I did, sweet pea. We were all watching. Me, your dad, Nana Joy and Grandpa Gary. You looked magnificent!"

Melissa beamed at her family. Then she pulled away from Carrie and ran to Dylan, who swept her up in his arms and spun her around, before planting a kiss on her forehead.

"Ahoy there, Cap'n Killigrew!" he said in a gruff pirate voice. "How's my ruler of the seven seas?"

"Good, Daddy! It was fun! Can I have ice cream?"

"Well, I don't know about that. Have you been a good pirate—plundering ships and stealing buried treasure?"

Melissa laughed and nodded. She twisted around in Dylan's arms to face her grandparents. "Did you see me, Nana Joy? I saw you and Grandpa Gary!"

Joy reached out and gently squeezed her cheek. "You were the best thing in the whole parade!"

"Oh, I don't know about that," Grandpa Gary said with a wry wink. "That big old devil over there was pretty impressive."

"Grandpa Gary!" Melissa cried, making him smile. She seemed to be the only one who could.

Carrie watched them, ignoring twinges of jealousy and guilt. Then she was looking beyond her daughter, scanning the crowds again, watching all the other, happier families, and missing Cal so much it hurt. She would go to see him again. Soon. She would—

A group of teenagers caught her eye. They were huddled together by the promenade railings, all wearing identical masks—

the grinning, maniacal face of the Devil.

"Carrie?" Dylan said. "You want to take her for ice cream, or shall I?"

The teenagers were unmoving, masked faces frozen on the crowds.

"Carrie?"

"What?"

"The ice cream?"

She stared at Dylan, then at Melissa, who wriggled impatiently in her father's arms.

"I'll go," she said. "You stay here with her."

"Okay. Anyone else for ice cream?"

Gary shook his head. Joy muttered no thanks.

"So, just me then," Dylan said, smiling.

Melissa pinched his nose. "And me, Daddy! And me!"

Now the masked teenagers were on the move, heading away and disappearing into the throng. *You're being paranoid*, Carrie told herself. *Paranoid and feeling guilty as hell.*

She glanced at Melissa, forced a smile. "Scoop or cone?"

"Cone, of course!"

"And a chocolate flake?"

Melissa raised her eyebrows. "Does a bear shit in the woods?"

"Melissa Killigrew!" Joy cried. She glanced at Gary, who was desperately trying not to smile, then at Dylan who was erupting with laughter. "Where did you hear such a horrible thing?"

Melissa shrugged. "School."

"Well, your Nana is right, sweet pea. We don't use that kind of language." Carrie glanced nervously at Joy, who didn't look away. It was a small reprieve, but it was a reprieve all the same. "I'll be right back."

Running a hand across Melissa's cheek, Carrie headed away from her family. Tears stung her eyes. If only she could love Dylan the way he loved her. She had tried, so many times. For a long while, she'd convinced herself that she was in love with him. Maybe she had been. But not now.

She still cared about him a great deal and together they'd produced Melissa—a child to replace the one she'd lost—how could she not feel gratitude for that? But their relationship had been borne from her grief. It had been a smokescreen. An intricately spun distraction.

When Cal had come back, the illusion had shattered. She and Dylan had hurt each other. They were both still reeling. Wasn't it better to end their marriage now than to drag it over broken glass?

Carrie glanced back at Dylan, who still had Melissa in his arms and was listening intently to her chatter. She smiled a sad smile, then headed for the ice cream van. There was a long line of people in front of her, all hot and red-faced and growing impatient. Some of them held cups of cider and were glancing down, tongues running over parched lips. But if there was one thing the British were good at, it was waiting for the right moment.

Which was almost upon them.

The marching band came to the end of their song and fell silent. The quiet was startling, almost physical. Even the jangly tunes of the fun fair had been cut short.

Carrie leaned to the left then to the right, straining to get a clear view of the beach through the bodies. A crackling shriek of feedback made the crowds collectively hiss and clench their teeth. Then Carrie heard the rasping voice of Mayor Prowse—a man mostly known for showing up drunk to his ceremonial duties. Today was no different.

"Is this thing on?" he bellowed over the portable PA system. *Not the most poetic start*, Carrie thought, then grimaced as Mayor Prowse cleared his phlegm-filled throat.

From somewhere to her right, a cry rang out. Startled, she turned to see what the trouble was, but now that everyone had stopped still for the ceremony, it was impossible to get a clear view of anything.

"Right, we'll begin," Mayor Prowse was saying, his words slurring together. Carrie wondered how long he'd been in the beer tent before making his way down to the beach. She stepped to the left, trying to get a better view, and saw glimpses of the beach. The three slipways. People gathered at the head of each one. Mayor Prowse swaying on a makeshift stage, microphone in one hand, the other raised above his head. She saw him turn to face the ocean before her view was obscured once more.

"Oh, Satan, purveyor of darkness, hear my plea! Take not our children but this offering to the sea. Close the gate for another year, let us keep our children, you can keep the beer."

Laughter rippled through the crowds. Followed by another cry, this time closer.

Carrie spun around.

On the other side of Cove Road, a man had collapsed and was having some sort of seizure on the ground. Two paramedics hurried towards him from a nearby ambulance. Carrie watched them with mounting concern, glad that she hadn't brought Melissa with her to the ice cream van. Heat like the town was experiencing today was unusual for this time of year; she was surprised more people hadn't been taken ill.

And yet, that uneasy feeling that had been trailing her through the town suddenly reappeared.

The paramedics were bent over the fallen man now. More curious onlookers gathered around, blocking Carrie's view. She turned back, noticing how nearly everyone in the crowd was watching the beach, cups of cider half raised, ready for the toast.

"Oh, Devil, master of all sin and atrocity!" the mayor cried dramatically, making the PA speakers rumble and pop. "We give you this offering and beseech that you leave us be!"

Something was happening. Some sort of disturbance further along the promenade. Carrie narrowed her eyes, straining to see.

Nat emerged from the throng, pushing and shoving, screaming at people to get out of her way.

Carrie sucked in a shocked breath. Nat was deathly white, her face dripping with perspiration, her eyes wide and startled—the expression of someone deep in shock. Leaving the ice cream van behind, Carrie headed straight for her.

"Nat!" she called, waving a hand as she ducked and darted through families and couples.

Startled, Nat snapped her head around and ran straight towards Carrie. They met, almost colliding with each other.

"What is it?" Carrie asked. Now she was close up, she saw that Nat's entire body was trembling uncontrollably. She glanced down and saw the knife in Nat's hand. "What the hell is going on?"

At first, it was as if unseen forces had sealed Nat's mouth. She tried to speak, but only a strangled choke came out.

"Breathe," Carrie urged. "You're scaring me."

Nat struggled to suck in a breath. Tears ran from the corners of her eyes.

"Where's Rose?" she gasped.

"She's—well, I guess she's somewhere on the beach. But what's happened, Nat? Why are you carrying a knife? Give it to me."

Nat pulled away from her, tried to leave in the direction of the beach.

Carrie shot out a hand and pulled her back. "Nat!"

"They're dead!" Nat sobbed, her face contorting into a terrible grimace. "They piled them all up at the holiday park!"

A chill pierced Carrie's heart. "Who's dead? What are you talking about?"

"They're here! I've got to find Rose! We've got to leave!"

Carrie's heart was hammering, her head spinning as adrenaline shot through her veins. "Who's here? You're not making any sense!"

But she already knew who Nat was talking about. She knew it in her heart. Deep down in the darkest recesses of her mind.

"It's them!" Nat hissed. "The Dawn Children!"

Down on the beach, the mayor had finished his speech and was nodding to the people by the slipways. One by one, they raised axes high above their heads, then together, brought them slicing down, piercing the barrels.

Foamy cider spurted from the wounds like arcs of blood. The barrels rolled forward, rumbling down the slipways gathering speed, heading for the ocean.

"Drink!" The mayor cried. "Let us toast the closing of the Devil's Gate for another year! Drink! Drink!"

At that exact moment, Carrie felt eyes on her. She looked up. And saw her. The young woman who'd been watching her from the crowd. She was smiling; a wide, toothy grin that sent shivers racing along Carrie's spine.

Nat had seen her, too.

"Rachel?" she gasped.

But it was as if the woman hadn't noticed her. Her eyes were fixed on Carrie, burning into hers.

"Rachel?" Nat said again.

"That's not her name," Carrie said as memories flashed through her mind. A young man and woman launching at her from the darkness, knives in hand. The same two, naked and sweaty, fucking on a mattress while she lay half-conscious, locked inside a cage. "She's called Morwenna. She's with the Dawn Children."

All around, hundreds of people were raising their cups in a toast. Down on the beach, the barrels had reached the tide. Waves crashed over them, foam spitting in the air.

Nat shook her head wildly, her eyes fixed on Morwenna, tears and snot wetting her face.

"No! That's not right!"

Morwenna had something in her hands. As hundreds of people tipped back their heads, as cider poured down their throats, she raised the red devil mask.

"You can thank Cal," she said, her face bitter and twisted. "He ruined everything."

She slipped the mask over her face.

Then she was gone, disappearing into the crowd, as if she was never there.

Carrie spun around, eyes growing impossibly round. People were laughing, wiping their mouths, crushing empty paper cups.

Nat was pulling away from her, running towards the beach.

Then smiles were turning into confusion. Confusion into panic. Panic into pain.

Carrie watched, mouth hanging open in a silent scream, as all around, faces turned red and people clutched their stomachs and clawed their chests and howled like animals.

Like dominoes, they all started knocking into each other.

Like bowling pins, they all fell to the ground. Hundreds of them. One after the other. Leaving scores of frightened children standing alone and shrieking in horror.

Carrie was paralysed, watching an ocean of convulsing bodies, ears ringing with guttural cries of pain.

It was happening everywhere.

All along the promenade. Across the street. Down on the beach.

People were dying.

Faces turning purple, now blue. Limbs shooting out, spasming, contracting. Fingers knotting and twisting.

"What. . .?" Carrie began.

She shook her head, over and over, turning around, scarcely able to comprehend what she was seeing.

Melissa swung into view. She was standing alone, screaming hysterically and tearing at her hair.

A lightning bolt of adrenaline struck Carrie.

She sprang forwards, dashing and weaving through a multitude of collapsed bodies.

Hands reached for her. Eyes pleaded for help. She kept on running, gaze pinned on Melissa, too terrified to let her slip from sight.

Joy and Gary were on the ground, faces the colour of nightshade, veins bulging from their temples and foreheads as they writhed in agony.

Dylan was next to them, knees pulled up to his chest, hands wrapped over his head, like a baby in the womb.

Empty cups littered the ground, tiny drops of poison already drying on the baked cement.

Carrie was frozen and helpless, not knowing what to do, not knowing how to make this stop.

Ignoring Melissa's screams, she dropped to her knees and placed a hand on Dylan's shoulder.

"No!" she sobbed. "Oh God, no!"

Dylan's hand shot out, his fingernails sinking into her wrist. He managed to look up and Carrie saw the unbearable pain that was consuming him.

"Get. . ." he managed to say. "Get her out!"

Then his eyes rolled back in his head. He was unconscious, convulsing on the floor. Pissing himself.

"I'm sorry!" Carrie shrieked. "I'm sorry! I'm sorry!"

Melissa's screams came back to her.

She staggered to her feet, spun a full circle, saw all the other children wailing and screaming, the ground littered with the dead and dying.

There were other adults, who hadn't drunk the cider, who were all paralysed, all sharing the same bewildered stare.

Then Carrie saw the masked devils.

They were scattered around, skipping and dancing around the bodies, knives in hands, blades glinting in the sunlight as they moved towards the surviving adults.

Down at Carrie's feet, Joy exhaled a final breath. Beside her, Gary was already dead, his hand forever reaching for his wife. Dylan was still clinging on, foam and spit and blood leaking from his mouth.

Her mind blank, her body taking control, Carrie lunged at Melissa and swept her into her arms.

Then she was running among the corpses.

Running for her life.

35

NAT RAN BUT it was like she was drowning. Her limbs pushed against unseen pressure. Her lungs couldn't get enough air. Blood pounded in her ears, muffling the chorus of screams.

The bodies were all around, thrashing and squirming, reaching for help. She stumbled through them, standing on arms, legs, chests, until she reached the promenade steps that led to the beach below.

Then it was as if she were no longer running underwater. Time caught up with her. Everything sped up.

Nat lost her footing on the second step, slipped and went crashing down, knees smashing on concrete, knife flying from her fingers, as she tumbled down to the hot sand.

What breath she had was knocked from her lungs. Grit flew into her eyes, making them burn. But she pushed herself up. Got to her feet. Started running again.

Pain shot up her legs. Her eyes were on fire, and she wiped desperately at them as she staggered forward, heading for the slipways.

Behind her on the promenade, people were shrieking and screaming. Hundreds of them. All screaming and dying. She was in a nightmare. One that she would never wake up from.

The crowd was thinner on the beach, with only town council members, the mayor, and a few festival organisers present for the offering ceremony. Now they were all doubled over or lying face down.

On the makeshift stage, Mayor Prowse was belly up, arms and legs punching and kicking, face as red as sunset.

A photographer stood to one side, a young man in his mid-twenties. He was motionless, camera in his hands, the strap looped around his neck, watching the mayor through glazed eyes.

The screams of the dying were reaching a crescendo, high-pitched and wracked with agony.

How was this happening?

The town was dying. People clawing at their throats and stomachs, faces contorted in awful grimaces. Only two minutes ago, they had been enjoying ice cream and riding on carousels, laughing and joking.

Now, it was as if the legend of the Devil's Gate had come true and the devil had stepped out to wreak havoc.

Except this time, he hadn't come for the children.

It was Rachel.

No. Not Rachel.

Morwenna.

She had tricked Nat. Fed her lies that she'd hungrily devoured because of her desperate need for attention. Morwenna had made her feel liked. Normal.

But it was all a ruse.

Like an idiot Nat had told her everything. Who was involved. How the offering ceremony played out. Where the alcohol was stored.

Morwenna had listened to every word and fed it all back to the Dawn Children. Somehow, they'd got to the cider before Rose had

267

served it up.

Now everyone was dying. Writhing on the ground, gurgling and choking, frothing at the mouth. Everyone except the frozen photographer.

And Rose.

Nat cried out in relief, dashing forwards and almost slamming into her. She wrapped her arms around the woman, squeezed tight, and sobbed into her chest.

"You're okay! You're alive!"

She pulled back to stare at Rose. Like the photographer, she was oddly emotionless as she stared at the people dying around her. They were her friends. Fellow townspeople. Her neighbours.

"I don't understand," she muttered and clutched at her chest. Behind her, the tide swept in, swirling with thick, creamy foam. The cider barrels bobbed in the water, heading out to sea.

"Did you drink the cider?" Nat cried.

Rose looked up at her with confused eyes. Her face was terribly pale, her eyes oscillating in their sockets.

"No, I never could stand the stuff. I switched mine for a cup of water."

"Thank God!"

A strangled, gurgling shriek rang up from below. Nat glanced down to see Marge Penshaw, who ran the bakery, expel a final, bubbling breath. Then she was dead, her eyes frozen on Nat.

On the stage, Mayor Prowse had grown still.

Rose was waking up, snapping out of her shock. She stared at the dead and dying on the sand.

"Dear Lord," she whispered. "Was it me? Did I do something wrong?"

She lunged forward, reaching out for one of the town councillors, who was curled up into a ball and quietly convulsing. Nat grabbed her, pulling her back.

"We have to go! It's not safe here!"

Rose's face was going blank again, her mind retreating to a safe place.

"Rose, come on! We have to leave!" Nat tried to pull away, but Rose held fast. The young photographer still hadn't moved a muscle.

"Hey you!" Nat called to him. "You need to go! Get out of town!"

The man stared at her, then back at the bodies.

Nat spun around, helpless and desperate. Spying one of the axes that had been used to open the barrels, she swooped down and scooped it up. It was heavy in her hand, but it made her feel a fraction safer.

She turned back to Rose. They needed to get out of here. Now. But both Rose and the photographer were resuming their frozen states.

Nat gave Rose a sharp tug. She stumbled, almost fell. But it did the trick. Rose blinked twice. Her face twisted with horror.

"What's happening?" she wailed. "Oh God, what's happening?"

Nat pulled her along. "We're getting out of here."

They started forward, heading back in the direction of the promenade, Nat's eyes wide and alert. From behind her, the photographer emitted a strangled wail. She stopped, glanced over her shoulder. Tears were running down his face. It was like he was awake inside, yet his body was in a coma. She couldn't leave him like this. Could she?

"Hey!" she yelled again. "Get moving. Now!"

But the photographer didn't get moving. He just looked around, eyes glazed, mouth half open.

Nat stalked towards him, Rose still in tow. On the sand, everyone was dead now. The screaming from the promenade had dampened to a disconcerting whimper.

"Hey, dick head!" she screamed at the photographer. "Get moving or I'll leave you behind!"

She let go of Rose, raised her hand, fully prepared to slap him hard if she needed to. Then she saw movement at the corner of her eye.

In the distance, two red devils were descending the stone steps of the promenade.

The Dawn Children.

Terror gripped Nat by the throat.

She turned back to the photographer. "Move!"

She struck him hard in the face. He staggered sideways, then went still again.

The Dawn Children were approaching, masks grinning from afar.

Nat spun on her heels. The Shack came into view. Grabbing Rose by the hand, she ran towards the beach bar. Reached the door, tried to shoulder it open. It was locked. Nat ran to the window, pressed her face against the glass. There were people inside, huddled together behind the bar.

Nat glanced over her shoulder. The Dawn Children had almost reached the photographer.

A cry escaped her throat. Grabbing Rose again, she dragged her alongside The Shack and pulled her around the corner, until they were hidden from view. Rose's eyes had glazed over again and she was mumbling incoherently. Nat clamped a palm across her mouth.

She counted to ten, then removed her hand. Rose was quiet, terrified, a sickly grey. Carefully, Nat peeked around the corner.

The photographer hadn't moved.

The Dawn Children stood in front of him, arms slung around each other's shoulders, knives swinging from their hands. It was a bizarre scene. The photographer lifted his camera, focused the lens, and snapped pictures of them. What the man had witnessed had broken his mind.

Nat watched in horror as the Dawn Children suddenly untangled themselves and pounced, knocking him to the ground.

Knives rained up and down in a frenzy. Blood spilled and spurted, soaking into the sand. The photographer's screams were snatched up by the ocean breeze. The Dawn Children stabbed and slashed, until the screaming stopped and the photographer lay still.

Getting to their feet, they wiped their blades clean on their clothes, then slowly turned to face The Shack, devil faces grinning wickedly in the sun.

36

CARRIE HAD MADE it across Cove Road and through the narrow alley that led to the town square. Melissa was in her arms, trembling and crying, her face buried into Carrie's shoulder, the horrors she'd witnessed burnt into her young mind forever.

As Carrie hurried towards Cove Crafts, her sandals slapping against the cobbled stones, she heard a sudden rush of running footsteps growing in momentum. She spun around, pressing her daughter protectively to her chest. A group of men and women, all in their late twenties, rushed past, arms swinging, lungs heaving, terrified whimpers escaping their throats. Carrie shut her eyes in relief, then opened them again.

Through the alley, she saw a glimpse of the promenade, of the bodies littered there. She watched the giant devil that had led the parade suddenly go up in flames. Three of the masked Dawn Children danced around it like minions worshipping a deity.

A survivor—a dark-haired man of indeterminate age—dashed past them, and the three gave chase, sharp blades raised high above their heads.

As the flames began to climb the devil's body, as thick smoke billowed in the air, Carrie saw young children wandering aimlessly among the dead.

They had let them live. They had let all the children live.

Guilt tearing through her, Carrie turned her back on them. She hurried across the square towards Cove Crafts. Melissa was holding on so tightly now, she was finding it hard to breathe.

"I need to move you, sweet pea," she gasped, trying to steady her. "Loosen up a little."

Melissa released her grip. Carrie shifted her around, balancing her on her left hip. Then she dug her free hand into her front jeans pocket. She found her phone, pulled it out, and wondered if anyone had managed to call the police. Because there didn't seem to be any officers around anymore. They'd all disappeared.

Carrie swiped the phone screen with her thumb, tapped 999 on the keypad, then realised there was no reception.

"Fuck!"

Stuffing the phone inside her back pocket, she slipped her hand inside the front one again and pulled out a small bunch of keys.

Melissa started howling. "I want Daddy! I want Nana Joy and Grandpa Gary!"

Carrie froze, key in hand, reaching for the door lock. She was having trouble comprehending that Dylan was dead. Gary and Joy, too. Along with everyone else.

That girl, Morwenna, she'd said it was because of Cal. That he'd ruined everything. Was it because he'd turned his back on them? Because he'd chosen to save Carrie instead?

All Carrie knew was that her daughter's life was in danger. All she knew was that she had to get Melissa out of this town alive.

Slipping the key into the lock, she opened the door.

Would hiding inside the shop be safe enough? Was there a hiding place secure enough where they could wait without fear of being found, until the madness stopped, until the police came. Because they had to come, didn't they? Mass murder had been committed in the blink of an eye. How could the police not know about it?

Carrie glanced over her shoulder and saw the empty square. Smelling smoke, she looked up and saw heavy, black plumes rising over the rooftops.

If hiding wasn't safe, what was the alternative? To run through Porth an Jowl while somehow avoiding the Dawn Children? To escape?

Carrying Melissa inside the shop, she shut the door again and locked it tight.

If they stayed here, they were going to die. The Dawn Children would find them. They would flush them out and make them pay for Cal's betrayal.

Hurrying down the far aisle with her daughter in her arms, Carrie shouldered open the storeroom door and ducked inside.

There was a small kitchen at the back. She hurried towards it, pulled open a drawer and pulled out a fruit knife. It was small, but the blade was sharp enough to do damage.

Slipping the knife into her back pocket, she returned to the shop floor and hurried behind the counter. Popping open the cash register, she pulled out some cash and stuffed it inside her left pocket.

Melissa was still sobbing, her tears splashing on Carrie's neck and soaking into her t-shirt. Setting her daughter down on the floor, Carrie crouched in front of her, both hidden by the counter. She gently wiped tears from the girl's frightened face, then kissed her on the forehead.

"Listen to me, sweet pea," she said. "We can't stay here. It's not safe."

Melissa shook her head, freeing more tears.

"It's not safe here," Carrie said again. "So we have to go outside. We're going to find a way out and we're going to get help."

"Then come back for Daddy? For Grandpa Gary and Nana Joy?"

Carrie felt her own tears dripping down her face. Felt grief rip her open inside. "We have to go now. I need to keep you safe. That means I need you to be brave and strong. And I need you to do exactly as I say. Can you do that for me, sweet pea?"

Melissa sobbed. Then nodded.

"That's my girl." Carrie reached up and tucked strands of hair behind her daughter's ear. "I promise I'll keep you safe."

Kissing Melissa again, she held her close and a little too tightly, then swept her into her arms. Reaching the shop door, she peered through the glass storefront and saw the square was still empty. Then she was unlocking the door and stepping outside, Melissa's arms wrapped tightly around her neck.

The smell of burning was sharp and acrid. The air was stifling and hot.

Carrie stepped forward and glanced down the alley towards the promenade. The giant devil was fully ablaze now, the sky turning black with smoke. Flames crackled. Children cried out for their parents.

They'll be safe, Carrie told herself. *They left them alive.*

But the fire, her mind whispered.

"Mummy. . ." Melissa whimpered in her arms. "I'm scared!"

"I know, sweet pea. I know."

Carrie turned, sucking in a trembling breath. Then she was leaving the square, carrying her daughter away from the promenade, and heading for the high street.

37

NAT GLANCED AROUND the corner of The Shack and was horrified by what she saw. The Dawn Children were on the other side now, reaching for the door. Shooting back, she pressed herself into the wall, holding her breath, trying to make herself small. She listened as one of them rattled the handle and found the door was locked.

On her right, Rose was panting heavily, her breaths growing erratic and more laboured with each inhalation.

On the other side of the building, the Dawn Children muttered to each other then started giggling. Hidden behind those demonic masks, it was hard to remember they were just kids.

Kids who had committed mass murder.

Nat turned to look at Rose and was shocked to see that her skin had turned a sickly, grey hue. She sucked in a ragged breath between clenched teeth and her face crumpled with pain.

"What's wrong?" Nat whispered.

Rose didn't look at her. "You should go. Leave me here. I can't outrun them."

Nat shook her head wildly from side to side.

Rose gasped, clutched a hand to her shoulder. "I'm telling you—go! Now!"

"Quiet!" Nat hissed. She was growing more terrified by the second. Something was wrong with Rose. She looked ill. Gravely ill.

Now, she could smell burning. Nat sniffed the air and recoiled at the sharp aroma of smoke. She heard the Dawn Children laugh again. Twisting around to face The Shack, she leaned out and saw a thin trail of smoke rising up from the other side of the building.

"Oh, shit!"

They'd set fire to the beach bar. They were going to burn it to the ground.

Terrified screams rang out from the people inside. Nat stood frozen, her mind racing. Then she lunged out and grabbed Rose by the wrist.

"Come on, we have to go!"

Rose pulled away from Nat. She moaned, clutching at her chest, pulling at the neck of her dress. Her skin had turned the colour of cement. "I . . . can't! It hurts! Please, Nat. . .Please go!"

Inside The Shack, the screams grew louder. There was a loud crash as something toppled over. More smoke billowed into the air, the stench of burning wood thick and pungent.

"Rose! What's wrong with you?" Nat gasped, unable to mask the fear in her voice.

But Rose's eyes were rolling in the back of her head. She cried out, raking fingers across her chest.

Nat froze, paralysed by fear. Rose hadn't drunk the poisoned cider. But the way she was clawing at her arm, at her chest. . .

She's having a heart attack!

This wasn't happening. None of it was real. Nat pinched herself hard. Then pinched again. But Rose was still in the throes of agony. The Shack was still on fire. And now, to Nat's horror, she saw the bright red masks of the Dawn Children, sharp teeth flashing, blood smearing their clothes, as one emerged on her left, the other on her right, carrying sharp knives and plastic water bottles filled with oily-looking liquid.

Rose cried out again as she slid along the wall. She went down, hitting the sand hard.

"Run!" she croaked.

The Dawn Children stood watching her, heads cocked to one side. Nat tried to move, but she was rooted to the spot.

"Rose!" she cried. "Get up! Please, get up!"

The kid on her left stepped forward. Nat twisted her head to the right and saw the other do the same. She gripped the axe in her hand, ready to fight or die.

"Please!" she cried. "Please don't hurt her!"

She shot another glance at Rose, who was propped against the wall, her eyes rolling in her head as thick smoke and flames rose up from the roof behind.

The masked devil on Nat's left raised the knife and lunged.

At the same time, a fire escape door was thrown open and people came spilling out. The door slammed into Nat's assailant, knocking him backwards. The people surged forward, pushing and shoving in blind panic. An elbow flew up and struck Nat on the jaw. She went down fast and hard, dropping the axe, landing on her back. Gasping for air, she tried to turn over.

The people from The Shack were running for their lives towards the promenade. One of the Dawn Children was in pursuit. Which left only one behind.

Nat saw him get to his knees. Saw the plastic bottle and the knife lying on the sand. She looked around for the axe, but it was gone. One of the people had taken it.

He was getting to his feet now, staring at her.

Nat lunged forward, reaching for the knife.

The kid was faster, grabbing the hilt. Then he was on top of her, knocking her back to the ground, driving a fist into her jaw.

The world went white, then red, then yellow.

Her vision doubled, then snapped back, in time to see the knife blade plummeting towards her throat.

Nat shot out a hand. The blade punctured her palm and slid straight through, emerging on the other side. She screamed as blood dripped from the wound. Then the masked devil was wrenching the blade out and raising it high above his head.

He struck again.

Nat brought up her forearm, blocking his attack, stopping the knife inches from her face. With her other hand, she clawed at the mask and tore it off.

He was just a boy. Maybe fourteen or fifteen years old. She imagined his face was once soft and cherubic. Now, it was clenched in a terrible grimace, his gaze feverish with blood lust.

He raised the knife again, this time wrapping both hands around the hilt. Nat's fingers scrabbled along the sand, picked up a handful and threw it in his eyes.

The boy screamed, dropping the blade and clawing at his face.

Nat twisted her body, bucking beneath him and throwing him off.

She scrambled to her feet, barely aware of the blood dripping from her punctured palm

The boy writhed on the ground, screaming in agony as he dug at his eyes.

Swinging back her leg, Nat shrieked and kicked his head with all her might.

The boy fell silent. Nat kicked again. His head ricocheted on his neck. Then he was still.

She didn't know if he was unconscious or dead. She didn't care.

Nat stumbled back, gasping for air. In the distance, she saw that some of The Shack escapees had made it to the promenade, while one unfortunate had been brought down. She watched his assailant squeeze the plastic bottle in his hand, drenching the man. He struck a match. There was an audible whoosh as the body went up in flames. Then the Dawn Child was running again, chasing after the other survivors.

Rose was on her back, head propped up against the wall. Clutching her bleeding hand to her chest, Nat sank down to her knees. She brushed fingers across Rose's cheek, felt the skin already cooling.

The Shack was ablaze, flames licking at the roof, smoke pouring into the blue sky. A loud crack splintered the air as something inside shattered.

Pulling with all her strength, Nat dragged Rose away from the fire. Her injured hand spasmed with white hot pain. She dug her heels deeper into the sand and mashed her jaws together, pulling Rose further and further away from the burning building.

Nat collapsed into a heap, panting and heaving and sobbing like a child. She leaned over Rose's body. Tears splashed on grey skin.

"Please," she whispered. She pressed fingers into the woman's neck. Felt nothing. "Please, wake up."

Rose lay motionless. Her kind, beautiful face soft and still.

"Please. I'm begging you. Please, wake up."

But Rose didn't wake up. She never would again.

As The Shack continued to burn and fall in on itself, the heat growing unbearably intense, Nat sat on the beach with Rose's hand lightly clasped in hers, quietly rocking back and forth.

38

THEY HAD MADE it onto Lavender Row. Carrie had deliberately avoided Cove Road. It was too open, making her and Melissa vulnerable. Easy targets that could be picked off in seconds.

The high street had been a war zone. Bodies on the ground. A car smashed through the window of the newsagent. Waste bins on fire. Hysterical survivors scattering in all directions, trying to find their way out.

Lavender Row was no different. Carrie hurried along the pavement, Melissa clutched in her arms, the child's face pressed into her shoulder, protecting her from the horrors that were all around.

Broken glass. Splatters of blood. Smoke pouring from a bedroom window. A desperate couple in their forties holding on to each other as they hid behind a parked car.

It had been less than ten minutes since everyone had died. Less than ten minutes to destroy an entire town.

There was no doubt in Carrie's mind—the attack had been carefully planned and coordinated. What terrified her the most was that it had been masterminded by teenagers. Kids like Cal.

A shriek shattered the air. Startled, Carrie spun around.

The scream had come from the cottage on her right. She didn't know who lived there. All she knew was that the scream had been wracked with pain. The ensuing silence was like ice piercing her heart. She quickened her pace, Melissa weighing down her arms, until she reached the end of the street

Behind Carrie, a door opened. She glanced over her shoulder and caught her breath in her throat.

Three children, wearing the now familiar red devil masks, filed out of the cottage where the scream had come from. They were small in stature, not tall enough to be teenagers, and they were soaked in blood.

Upon seeing them, the couple who had been hiding behind the car jumped to their feet and started running in the opposite direction. The Dawn Children chased after them.

Terrified, Carrie turned on to the side path that connected the streets and began climbing. The sharp ascent made her calf muscles burn.

On her left, the rocky cliff face climbed into the sky, Desperation Point jutting out in the distance high above.

Children.

How could children be capable of such brutality? Of inflicting hurt and pain? Of committing murder?

Cal had been capable of all those things. Grady Spencer had spent years breaking him down and building him back up again, poisoning his mind, twisting it until it was disturbed and filled with hate. Had these children been moulded by the same inhumane methods?

The video that Carrie had refused to watch had shown Cal stab a man to death inside a circle of children. Her solicitor had described their faces as blank and emotionless, as if cold-blooded murder meant nothing to them.

Who were these children? Why had they been trained to kill?

She climbed higher, her limbs burning.

Who knew why people did evil things?

Every day around the world, children were beaten, raped, and murdered, their innocence torn away. And there was only one reason for it—to make their abusers feel powerful. But these children here, they were taking the power back. Punishing the world for all the wrongdoing that had been done to them.

Carrie's muscles were screaming. She slid to a halt. "I have to put you down, sweet pea. I can't carry you anymore."

She wondered if, given the right circumstances, her daughter could become a killer, too.

Lowering Melissa to the ground, she grasped her hand and got moving again. They reached the corner of Clarence Row. The street where they lived. In a town that was meant to be safe. Rounding the corner, Carrie clutching tightly to Melissa, she wondered if they would ever feel safe again.

There was a body on the pavement. It was Carrie's neighbour, Dottie Penpol. Somehow, she had made it up here from the promenade, no doubt listening to the same dangerous voice that was whispering in Carrie's mind. *Get home. Lock the door. Wait until the monsters go away.* Dottie was dead now, face down on the ground. Head turned to the side, lifeless eyes staring at nothing.

"Don't look," she told Melissa, but it was too late.

Guiding her around the body, Carrie hurried along until they were standing outside their home on the opposite side of the street. The front door was open. She heard movement from inside. Crashes. Furniture being turned over. All their home comforts being destroyed.

Carrie's eyes found her car, which was parked in front of the garden gate. She had the keys in her pocket. Cove Road lay just ahead. They could get in the car, drive to the top, and get out of the town. But it would mean leaving everyone behind. All those children wandering on the promenade, orphaned and alone.

It would mean getting inside the car without disturbing whoever was inside her home.

She glanced back down the street. Saw Dottie's legs sticking out from the kerb.

Carrie squeezed Melissa's hand. "Come on. We're getting out of here."

They crept across the road, Carrie lifting a finger to her lips. Reaching the vehicle, she pulled the keys from her pocket and pressed the unlock button. All the door locks snapped up with a heavy clunk.

Carrie glanced at the house. Something smashed inside.

Moving quickly, she opened the back door and lifted Melissa in, strapping her to her booster seat. She shut the door again, making another loud clunk. Then she was moving around to the driver door and climbing inside.

The door slammed loudly behind her.

She shot another glance towards the house.

With a trembling hand, she slipped the key into the ignition.

In the backseat, Melissa was silent. She hadn't spoken a word since leaving the square.

Carrie twisted the key.

The engine roared to life.

She worked quickly, manoeuvring the vehicle away from the kerb, pressing down on the accelerator. She checked the rear-view mirror, staring at the open door of her house, waiting for someone to come. Then she was rolling onto Cove Road, turning left, shifting gears, and driving up the hill.

"Oh God!"

She slammed on the brakes. Melissa gasped, jolting forward, caught by the seatbelt.

Cove Road was littered with bodies. Some were on fire. Ahead of Carrie, on the left, a police officer lay, unmoving, in a pool of congealing blood.

But it wasn't the bodies that horrified her the most. It was the carnage that lay beyond.

A large white van had been parked horizontally across the road. Other vehicles had been stationed behind and to the sides. In a bid to escape, people had tried to drive through the blockade and had only succeeded in making it worse. There were bodies hanging out of shattered windscreens. More on the ground. Some of the cars were on fire.

At the very top of the roadblock, standing guard, were the Dawn Children.

Carrie's hand flew to her mouth. She counted at least fifteen of them, red devil masks appearing between the flames, like she'd driven straight into Hell.

This was the only way in and out of town.

Their only escape.

Hopelessness flooded Carrie's mind, paralysing her limbs. She glanced up at the rear-view mirror, saw her daughter's deathly-pale face and haunted eyes.

Up ahead, one of the masked children had noticed the car through the smoke and was alerting others. A row of smiling demons turned in her direction.

Carrie stared at them. They stared back.

And then it came to her. There was another way out of here. Another way to get Melissa to safety.

The Dawn Children were coming for her. Climbing over the blockade. Trampling over the dead.

Carrie shifted the gearstick, reversed down the hill and executed a three-point turn. The Dawn Children were running now, blades in hands, gathering speed.

Carrie slammed her foot down on the accelerator pedal and the car took off, back along Clarence Row.

39

THE SHACK WAS burning out of control, a bright inferno that turned the sand around it to glass. Nat sat by Rose's side, knees pulled up to her chest, arms wrapped around her shins, her bloodied hand dull and throbbing. She didn't know how long she'd been sitting like that. Perhaps minutes. Perhaps hours. There was an emptiness inside her, a black hole that had consumed her being.

Rose was dead. Without her, life had no meaning. She had been the only one in this world to give Nat a chance. The only one in this world who'd truly loved her. Who had protected her. Now Rose was gone and Nat was alone.

She stared at the ocean, watched the waves rolling in, saw the cider barrels floating further and further away, passing by the Devil's Gate, missing it completely. Above her, seagulls floated on the breeze, their cries soaring high.

A deafening crack made Nat blink. Slowly, she turned her head, saw The Shack collapse in on itself, sending thousands of bright red sparks into the air and hot flames licking the sky.

She turned back to Rose. Stared at her pale, lifeless form.

She lifted her wounded hand, turned it over, examining the raw, bloody puncture in the centre of her palm. It was still bleeding, but the blood was congealing now, the flow slowing down.

The boy she had killed lay on the sand, next to the burning remains of the bar. A length of timber had fallen across his legs, the wood charred and smoking, the edges glowing red.

Nat returned her gaze to Rose, reached out with her injured hand and stroked the woman's face.

The grief was coming. She could sense it climbing out of the black hole like a monstrous beast, thick, razor-sharp claws sinking into her flesh.

It was coming, and it would tear her apart.

She couldn't let it happen. Not yet.

When the time came, she would embrace it fully. Would let it eat her alive.

But not now.

Sitting up on her knees, she shut her eyes and willed herself to be numb, coaxing the beast back into its hole. Leaning down, she kissed Rose on both cheeks, then on her forehead. Then on her mouth.

"You were my real mother," she whispered. "I never told you that. But I hope you knew."

Slipping fingers into Rose's dress pocket, she pulled out the handkerchief that she knew would be inside, shook it open, then wrapped it tightly around her injured hand. Once it was secure, she got to her feet.

Her eyes found the dead boy again. Saw the knife on the sand. The bottle of fuel he'd used to set fire to The Shack. The devil mask that had looked so terrifying not so long ago, now lay half buried in sand, nothing more than cheap plastic fancy dress.

Nat turn ninety degrees and stared up at the town. What she saw took her breath away. Devil's Cove was burning, smoke billowing in thick, black plumes.

Nat was alone. In hell. Just like she was meant to be.

She didn't care if she lived or died. Everything she loved had been snatched away. But if she was going to die, the Dawn Children would be coming with her.

40

THE CAR SHOT along the street, Carrie's eyes sharp and focused on the turning up ahead. Out of nowhere, a masked teenager sprang through the air and lunged at the car. Carrie swerved. The girl slammed onto the bonnet then went up and over the roof. Shrieking, Carrie swerved again, almost colliding with a row of parked cars. Her eyes shot up to the rear-view mirror and she saw the girl hit the tarmac, then bounce and roll.

I've killed a child! she thought, as Melissa screamed in the backseat.

But she had no time to process it. The Dawn Children were turning off the hill and entering Clarence Row behind her; a vicious mob of red devils.

"Hold on!" Carrie cried.

They reached the end of the row and she spun the wheel, turning onto the path that ran alongside. It wasn't made for cars and was just wide enough to squeeze the vehicle through.

Gears crunching, paintwork scraping against the barrier, Carrie drove on until she reached the top. She spun the wheel again and turned onto Grenville Row, where she slammed on the brakes.

Without turning off the engine, she threw open the door and climbed out, then went around to the back and freed Melissa from her booster seat. Scooping her up in her arms, she turned and ran.

She reached the pavement, pushed open the gate of the first house on the left. As she hurried along the garden path, she risked a glance over her shoulder. She heard shouts and running.

The Dawn Children had reached the end of Clarence Row and were entering the side path. She had a minute, maybe two, before they'd appear around the corner.

Carrie glanced down the length of Grenville Row, which was so dangerously close to the blockade, and saw one of the Dawn Children moving along the street.

Heart leaping into her throat, she tightened her grip on Melissa and continued along the path, through the garden and along the side of the house. She didn't know the woman who lived here—only that she was called Jane. To Carrie, she was just a face she sometimes saw around town, or a name Rose sometimes mentioned because Rose knew just about everyone. *Oh, Rose! I hope Nat found her. I hope they're safe!* If Jane was inside the house now, she was staying deathly silent.

Carrie slid to a halt. The backyard was paved and empty, weeds growing up through the cracks. A tall, wooden fence ran along the length of the yard and continued on, bordering the backs of all the houses on Grenville Row. On the other side, a thick canopy of leaves towered over the roofs.

Briar Wood.

This was their way out. The only way to escape the town.

Putting Melissa down, Carrie hurried over to the fence and tested each vertical board, slipping her fingers between the tiny gaps, attempting and failing to pry one free.

Panic rising, she stepped back.

The fence was six feet tall. She could reach the top with her hands and pull herself up.

But what about Melissa?

She crouched down and stared at her daughter, who was pale and trembling.

"Listen to me," Carrie said, any pretence at calm long gone. "We have to go over the fence. I'm going to put you on my back and you'll put your arms around my neck. Just like a piggyback ride. I'll climb to the top, then swing over. You're going to hold on as tight as you can and you're not going to let go."

Melissa's eyes grew round and scared. "No, I—"

"It's not up for discussion. You need to do exactly as I say. We're going over the fence. You and me, together. Understood?"

Melissa didn't move, just stared.

"Understood?" Carrie said, raising her voice, hating herself for it.

Melissa nodded. Tears slipped from her eyes.

"Good girl. That's my sweet pea." Carrie kissed her hard on the cheek, then twisted around. "Climb on."

She felt Melissa's body press against her back, felt her tiny arms wrap around her neck and her frightened breaths on her hair. Carrie stood and Melissa wrapped her legs around her mother's waist.

"Hold on tight," Carrie said.

She approached the fence. Reached up and grabbed the top with her fingers. She hoisted herself up, shoes pressing into the wooden boards, her aching muscles complaining in her arms.

Melissa squealed and squeezed Carrie's neck, choking her as she clumsily swung her right leg up and over.

"I'm scared, Mummy!"

"You're doing great, sweet pea. We're almost there," Carrie gasped.

She was straddling the fence now and peering through the trees of Briar Wood. It was quiet and still out there, rays of sunlight piercing the canopy and illuminating the ground.

"We're going to climb over. You need to hold on tight. There's a drop. Not a big one, but I'll try to land on my feet, okay?"

"No, I'll fall!"

"Remember what I told you. You need to be brave. You need to do exactly what I say."

"Okay," Melissa sobbed.

"Good girl. You're my little angel. I'm going to swing my other leg over right now. Then we'll—"

White hot, searing pain ripped through Carrie's left leg.

She screamed in agony. Looked down and saw a hunting knife buried deep in her thigh, right up to the hilt.

She saw Morwenna, mask-free, staring up at her from the yard and grinning wickedly.

Without thinking, Carrie twisted her upper body, grabbed Melissa's wrist and wrenched her from her back. Melissa dangled in mid-air for a second, shocked eyes staring at her mother.

Then Carrie let her go.

Melissa fell, hitting the muddy ground of Briar Wood.

"Run!" Carrie screamed. "Run as fast as you can!"

Morwenna grabbed the hilt of the knife and twisted it. Carrie shrieked again in pain. Her vision turned white. Then she was dragged from the fence, back into the yard.

CARRIE HIT THE ground hard, landing on her back and knocking the air from her lungs. Morwenna was on top of her, fists raining down on Carrie's chest, nails scratching at her face and neck, clawing at her eyes.

She was laughing, her face contorting into a terrible grimace. Then she was wrapping fingers around Carrie's throat and choking the life from her.

"This is what you get!" she hissed, her face coming close to Carrie's. Her eyes were wide and rolling, the pupils grossly dilated. "This is what you get for raising a monster!"

Her hands squeezed tighter.

Carrie grasped Morwenna's wrists and tried to prise them away. But the young woman's grip was like iron.

Her vision was turning red.

A pulsing started in her temples, growing more intense by the second, until it was pounding like a kettle drum.

She kicked out. The hilt of the knife that was still buried in her leg hit the ground. Lightning bolts of pain shot through her thigh and she almost blacked out.

"Your son ruined everything! Jacob had a plan. You and your stupid son ruined it all!" Hands still gripped around Carrie's throat,

Morwenna bent down and sank teeth into her face.

Fresh pain ripped through Carrie's cheek. Blood and saliva ran down her neck.

Morwenna sat up again and pressed her weight on Carrie's throat.

Carrie thrashed and bucked her hips. Managed to get a foot on the ground.

Morwenna held fast.

Everything was going dark.

Yellow spots speckled the shadows.

The pounding in her head crashed like thunder.

From beneath it all, Carrie felt something pressing into her skin. Something in her back pocket.

As Morwenna throttled the life from her, as everything began to fade away, Carrie reached beneath her bucking body and pulled out the fruit knife.

She swung her arm, slicing the blade across Morwenna's face.

The young woman shrieked. Released her grip on Carrie's throat. She fell back, grasping the open wound on her cheek.

Choking and gasping for air, Carrie scrambled away on her elbows.

"You fucking bitch!" Morwenna screamed.

She sprang forward like a wild animal, hands curled like sharp talons, spittle flying from her mouth. She landed on top of Carrie. Raised a fist. Brought it down hard on Carrie's chin.

Blood rained from Morwenna's cheek as she struck again.

With an anguished scream, Carrie lashed out.

The fruit knife punctured Morwenna's throat. Her eyes grew round with surprise. The women stared at each other in horror.

Then Carrie pulled out the blade.

Blood pulsed from Morwenna's neck. She clutched a hand to the wound and slipped to the side, rolling from Carrie's body, where she lay on the ground, choking and spluttering, a pool of blood widening beneath her.

Then she was silent and still.

Carrie gasped and wheezed. Her throat was on fire. Her leg was a mess. But now footsteps were stampeding towards her.

Adrenaline shooting through her body, she dragged herself to her feet. The blade was still embedded in her thigh, the wound pulsating all the way down to her feet.

She clenched her jaw, grabbed the top of the fence and hoisted herself up once more. With a terrible, agonising cry, she swung her injured leg over until she was straddling the top.

The Dawn Children entered the backyard, masked faces staring up at her, then down at Morwenna's lifeless corpse.

Carrie swung her other leg over and jumped to the ground.

White hot pain incinerated her nerve endings. She fell to her hands and knees, vomit bubbling in her throat. She managed to pull herself up then looked wildly around.

Melissa wasn't here.

"Sweet pea!" she cried, her voice broken and strangled.

Behind her, the Dawn Children were climbing the fence.

Carrie staggered forward. Blood soaked her leg.

Her throat burned as she called Melissa's name.

She turned a full circle. Saw the Dawn Children leaping from the fence and hitting the ground. Saw more of them appearing through the trees up ahead, coming from the direction of the roadblock.

They came closer, surrounding Carrie in a perfect circle. Just like they'd done to the man in the video.

And then she saw her. Melissa.

But she wasn't alone.

Carrie stared at the young man who had an arm around her daughter's shoulder. He smiled at her—a sweet smile for someone so dangerous—then waved a hand through the air.

The Dawn Children began removing their masks.

Carrie gasped. They really were children; some as young as five or six, others in their teens. They all shared the same blank expression —the one her solicitor had described from the video.

"I know you," Carrie said through clenched teeth, as she turned back to their leader. "Your name is Heath. You were in my house that night. You took me to Burnt House Farm. Poured petrol everywhere and left me to burn to death inside a cage."

Heath nodded, his arm still hanging over Melissa's shoulder. "It's true, I did. But I was saving you. Saving you from this world. But your son decided to keep you here."

"He saved me!" Carrie spat. "Cal got me out of there. I'm alive because of him."

The pain in her leg was becoming unbearable. The blade was keeping the wound sealed, but she felt as if poison was spreading through her veins, turning them rotten.

"Yes, you are. But at what cost?" Heath said. "We had a father once. His name was Jacob. He was the only one who cared for us. The only one who understood how dangerous this world is for children like us. He had a plan. He wanted to cleanse the world and make it safe again. But Cal ruined it. He clouded Jacob's mind. Made him confused. Jacob chose Cal to lead the New Dawn. But he should have chosen me."

There was madness in Heath's eyes. Whatever had been done to him as a child, it had damaged him beyond repair. The darkness inside him was rotten and all consuming, eating away all the goodness until only anger and rage and the desire to hurt remained.

Carrie stared at him, then shot a glance at Melissa, who was deathly pale, her face growing as expressionless as the other children as shock set in.

"This is what it's all about?" Carrie said. "All these people dead"—Dylan's face flashed in her mind. Joy's and Gary's—"all these people gone because you were jealous? Because Jacob picked Cal and not you?" Her voice trembled with anger and grief. "How very fucking mature!"

Heath smiled, exposing his teeth. "You don't understand. This was always Jacob's plan. To cleanse the world of poisonous adults. That's why he had Cal execute that pervert of a councillor. That's why all the others had to die."

"The people in this town are innocent!" Carrie raged.

A wave of nausea hit her, making her suddenly dizzy and weak. She glanced around the circle, saw the empty faces of the Dawn Children.

What had happened to them all? Where were their families?

Heath shrugged, ran a finger along Melissa's cheek. "Every war has its casualties. Besides, this town needed to be razed to the ground. This was Grady Spencer's home. The greatest monster of them all. He murdered children. Tortured them. Fed them to his dog. See what he did to your son! See what he did to his own son!

"I suppose we should thank him, really. Without him, Jacob would never have seen the light and become our father. He would never have saved us. There would be no Dawn." Heath's eyes grew dark and violent again. "But then Jacob was taken away from us. Along with everything he'd planned."

Carrie shook her head, tears rolling down her face. "Please. Let my daughter go."

But Heath wasn't listening. He was frowning, searching the circle. "Where's Morwenna?"

One of the children, a boy no older than ten with a shock of red hair, pointed at the fence. "She's dead. The lady killed her."

Carrie glanced at her daughter. At the hand that was now wrapped loosely around her throat. She had expected to see grief in Heath's eyes. But there was only a void.

"Then she is at peace," he said. "Morwenna has crossed over into the New Dawn."

In the near distance, quiet at first, but growing louder, came the sound of sirens.

The Dawn Children stared at each other.

Heath grinned widely, releasing Melissa and stretching out his arms into a cross. "Salvation is at hand!"

"It's over," Carrie said. "The police are coming. You'll be arrested. All of you. It doesn't matter that you're children—you'll all go to prison. You'll spend the rest of your lives regretting what you've done."

Heath shook his head. "No. We won't. We will all go into the New Dawn." He addressed the group now, his eyes sparkling darkly. "Our father, Jacob, he saw us ruling this world free of pain, standing on the corpses of slain monsters. But this world is not for us. This world is dark and it's twisted and full of hate. This world wants to devour us. To tear the meat from our bones. To suck the marrow dry.

But we won't allow it. We will set ourselves free."

He turned and nodded to two boys who were barely in their teens. Both carried backpacks on their shoulders. Carrie watched as they removed the bags and pulled out plastic containers, along with tubes of paper cups.

One by one, they filled each cup with glistening liquid and passed them around the circle, until every child held one in their hand.

Carrie's blood ran cold. The children stared at the cups, then uncertainly at each other.

"What are you doing?" Carrie's voice trembled. She tried to take a step forward, but the blade bit deeper into her flesh, making her scream.

One of the boys handed a cup to Heath, then entered the circle, bringing a second cup to Carrie. Keeping his distance, he held it out.

Carrie stared at it, mouth hanging open. "I'm not drinking that."

Heath smiled, pulled a knife from a sheath strapped to his waist and put it to Melissa's throat.

"Yes, you will," he said. "Our parents are dead. We need a new mother in the Dawn. I choose you."

Carrie shook her head, over and over. "No. I can't."

"You can. It's easy. Just lift it to your lips and tip it back. Pretend it's wine, if you like."

"No. Please. Let my daughter go."

The sirens were getting louder. There were several of them, all melding into one cacophonous wail.

Tears splashed down Carrie's face. She met Melissa's blank gaze. "Sweet pea. I'm so sorry!"

"Don't be," Heath said. "Drink and you'll see her on the other side." He turned to the children. "Drink! We'll all go together, hand in hand, into the New Dawn."

The children stared at the cups, then around the circle. No one drank.

Heath's face grew dark and thunderous.

"You're making them doubt!" he hissed at Carrie. "You're making them confused, just like Cal did to Jacob!"

He grabbed Melissa's hair and pulled her neck back, pressing the blade against her skin.

"Drink!" he screamed.

Carrie's whole body trembled as she stared into the cup, at the sticky liquid rippling inside. She stared at her daughter, at the blade pressed to her neck.

Sobbing, she tried to raise the cup to her lips, but her body betrayed her, its survival instincts kicking in.

"Then she fucking dies!" Heath screamed.

One of the teenagers, a girl no older than fourteen, shook her head.

"Children are sacred," she said. "Children are the New Dawn. That's what Jacob said." The other children murmured and nodded. "We don't hurt each other."

It was as if Heath couldn't see her. His eyes were burning into Carrie's, seething with hate.

"Children are sacred," the girl repeated. "Children are—"

"*Shut your fucking mouth and drink your fucking drink!*" He turned on the circle, face flushing the colour of blood. "Don't you understand? They're coming for us! The monsters are coming to tear us all apart! Save yourselves before it's too late! Drink and go into the New Dawn!"

A boy, no older than ten, raised the cup to his mouth.

"No!" Carrie screamed. "You'll die!"

The others copied the boy, their blank expressions returning.

"Now you," Heath said, staring at Carrie. He pulled Melissa's head back further, pushing the blade against her neck.

Carrie raised the cup.

"I'm sorry, sweet pea!" she screamed. "Close your eyes for Mummy!"

She pressed the cup to her lips.

The Dawn Children did the same.

And then the Devil stepped out from behind a tree.

Heath turned in surprise. Saw the Devil lift a hand and squeeze. Lighter fuel spurted over Heath's face and rained down over his clothes.

Carrie tossed the cup to one side. She leaned forward, grabbed the hilt of the knife with both hands and wrenched it from her thigh. Pain shot up to her head and down to her toes. Blood spurted from the wound.

Heath dropped his blade and staggered backwards, rubbing his eyes with one hand, dragging Melissa behind him with the other.

The Devil stalked after him, yellow eyes glowing, sharp teeth flashing. It struck a match against the side of a tree and a flame sparked to life.

Carrie stumbled forward, knife raised. She plunged the blade into Heath's wrist.

He screamed and let go of Melissa.

Carrie pulled her daughter away. Blood gushed from her thigh and drenched her leg.

The Dawn Children stared, cups still poised at their lips, mesmerised by the Devil. Who was reaching up and pulling off its mask.

Nat stared at Heath. Her face twisted with burning hatred.

She flicked the match.

Carrie watched it sail through the air. Listened to the *whoosh* of igniting fuel.

Then Heath was burning. Screaming at the top of his lungs. Spinning in circles.

The Dawn Children sprang back, dropping their cups to the ground. They watched in horror as their leader was engulfed in a ball of fire.

Heath ran. Made it five steps. Then he went down. Quiet and still. His body consumed by flames.

The Dawn Children scattered, running in all directions.

There were other voices now. Adults, shouting instructions, coming through the trees.

Carrie held onto Melissa, pressed her daughter's face into her stomach, shutting out all the horror.

Nat stood, perfectly calm, watching Heath burn, flames dancing and shimmering in her eyes.

The day was growing dim; thick smoke from a burning town smothering all light.

Carrie glanced down at her leg, saw how much blood she'd lost.

She was cold.

Growing weaker by the second.

She held onto Melissa, stroked her hair.

"You're safe, sweet pea," she whispered. "You're safe now."

Then Carrie fell.

The world turned red.

Then white.

Then gold.

Like a New Dawn.

SIX MONTHS LATER

NAT SAT IN the cramped living room of the second floor flat, traffic noise from below rattling the windows. Pencil poised, she looked up from her sketchpad and stared at her subject. Then let out a frustrated sigh.

"I wish you'd stop moving. Do you have ants in your pants or what?"

Sitting on a stool in the corner, arms wrapped around a soft brown bear, Melissa stared at her in silence. She was too pale, the light gone out of her eyes. She shrugged, squeezed the bear to her chest, and looked out the window. "I want to watch TV."

"Everything okay in here?" Carrie appeared in the doorway, running a brush through her hair.

Nat pulled a face. "Ask Miss Thing over there. Apparently posing for a portrait is boring."

Carrie limped into the room, favouring her right leg. Dropping the brush on the table, she swept her hair back into a ponytail as she glanced down at Nat's sketchpad. "That will look nice in a frame when it's done."

"The only place this is going is in the bin."

"Like hell it is. I'll hang it in my bedroom so you don't have to see it." She glanced over at Melissa. Felt a twinge of worry. "You okay, sweet pea?"

Melissa nodded. "Fine."

Carrie's gaze shifted to Nat, saw the same haunted expression. It was a familiar look. All three of them had been wearing it lately.

"Well, I'm heading out," Carrie said, bending down to ruffle her daughter's hair. She winced as dull pain shot through her thigh. "I won't be long. Two hours max. You sure you're okay to watch her?"

Nat rolled her eyes. "I can take care of a five-year-old brat. It's not rocket science."

"No, but you'll be seeing stars if you call my daughter a brat again." Carrie shot her a wry smile. Nat only stared. "Are you sure you're okay? You seem glummer than usual."

"I'm fine."

"And I'm a master at seeing through crap. What's wrong? Is it the will? Because if you don't want the money, I'll gladly take it off your hands."

Nat opened her mouth. Shut it again as she slowly shook her head. "I still can't believe she left me everything. I don't understand why."

"You don't?" Carrie rubbed the side of her leg. Physiotherapy was helping, but it still hurt like a bastard. "Rose left you that money because she loved you. Because in her eyes, you were her daughter. Why *wouldn't* she leave you that money?"

She stared at Nat, whose eyes were wet and glossy. She looked away, covering her tears. Carrie shuffled over and placed a hand on her shoulder. Nat flinched.

"When I get back, we'll get that application done and sent off tomorrow."

"Yeah, about that..."

"No. I don't want to hear any excuses. We both know art school is what you want. Rose did, too. So get over your 'I don't deserve this. I'm a terrible person' bullshit and let's get that form finished tonight. We're almost out of time."

Nat shrugged and wiped her eyes, exposing the ugly scar tissue on her right hand. "Whatever."

"Now I'm really off this time," Carrie said, returning to Melissa and stroking her face. "I'll be back soon, sweet pea. Be good for Nat. Maybe I'll bring you back an ice cream. Maybe I'll even let you eat it before dinner."

Melissa stared at her, blank eyes round and hollow. Carrie straightened, made it over to the door before she turned around again. "Are you sure you'll—"

"My God, woman! Just go!"

*

The hospital was a ten minute drive through busy city streets. Carrie was still getting used to life in Bristol. She'd been so busy that there'd barely been time to explore her new surroundings. All she knew was that any place was better than the hell she'd left behind.

The trial had come and gone last month. Cal had been lucky. The defence team had presented enough compelling evidence to convince the jury that he hadn't been in control when he'd killed John Beaumont and stabbed his grandmother. The verdict had been what they'd hope for—manslaughter due to diminished responsibility. Even better, instead of serving his time at a young offenders institute, he'd remain at the hospital, under the care of Dr Jensen and a team of specialists, where he'd continue to receive treatment, until it was deemed that he was well enough—and safe enough—to be released. No one knew when that would be. A year. Two. Maybe never. Only time would tell.

Strangely enough, the massacre at Devil's Cove had helped his case, the defence using it to demonstrate how a child's mind could succumb to severe mental abuse and manipulation. How a child could be coerced into committing murder.

Eight hundred and twenty-six people had been murdered that day, the poison killing half of them, the fires finishing off the rest. Not quite beating Jonestown on the scale of cult massacres but coming damn close. Eight hundred and twenty-six people, including Dylan, his parents Joy and Gary, and poor, dear Rose. Carrie was still having trouble processing their deaths. She knew the grief would come and when it did, it would floor her. But right now, she was focused on her children.

Melissa was in therapy. Cal was in the hospital. All she wanted was for them both to be well.

As for Porth an Jowl, it was a ghost town. The survivors who hadn't lost everything in the fire had abandoned their homes and moved elsewhere. Now the Devil was free to roam the empty streets as he pleased.

With Heath dead, the remaining Dawn Children had run. But they hadn't got very far. Most of them were currently locked away in secure homes and institutes, their fates still unresolved. In an atrocity like this, how did you prove who was a killer and who was a victim? Could a five-year-old even be charged with murder? The judicial system was wringing its hands.

Two minutes had passed since Carrie had parked in one of the visitor bays. She sat behind the wheel, staring up at the hospital, sucking in deep breaths and letting them out in steady streams. She glanced up at the rear-view mirror, at her washed out, gaunt reflection.

"You can do this," she whispered, like she did every time she came here. "Do it for him."

Leaving the car, she entered the hospital and went through the usual security checks. Now she sat at a table in an empty room, not a sharp object in sight. A door opened and he was brought in.

Cal. Her son.

His hair had grown since she'd last seen him. He'd put on a little weight, too. He was still short for his age, probably always would be. But he was alive. He sat across from Carrie, his large, haunted, beautiful eyes staring straight at her. By the door, the usual tall nurse stood with his arms folded across his powerful chest, his gaze fixed on the window in an attempt to give them at least the impression of privacy.

Carrie stared at Cal. Stared into his eyes. Sometimes it was like staring into space, thousands of glittering stars staring right back.

She smiled at him. "How is my favourite son?"

Nothing. No response. At least he was looking at her this time. She shifted on the hard plastic seat, a dull ache in her thigh waking up.

"Well," she said. "We're all moved into the new flat. It's okay, I suppose. A little cramped and it could do with a lick of paint. The street's not exactly quiet. But it's home for now. When you get out, we can find somewhere bigger. Somewhere with enough room for us all."

She leaned back. Glanced at the nurse by the door, feeling awkward and lost for words. Cal was still staring at her, eyes piercing her soul.

"I spoke to Dr Jensen this week. She said she's feeling really positive about the outcome of the trial, and that she's happy you get to stay here. In fact, she said she's quite confident that she can help you. That's good, isn't it? It's good to have someone else on your side."

Cal stared, unblinking.

Carrie squirmed on the chair. The throbbing in her thigh intensified as she shifted her weight. "I heard your dad came to visit. That's great! I also heard he got a little upset, but not because of you. He's just a little overwhelmed, that's all. Probably needs some more time to get used to seeing you here. But he'll come around."

She stared at her son. At Cal. Feeling a sudden desperation tightening her chest. She glanced at the nurse, who was still gazing at the window, then placed a hand on the table.

Come on. Think of something else to say.

"Oh, I almost forgot. I had a postcard from Sally the other week. She and your grandfather are heading out to Australia. Can you believe it? I swear one day they'll sail off the edge of the world."

Her chest was growing tighter. The air in the room thinner. She leaned forward, staring into her son's dark eyes.

"Please, Cal," she whispered. "Please, say something."

A small crease appeared between his eyebrows.

"Are you in there? Is my boy still in there?"

His nostrils were flaring now. The frown pressing deeper into his skin.

"I miss you so much. So much. Won't you say anything?"

Tears ran down Carrie's face and hit the table in pitiful drips and drops. Cal stared at her, his chest heaving up and down. She was making him angry. Getting him worked up. Doing all the things Dr Jensen said she shouldn't do.

Carrie leaned back and tried to centre herself.

Was it pointless? This coming here every two weeks, trying to reach him, over and over, only to fail, over and over. Her son was gone. Just like she'd told poor, dear Rose that afternoon at the town hall. She was talking to a shell. The grief in her heart would never leave her.

Not until she said goodbye.

Not until she set him free.

Wiping her eyes, Carrie sucked in another breath and forced a smile to her lips. Inside, she was dying.

Go on. Be brave. All you're doing is killing each other.

"Well, I should probably get back. Nat's looking after Melissa and I'm not sure I trust the two of them alone for more than an hour."

Nothing. Even the frown had disappeared. The breathing returned to normal.

Do it now. Let him go. Walk out of here and never come back.

Her heart splintering all over again, Carrie cleared her throat and caught the nurse's attention. Time to go. Now. Before she broke down.

"Well, you take care of yourself, Cal. I'll see you again soon."

She placed her hands on the table and pushed herself up.

Cal struck like a cobra, fingers shooting out and wrapping tightly around Carrie's wrist. Shocked, she stared down at her son's hand, then into his wide, frightened eyes.

The nurse started forward. Carrie shook her head.

"It's okay," she said.

She turned back to Cal, who opened his mouth, exposing all his teeth. Tears ran from the corners of his eyes. The grip on her wrist became unbearably tight, nails digging into her flesh, tiny drops of blood welling, pain shooting up to her elbow.

"What?" Carrie said. "What is it?"

A strange, strangled noise rose up from his throat.

Carrie stared at him, hopeful, desperate, unable to look away. "What is it?"

Cal's face turned red. And then he spoke.

Just four words. Barely whispered.

"Mum," he said. "I love you."

DEAR READER

And so the Devil's Cove saga comes to a bitter-sweet end. I hope you've enjoyed the journey and found it to be a wild, grisly, moving, nerve-shredding ride. If you did, I'd be hugely grateful if you'd spare a minute or two to write a review on the website you purchased the books from. Just a few words will go a long way to help new readers decide to give the Devil's Cove trilogy a try.

If you ever find yourself in Cornwall, do visit St Michael's Mount, Penzance, St Ives and Falmouth—they are all lovely places with not a murderous cult member in sight. Porth an Jowl aka Devil's Cove is entirely fictional, but if you pay a visit to the beach town of Perranporth, you'll get a good look at the place that inspired its look and feel.

As they say in Cornwall, *yeghes da!*

Malcolm, August 2019.

ACKNOWLEDGEMENTS

Thank you as always to my editor Natasha Orme, who always manages to polish the heart and the darkness in my stories; to J. Caleb Clark for another breath-taking cover design; to all the professionals who helped me shape this trilogy into something believable: Andrea Lydon, former CSI, Philip Bates, DI Gail Windsor, Rebecca Bradley, Sarah Grey, OT; thank you to my Read & Review team—I'm lucky to have my own cheerleading squad; and to my friends and family, who still like me despite my 'dark personality'; and lastly, as always, to Xander, who sticks around despite my alarming internet history. It's research, honest.

CPSIA information can be obtained
at www.ICGtesting.com
Printed in the USA
LVHW021524180620
658424LV00005B/1192